WELCOME TO THE DUNGEON

It is a fantastic world where measure knows no proportion and time has no bearing.

It is a shattered city littered with the rubble and refuse of an unknown apocalypse.

It is a maze of passages where men live in the walls like mice.

It is a game of mockery in which everyone is a player but no one controls the moves.

From the streets of the Dives to the depths of the Underground, this is the quest of Clive Folliot, explorer and hero.

Don't miss any of the exciting volumes in
Philip José Farmer's THE DUNGEON!

THE BLACK TOWER
THE DARK ABYSS
THE VALLEY OF THUNDER
THE LAKE OF FIRE
THE HIDDEN CITY
THE FINAL BATTLE

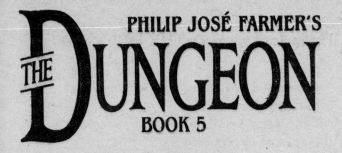

PHILIP JOSÉ FARMER'S
THE DUNGEON
BOOK 5

THE
HIDDEN
CITY
■
Charles de Lint

BANTAM BOOKS
NEW YORK · TORONTO · LONDON · SYDNEY · AUCKLAND

Special thanks to Lou Aronica, Betsy Mitchell, Richard Curtis, David M. Harris, and Mary Higgins.

THE HIDDEN CITY

A Bantam Spectra Book / March 1990

THE DUNGEON is a trademark of Byron Preiss Visual Publications, Inc.
Cover and interior art by Robert Gould.
Book and cover design by Alex Jay/Studio J.

ISBN 0-553-28338-3

Published simultaneously in the United States and Canada

Bantam Books are published by Bantam Books, a division of Bantam Doubleday Dell Publishing Group, Inc. Its trademark, consisting of the words "Bantam Books" and the portrayal of a rooster, is Registered in U.S. Patent and Trademark Office and in other countries. Marca Registrada, Bantam Books, 666 Fifth Avenue, New York, New York 10103.

---

for Bruce

(we've got to stop meeting
in these kinds of places)

with special thanks to David

(not just for the candy, but for
holding the whole thing together)

■ FOREWORD ■

"Heaven reveals nothing.//"Earth keeps its secrets to itself."

So wrote Li Ho, ancient Chinese poet (A.D. 791–817).

The final line of his poem goes somewhat like this: "See the man who raved while writing on the wall his questions to heaven."

Li Ho refers here to Ch'u Yüan, who lived during the third century B.C. Ch'u, while wandering through the ruins of the palaces and tombs of long-dead kings, went mad, and he wrote his questions beneath some murals. We do not know what the questions were. They must have been the same sort that drives the thinking person nowadays to despair or near frenzy. I say "nowadays" though these questions have always been asked.

Why are we here? Why do we have to suffer? Why is there such injustice? Where do we go from here? Who is pushing us around?

The ancient Greeks believed that the Olympic gods interfered in human affairs, but that this interference was sporadic and usually for the personal benefit of a god or goddess. Never mind what happened to the unlucky man or woman or child who got in the way. The Greeks did not believe, however, that the deities conspired to wreak havoc, misery, and death among humankind, but that, generally, Chance or Fate determined the lot of the members of Homo sapiens. That this seldom resulted in good for Homo sapiens was just the way things were. Though the gods occasionally took a hand in man's destiny, the universe was a machine that cared nothing for what happened to the living. Or for that matter, the nonliving: the destruction of a mountain was as significant, or as insignificant, an event as the death of a mouse.

Other ancient cultures seemed to have much the same attitude, although the Egyptians and the Hebrews were exceptions. They seemed to believe that the gods monitored closely the lives and attitudes of their worshipers. In other words, they cared about humans. The Hebrews may have gotten this concept from the Egyptians while in servitude to them. But their idea of one God eventually evolved from the idea of many gods, though this may also have been the influence of Ikhnaton, the pharaoh who conceived monotheism.

The concept of a vast plot against humanity seems to have originated with the early Christians. This was probably influenced by various then-contemporary religions, most notably that of the Persians, from whom the modern Iranians are descended. The Buddhists did not blame other people or higher beings for the good or bad lot of individuals, and believed in no cosmic conspiracy against them. Every individual was responsible for his or her own fate.

The seeds of the conspiracy concept lay in the ancient Hebrew religion. The early Christians nourished this idea with Persian ideas, and the concept eventually grew into that of the great evil being, the superhumanly powerful anti–human being, the fallen angel called Lucifer, Satan, the Devil, and Old Nick.

In reality there is no abstract evil, no malignant, pervasive, ectoplasmic cloud floating around causing bad things to happen to us powerless humans. Evil is not a Platonic idea. The old folk saying, "Evil is as evil does," describes the nature of evil. Evil is what happens and what is caused to happen. What happens is the result of accident or chance or the deliberate action of human beings. The only conspiracy in this universe is that among sentients. It is not necessary to invent the devil to account for bad things. The philosophical and logical tool, Occam's Razor, cuts the devil out of the scheme of this world. The Englishman William of Occam, born A.D. 1285, gave his name to this principle, though others before him had stated it in various forms: "Entities are not to be multiplied beyond necessity."

That is, cut out the crap. Use the simplest explanation. Thus Satan is a fantasy, a totally unneeded accretion to the explanation of evil actions and reactions.

Even in this modern age, many people still believe in the existence of Satan as a living entity who personally begets all the evil thinking and behavior on Earth. "The Devil made me do it!" In 1990 there are many who think just as their Old Stone Age forebears did. They sincerely believe that "evil" is the afflatus spawned by the great conspiracy against "good" by Satan and his legion of devils, the lesser fallen angels.

But sincerity, as we know, is not confined just to "good" people. Nor is sincerity the test of validity. Hitler and Stalin and Jack the Ripper and the Inquisitor, Torquemada, were sincere. Nevertheless, the history of conspiracies generated by human beings is long and authentic. Extrapolating, we may safely assume that other sentients, those on non-Terrestrial planets and in other dimensions, must also have their history of conspirators.

The Dungeon series is based on, among other things, a Big Conspiracy. Richard Lupoff's Volume One contained the first hints of it, and Volume Five, by Charles de Lint, develops the idea tenfold. Though there are demons and references to Hell's Sire in this series, they obviously are not the Bible's, Milton's, or Dante's demons. Their origins and motives are based on reality, albeit reality in fictional form. They are flesh and blood, these demons and mysterious powers, and are not immortal. The Great Satan behind this conspiracy (or collection of conspiracies) is not the metaphysical creature invented by ancient theologians.

On the other hand, while previous books in the series did hint at or imply metaphysical situations, Volume Five dives headlong into metaphysical waters. I cannot elaborate without spoiling your sense of anticipation and surprise. You will recognize these excursions into the lands beyond physics when you encounter them. De Lint, I am sure, is not asking the reader to accept the ancient theology on which these episodes seem to be based. He connects the latest thinking of physicists to these theological/mythological ideas. He implies that such concepts as *heaven, hell,* and *limbo,* though presently religious in nature, may become physical in nature.

At one time physicists considered parallel universes and "other dimensions" to be the fantasies of romantic writers. Most physicists in the early twentieth century also regarded travel to the moon and the planets as impossible, as fiction writers' wild and irresponsible imaginings. Nowadays the more progressive physicists are not backwards about recognizing the possibility of such things as parallel universes, other dimensions, and interdimensional travel.

De Lint is saying that the concepts of *heaven, hell,* and *limbo* were derived from real worlds, the nature of which were unknown. The theologians embroidered on these concepts for their own uses. These other-worlds may become, however, much better known. They may someday be classed with the phenomena of black holes, wormholes, cosmic strings, chronons (wave particles of time), and the like. Their true nature will eventually be revealed as quite different from that portrayed by the theologians and metaphysicists.

De Lint includes several original concepts in this novel. If you do not agree with me on their originality, you will at least agree that his use of these concepts is novel. One scene herein raised the hairs on the back of my neck and chilled my skin. This does not often happen to me when I read a story. I hope that you will react as I did.

Another phenomenon accepted as possible in this series is telepathy. My personal attitude toward this, after reading much of the pro and con literature of psionics, is that the existence of telepathy has not been proved. Until it is, I remain a skeptic. If telepathy does

THE HIDDEN CITY ■ 5

exist, I believe it is quite rare, perhaps because very few of us have descramblers for telepathic messages in the receiving part of our brains. Only a tiny minority may have the power to receive, and that talent is probably intermittent and undependable.

Our band of adventurers develop both transmission and reception, the inference being that all sentients have, or have had, this power. Or perhaps, that one of their number is giving them this talent for his or her own (possibly sinister) purpose. There is no doubt, however, that this series is based on the premise that all sentient beings, human or otherwise, share a common substratum of icons and emotions. It also implies that all sentients have a basic need for companionship, affection, and approval. That seems valid to me. Certainly the "higher" animals on Earth share this need with Homo sapiens. It seems likely that not only mankind and the animals, but all sentients and the "higher" animals on their worlds, are born with this need. It is something that evolution or God, whichever you prefer (and you may like both), has endowed life with. Everywhere.

Meanwhile the band struggles against such harsh and cruel perils, both physical and metaphysical, that it is a wonder it has not broken down completely. Its trials far exceed those of rats in a maze or rats presented with seemingly insoluble problems in a laboratory. Alone, its members might go crazy. But they are together, and they share by this time a genuine companionship, affection, and approval. It was not so in the beginnings of their acquaintanceship.

Unlike the man about whom Li Ho wrote, our heroes have not gone mad. Made of stout stuff, reinforced by one another, they keep their sanity. And unlike Ch'u Yüan, they expect answers to their questions. This is in the spirit of my writings, especially those about Sir Richard Francis Burton of my *Riverworld* series. He plunged into the unknown after his involuntary journey into an alien world. He went into the deeper unknown because it was the unknown, and he wished to make it the known. And he not only expected answers to his questions. He demanded them.

We shall see what the answers are in the next and final book of *The Dungeon*.

—Philip José Farmer

▪ CHAPTER ONE ▪

The Dungeon was playing havoc on Annabelle's acrophobia.

Her fear of heights wasn't so much a fear of falling as a reaction against the desperate need that grew, whenever she was perched on some precarious elevation, to throw herself out into space. To simply let herself go tumbling over the edge and then let gravity take control.

And then you hit the ground.

And then you died.

But no matter how surely she knew that to be the logical conclusion, it didn't stop the terror.

In her own world only the small voice of logic, crying out under the unreasoning panic, could stop her from the simple process of shutting down all of her body's motor functions. The trouble with the Dungeon was that, time and again, as they went through the gates separating the various levels, the authority of that small voice of reason eroded as she fell incredible distances— at least through what felt like incredible distances— without physical harm.

Do you see? the heights appeared to ask her. *There was never any harm in just . . . letting go. . . .*

The voice of reason, presented with the irrefutable proof of her constant survival, was rapidly deteriorating.

Perhaps I was wrong . . . , it told her.

And that was more frightening than anything the Dungeon had thrown at her to date, because all that kept her sane when she was caught in the grip of her acrophobia was the knowledge—deeply hidden at times, it's true, but present all the same—that the base instinct of her sense of self-preservation would keep her safe, no matter how ardently the depths beyond her perch called out to her.

Because it *wasn't* safe.

Not for a minute.

It was true that the chance of being hurt was minimal, floating down through a gate as she was now—from the literal hell of the seventh level to who knew what awaited them on the eighth, Finnbogg's pawlike hand gripped in one of her own, Horace's in her other —but what if the next time their adventures took them to some precarious perch? A time when the curious cushioning that existed in many of the gates was absent and gravity merely hungered to draw her down to her death? If her self-preservation didn't cut in, if there was no one to help her . . .

Her boots came into contact with something hard at that moment, cutting off her train of thought with more pressing concerns.

"Heads up," she called softly to her companions. "Here we go again—"

She braced herself, but there was no real need. The surface underfoot was hard as pavement, but they landed as gently as feathers. Then one foot slipped on something greasy. She would have fallen, but Finnbogg and Horace kept her on her feet. The gray gauze of the gate that had blinded their vision as they fell drew away, and slowly their surroundings came into focus. A noxious odor clogged their nostrils before they could really register exactly where this gate had dumped them.

"Smells bad, very bad," Finnbogg said, his bulldog-like features wrinkling.

Annabelle nodded. And if it smelled this foul to her, she couldn't imagine how bad it would be to the dwarf's sharper olfactory senses. She looked down at what she'd slipped on and grimaced at the puddle of vomit that lay there on the pavement.

Pavement? She thought, then looked around.

They stood in an alleyway, brick walls rising on either side of them. There were garbage cans and litter strewn up and down its length. Through the mouth of the alley she could make out a vista of broken-down and burned-out buildings under a sullen sky that reminded her of nothing so much as the South Bronx.

Had they made it home? To the homeworld that she and Horace shared, at any rate?

She moved away from the disgusting puddle underfoot and cleaned her boots as best she could in the refuse spilling out of a garbage can. Her stomach fluttered and an unpleasant taste rose in her throat.

Get ahold of yourself, Annie B., she told herself. You've seen worse.

Good advice, but it didn't make their present surroundings any more appealing. Still, they *were* alive. And at least there didn't appear to be any immediate threat.

She looked at her companions. As she took in Horace, standing there with a shirt wrapped around his waist, a cloak overtop and nothing else, his head shaved bald under the black top hat he was wearing, his mustache and beard gone with his hair, she had trouble suppressing a grin. Quartermaster Sergeant Horace Hamilton Smythe, the queen's own man and at one time, before he was promoted, her many times great-grandfather's loyal batman. Right now he looked like a leftover extra from one of those old Monty Python flicks.

"Christ," she said. "Don't you look a sight."

Smythe wouldn't turn his gaze her way, which prompted Annabelle to realize that she didn't look much better herself. Having lost her shirt, all she was wearing were her boots and black jeans, with her leather-jacket overtop. Unzipped. Which was what was bothering Horace. She zipped the jacket up.

"Okay, Horace—I'm all decent now."

"I wish I could say the same," Smythe muttered, drawing his cloak tighter around himself.

He hadn't landed in the same puddle of vomit as she

had, but he was barefoot. Annabelle didn't envy him that—not here.

"Finnbogg hates this place," their other companion complained. "Hates it bad—not okay."

"Gotcha," Annabelle said. "We'll get moving as soon as the others arrive."

Which should have been only moments after their own arrival. What was keeping them? If Clive and the others had come through the mirror immediately after they had, they should have been here by now.

"I'm starting to get a bad feeling about this," she said. Her companions nodded glumly.

"Only some new danger would have kept Clive from joining us," Smythe said.

"Or some caprice of the gate," Annabelle added grimly.

As soon as she'd spoken, she wished she hadn't. Finnbogg's long look grew longer, the worry in Horace's eyes deepened, while Annabelle had the unhappy thought that simply by voicing her concern aloud, she'd made it real.

"They'll be along real soon," she said.

"Real soon," Finnbogg repeated mournfully.

"Any minute now," Horace agreed.

But not one of them believed it for a moment. Not as time dragged on and there was still no sign of the rest of their party.

"Shit," Annabelle said. "Just when it seemed like we were really starting to get somewhere. . . ."

Now they were back to square one again.

A similar concern for their own missing companions troubled Sidi Bombay.

He and Tomàs had also arrived in a ruined cityscape, also alone. But while the other three had arrived in an alleyway, the Indian and his companion had landed on the roof of a building that towered a good hundred stories into a sky dirty with gray clouds.

On all sides of them spread a panoramic view of the desolate city to which the gate had brought them. They looked out over miles upon miles of blocks littered with ruined buildings, streets overgrown with dense vegetation and choked with the rubble of tumbled-down structures and abandoned vehicles. From their bird's-eye view it all appeared more like a map than an actual center of habitation.

"*Madre de Dios,*" Tomàs said softly, looking over the edge of the roof and down, down, down to the street below. "This is not a place for Annabelle, *sim*?"

Sidi nodded. "Although the real question that comes to me just now is *where* is Annabelle? Where are the others? Why have we arrived here alone?"

"Could they have abandoned us?" Tomàs asked.

"Not through any choice of their own."

"That does not comfort me."

"Nor does it comfort me," Sidi said.

He glanced at his companion to see Tomàs checking his pockets.

"What have you lost?" he asked.

"The pistol I had. That . . ."

"Laser," Sidi said, supplying the word as he remembered the deadly weapon.

"*Sim,*" Tomàs said. "From the Palace of the Morning Star. It is gone."

"You must have dropped it."

"Or it was stolen from me—as the Dungeonmasters stole the white suits from us."

Sidi nodded. "Or it was stolen," he agreed.

He remained by the Portuguese's side for a few moments longer, looking out over the city, then turned away.

"Where are you going?" Tomàs asked.

"To find a way down from this mountain of a building."

Tomàs looked down at the street far below once more, eyes narrowing as he tried to close the distance.

"What if when they arrived . . . ," he began.

"Yes?" Sidi prompted the Portuguese when he hesitated.

Tomàs turned once more from the view and leaned

against the balustrade. "What if there was not a rooftop awaiting them? What if they appeared in the air"—Tomàs waved in the general direction beyond the safety of the roof—"and fell to the streets below?"

"That is a terrible thought, Tomàs."

"*Christo!* Do you think it appeals to me? But we are alone here, we two—*sim*? If the others could come, they would be here with us—*sim*?"

Sidi knew that the anguish in his companion's features mirrored his own. He looked across the cityscape once more, then turned away again. The gravel footing of the roof rattled under his shoes as he made his way across to where a small structure stood.

"If we are lucky," Tomàs said as he caught up to the Indian, "there will be one of those 'elevator' devices such as they had in Dramaran. I do not look forward to walking down so many flights of stairs."

Neither did Sidi. The door in the small structure opened easily at his touch, but inside—whether there had been stairs or an elevator once—there was only a dark well now that descended for as far as they could see. The Indian kicked a piece of gravel down. It bounced against the walls as it fell, but though they listened for a long time, they never heard it land.

"We are trapped," Tomàs said. He looked about the rooftop. "Without food or water or shelter from the elements."

Sidi nodded. "Unless we find our own way down."

"But you can see for yourself—there are neither stairs nor device."

"I said our own way—by which I mean another way."

Tomàs regarded him for a long moment, then slowly shook his head. "Oh, no. You won't catch me trying to climb down the wall like a bug."

"Do you have a better suggestion?"

"*Sim.* We wait to be rescued."

"You said it yourself. We have no food, no water, no shelter. What if we must wait days? Weeks? Can you fast that long, Tomàs? And what if we are never rescued? What then?"

"*Asno*," Tomàs muttered. "I didn't say you were wrong—only that it is *muy peligroso*. Very dangerous."

"I have climbed mountains in the Himalayas, while moving through a ship's rigging is almost second nature to you. I think we are better equipped for the adventure than you believe, Tomàs."

Returning to the balustrade, they both looked down. The building's face was not as sheer as it appeared on an initial glance. There was a webwork of cracks—due to weathering, no doubt. Faint in places, but present all the same for as far as they could see.

"You see? There are handholds," Sidi said.

"For a bug, perhaps."

"We need only go down to the next level. Perhaps we can find a stairwell there that hasn't collapsed."

"And if we don't?"

"We go on until we do."

Tomàs shook his head unhappily.

"I will go first to show you the way," Sidi said.

He removed his shoes and thrust one into each pocket of his jacket, then swung himself over the balustrade, toes reaching for the first series of cracks in the stone that he'd spied when he'd looked down.

"*Buena suerte*," Tomàs said. "You are very brave, Sidi. I will say a prayer to the Virgin that she look after you."

The Indian nodded, knowing that Tomàs meant well. But among his own people a virgin deity was but an aspect of Shiva, and she preferred to see a man make his own way in the world.

"Don't keep me waiting too long," was all he said by way of reply.

Tomàs watched as Sidi inched his way from crack to crack, slowly making his progress away from the roof. In fifteen minutes he had gone no farther than a half-dozen feet. Tomàs imagined the cramps that the Indian would be feeling in his fingers and toes; all the weight of his body—no matter how slight—rested on those frail appendages.

Finally he stood back. He made the sign of the cross on his chest, promised a thousand candles to the Virgin if she would see him through this latest trial, then swung over the balustrade himself.

This was not encouraging, thought the eldest son of Baron Tewkesbury as he studied what there was to be seen of the Dungeon's eighth level.

He and Shriek had also arrived in a ruined city, but while the others had at least come to a place scaled to their own size, Neville Folliot and his companion had landed in a metropolis that must once have housed giants, for the pair were dwarfed by the immensity of their surroundings.

The buildings around them were made of brick. The windows, where they weren't broken, were glass. Vegetation had cracked through the pavement on the streets and sidewalks. Abandoned metal vehicles were scattered the length of the street. But whatever they laid their gaze upon was of such a gigantic scale that the pair had only a mouse's-eye view of it all.

They were no taller than the bricks that made up the walls of the nearest building. The clumps of weeds were small forests. The abandoned vehicles must once have been conveyances for creatures so large that just imagining the size of the city's previous occupants left their heads spinning.

Neville began to get an inkling as to how Jonathan Swift's hero must have felt when he first reached Brobdingnag.

"In a place such as this," he said to his companion, "we'd be considered no more than vermin, scurrying about in the shadows of those who created the place— an unpleasant concept for a peer of the realm."

Shriek regarded him with what passed for amusement on her alien features. *In the eyes of the Dungeonmasters, indubitably we* are *no more than vermin, Being Neville.*

"That, my dear spider woman, is an equally unpleasant concept, made more so by its obvious veracity."

Of more concern to this being is the whereabouts of our companions.

Neville nodded. "We appear to have been deserted."

The Clive Being would not do so willingly.

"That is only your opinion, madam. Myself, I would not be surprised."

Then you show only how little you know your brother.

Neville considered that for a moment, then shrugged. "I stand corrected. And since we are bowing to your wisdom, Mistress Shriek, perhaps you would care to offer a plan of action as to what we should attempt next? Press on? Or wait here for my ever-faithful sibling? I leave the choice up to you and will gracefully follow your decision. However, if I might make a suggestion, it would be to retreat to a more easily defended position for the nonce."

Little about their new environment put him at ease. They were too small, too easily prey to what in their own world would be considered no more than a nuisance. Here even an insect, in the scale of this immense city, could present a danger impossible for them to deal with—Shriek's hair spikes and his own sword notwithstanding.

Imagine a hunting beetle the size of a cart, armor-plated. A bee with a stinger the length of a spear—or worse, a swarm of hornets, each the size of a large dog. . . .

It didn't make for pleasant conjecture, Neville decided.

"Well, madam?" he asked.

Shriek merely regarded him. *I see yet again why Being Clive is of two minds with you.*

"And why would that be?"

But the alien merely shook her head. *I agree with your counsel, Being Neville. We will seek a more advantageous vantage point and make further plans once we have—*

Her mental voice broke off as suddenly as if a switch had been thrown, cutting her off. The sudden silence jolted Neville. He had been studying the height of the lowest step leading up to the monstrous portal of the nearest building. Now he turned to see Shriek standing with her head cocked to one side, listening. One hand of four reached toward the hair spikes that covered her torso.

"What is it—" he began, but he got no further.

Hist, Being Neville. There is danger near. Mindspeak if you wish to communicate. Or else be still.

He couldn't mindspeak, Neville wanted to tell her, but he kept his own counsel this time. His time in the Dungeon had taught him this much: there was danger at every turn. If the alien perceived what he could not, he was more than willing to bow to her superior senses —with all honesty, rather than with the exaggerated civility he had offered her so far that owed a great deal more to sarcasm than to courtesy.

He waited patiently while she scanned their surroundings, his own head cocked. He heard nothing but remained quiet. It was only when the alien turned on him suddenly, upper arms pulling him close to her chest, that he could no longer refrain from speaking.

"Now you go too far, madam!" he protested.

Will you be still?

Her voice rang like thunder in Neville's head. With her lower arms she drew a thick silk thread from her spinnerets and tossed it to the top of the enormous step. No sooner had it attached than she drew herself up along its length, bearing Neville as easily as she might have a child.

Watch, she said when they were safely on the step, drawn back far enough from its lip to still see below.

Her voice was its usual volume now—no louder than spoken words, though for Neville still as disconcerting as having another's voice speak to one in one's own mind would always be. She loosed her grip on him, steadying him when he would have stumbled.

Take care, Being Neville. They are very close now.

Neville nodded. Close enough for him to hear, as well, what had first alarmed his companion. He peered over the edge of the step and looked toward the thicket of weeds from which issued the unmistakable sound of conversation and harnesses jingling. His sword hand drifted to the hilt of his saber, then fell numbly away as the party rode forth.

It was all Neville could do to stifle a cry of amazement.

Fairies, was all he could think to call them.

For they rode on rats—not the scurvy creatures to be found in any dockyard from London to the ports of Africa, but sleek, groomed creatures, their fur a pure white, their harnesses silver and gold, noses and tails the pink of a newborn baby's skin. And the beings themselves—how could he not call them fairies? They were slender, graceful creatures, men and women both in the small company of ten that rode forth; cheekbones high, ears topping to fine points, hair like a waterfall of fine golden fillets held back with jeweled tiaras, eyes dark like deep forest pools; the men in jackets, trousers, and boots all of green, weaponed with delicate épées and bows; the women in gowns like shimmering gauze that clung to their every charm. . . .

What else could they be but fairies?

Except . . . except . . .

They weren't the diminutive creatures of folklore and tale. No matter their appearance, nor their choice of steeds, the company was composed of beings the same size as he himself. Yet if one took in the scale of this city, they *were* diminutive.

As was he.

It all became a little too confusing at times. But this *was* the Dungeon, he reminded himself. Not England. Here the impossible was possible. If he could travel with an intelligent spider, then why could there *not* be fairies here as well, diminutive or not?

You know these beings? Shrick asked.

He turned to his companion and shook his head.

There was a look in your features . . . , Shriek began, then gave a mental shrug. *I still find it difficult to read the faces of your kind.*

Neville opened his mouth to explain the simple *wonder* of what he saw, but the alien laid one of her oddly shaped fingers against his lips.

Mindspeak only, she warned him yet again, but then she remembered that he had yet to be drawn into the neural web of communication that she shared with the lost members of their company. He *couldn't* mindspeak.

Before Neville knew what she was about, she had entwined her fingers with his, and their minds were in contact. More quickly than Shriek would have thought possible, more quickly than any untrained nontelepath with whom she had ever come into such intimacy with, Neville erected barriers between their minds. But the line of communication remained open—a gossamer thread running between them along which Neville sent his thoughts.

Ah, he said in her mind. *Now I see the trick of it.*

You cannot tell me that you are unfamiliar with this process, Being Neville.

I am merely a swift learner, Neville replied.

But to erect such barriers, so quickly . . .

I also value my privacy, madam.

They studied each other for a long moment, each trying to read the other's alien features, neither succeeding in breaching the other's barriers. Finally Shriek gave a mental shrug.

You recognized these beings . . . , she began again.

But then they both realized that during their time on the neural web that now linked their minds, they had been discovered. Two archers stood on the step above them, bows drawn taut, shafts aimed at their hearts. Below, the remainder of the party sat quietly on their mounts, looking upward. One stepped her rat a pace or two from her companions.

She spoke a few words in a completely foreign

tongue that utterly charmed Neville with its sweet, bell-like sound.

"I'm afraid I don't understand you," he replied in the common patois of the Dungeon.

"I asked," the woman replied in kind, "are you aligned with the Ren or the Chaffri?"

Neville and Shriek exchanged worried glances.

We must tell her the truth, Shriek said. *That we belong to neither.*

And what if she does?

What do you mean? Shriek asked.

Does the expression 'our goose will be cooked' mean anything on your homeworld?

I wish Being Clive were here, was all that Shriek could say then.

Looking at the fierce faces of the fairy woman's guard, Neville surprised himself by realizing that he too wished his twin were present. Weighing both their experiences in the Dungeon thus far, he was loathe to admit it even to himself, but for those keeping score— like those damnable Dungeonmasters—so far Clive had met with far more success than ever he had.

Clive had kept his party intact, while Neville had never managed to gather steady companions about himself.

Clive had that damned undefeatable optimism of his that kept him always pushing ahead, no matter what the odds—and what made it worse, his concern in doing so was never so much for himself, but for others. Coming in search of his twin, risking his life time and again for the motley crew of aliens and time travelers he'd assembled about himself . . .

Clive hadn't been reduced to being merely dinner for the Lords of Thunder.

But Clive was nowhere near to help them at this moment.

They had only themselves.

"Has anyone ever told you how radiant you look in that gown?" he asked the woman awaiting their reply below.

She regarded him for a long, cool moment, then made a quick motion with one delicate hand.

"Take them captive!" she told her guards. "But gently. I would question them while they are still in one piece."

What now, Being Neville? Shriek asked.

I believe that in a case such as this, he replied, his gaze never leaving that of the woman below, *discretion would prove to be the better part of valor—don't you think?*

Shriek sent only a wordless grumble into his mind.

Don't care for the Bard, do you, madam?

Don't care for you, Shriek replied.

Only the fact that his hand was clasped around that of his companion told Baron Tewkesbury's youngest son that he wasn't alone in this gray void between the Dungeon levels.

But Clive Folliot was less concerned with his immediate situation than perhaps he should have been. It was true that there was nothing to see—and as little to hear, or taste, or touch, save Chang Guafe's metallic grip in his own—yet he should have been concerned with their destination. The Dungeon was not a place where a man could let down his guard for an instant—not and survive as well. Yet Clive's mind churned with other worries.

As they fell through the gray, flickers of a brilliant blue flashed in his mind—reminding him of that earlier gate they had taken, after which their company split in two. The blue flashes brought him a nagging feeling that he was forgetting something of importance, but they did no more than that. They revealed nothing. They opened no doors in his memory. But they would give him no rest either, teasing and flickering behind his eyelids like torch shadows in the wind, and they quickly brought on the dull beginnings of a headache—an all-too-familiar sensation in the Dungeon.

But when he worked to put that nagging feeling from his mind, he saw instead the chess set placed on the board in the chamber they had so recently quit by stepping through a looking glass. The white pieces had included models of himself and the others of his party, but that was not what had so upset him.

It was the red pieces.

The half of the set that obviously represented their opponents.

It was the fact that among them stood miniature replicas of Sidi Bombay and Clive's current companion, the cyborg Chang Guafe.

Did their presence on the opposing team mean that all along the two waited only the proper moment to betray him? Were they working with the enemy—whoever that mysterious enemy might be?

Clive refused to believe it. It had to be yet another trick of the Dungeonmasters. But still . . . what did he know of either? Guafe was an alien—more so even than Shriek or Finnbogg, to Clive's thinking, for his thought processes were based on cold logic, nothing more. As for the Indian . . . Sidi Bombay remained the same enigma he had been from the moment he had come out of the darkness on that African night so long ago to join his party.

Clive's heart told him that neither would betray him. After all they had been through together, they were his friends now. He would trust them with his life.

Wouldn't he?

Damn these Dungeonmasters for the games they played with his mind. They made a mockery of everything he believed in. They gave lie to so much that it was next to impossible to trust one's own senses.

The pretenders to his twin's name and face that he had met throughout the upper levels of the Dungeon . . .

The vision of his fiancée in the molten pool . . .

The time he had spent reconciling with his father . . .

Lies.

All damned lies.

And now these chess pieces, so casually set out for him to spy.

More lies.

It had to be another lie. For if it wasn't, then who was to say that any one of his companions could be trusted? God help him, could he even trust himself? When he thought of what the Dungeonmasters had already done to Smythe . . . placing the implants in his mind to make him bow to their damnable will, an enslavement that only Horace's constant vigilance could keep at bay . . .

Who was to say they hadn't planted similar devices in each and every one of them? Would he turn on his companions at some moment of crisis? Would Annabelle?

God, he hated the creators of the Dungeon for what they did. To them it was all part and parcel of some complex game. An amusement, nothing more. But for him and his companions it undermined the very basis of their beings. Eroded loyalties. Made a mockery of truth. Challenged every perception.

In a place such as this how was a man ever to know what was true and what was not when he could not trust even himself?

His companion's metallic fingers tightened on his own just then, drawing him back to their present situation. A moment later, as he felt a solid surface under his boots, he realized that Guafe was merely warning him that they had arrived.

They landed in what appeared to be a central square of a large metropolis. Ruined buildings lay all about them, along with the metal shells of abandoned vehicles. Vegetation ran rampant, a jungle of growths that cracked their way through the stonework. Overhead was a dismal gray sky.

Clive blinked as he studied his surroundings. There was something wrong about what he viewed. Not just the desolation of the city—more as though his senses had gone subtly askew.

"It appears," his companion remarked then, "that

the original inhabitants of this place were only half our size."

That was what was wrong, Clive realized. When he looked at the nearest building, its doorway was sized down to a being that had only half his own height. It gave him an odd feeling, standing here as he was, too tall for his surroundings.

"And," Guafe added, "we are also alone."

And so they were. There was not a sign of any of the others who had gone through the looking glass before them.

Clive shot the cyborg a considering glance—Was this the beginning of the betrayal? he couldn't stop from asking himself—then firmly shut that disloyal thought away. He was damned if he'd play the Dungeonmasters' game.

"What could have happened to them?" he asked as he slowly looked about, scanning the deserted streets that led away from the square where they stood.

"Considering the spatial and temporal paradoxes we have encountered thus far in the Dungeon," Guafe replied, "they could be anywhere . . . or anywhen."

Clive's shoulders sagged as the reality of the cyborg's observation struck home. But when Guafe turned to look at him, he quickly straightened himself and gave a brusque nod.

"So be it," he said. "Then our first order of the day will be to discover the whereabouts of the others."

The red facets of the cyborg's eyes glittered as he continued to regard Clive, but he said nothing.

"Do you disagree?" Clive asked him, doubts arising once more no matter how he tried to keep them at bay.

Guafe shook his head. "On the contrary, I can but admire your loyalty to our companions."

"They have earned my loyalty—each one of them."

"Even your brother?"

When Clive thought of his twin, it was difficult to sort through the bewildering battery of conflicting emotions that helter-skeltered their way through his mind. Their differences were many. Neville had treated him poorly—to put it mildly—but he was still Clive's brother, and the more time Clive spent with him of late, the better he was beginning to understand some of what had driven Neville to do all that he had done.

Neville was haunted by his own private demons; the baron had compelled him as much as Clive had driven himself to compete against his brother.

He met the cyborg's steady gaze and finally nodded. "Even my brother," he said.

"I believe I am finally beginning to understand the Dungeonmasters' fascination with your family," Guafe said mildly, "particularly as it is embodied in you."

"I am no one special," Clive said.

"On the contrary, Clive Folliot, from my observations of your race to date, I would consider you very special indeed."

Clive couldn't control the sudden heat that rose up his neck and reddened his cheek.

"Yes, well," he said, "that's all well and fine, but it brings us no closer to finding the others. What can your sensors tell us of this place?"

Guafe remained quiet for a long moment before speaking.

"Simple observation on primary data-infeed levels indicates that this city fell victim to a localized disaster of major proportions—the detonation of a nuclear device, I believe, as I can still detect a faint radiation level —which is no longer harmful, I should add. The site of the blast must have been a few kilometers distant, hence the relative stability of the structures still standing about us. I would place the time frame for the disaster at approximately one hundred and thirty years as you count them. There are no life-forms in the immediate vicinity."

"What of the buildings themselves?" Clive asked. "Do you sense the same—circuitry I believe you named it—as there was in my father's . . . in the building on the previous level?"

"Negative. These structures are devoid of such apparatus. Below, however . . ."

Clive had a sinking feeling. Their worst moments in the Dungeon had inevitably occurred in its subterranean levels.

"Below?" he prompted.

"My sensors indicate considerable activity—electronic as well as mechanical."

"Which means?"

The cyborg shrugged. "Unfortunately there is insufficient data to elaborate further at this moment."

Clive took a last look around at their surroundings— all scaled to half their size. What manner of beings had dwelt here? Humans, such as himself? He wouldn't be willing to wager on it—not with all the varied races they had encountered thus far in the Dungeon. But that wasn't material at the moment. Finding their companions was the first priority. Once they were all together again, they could see about confronting the monsters who had created this hellish place for their own singular amusement.

There were debts to be paid; let the Dungeonmasters take note.

Enormous debts.

And Major Clive Folliot, presently on leave from Her Majesty's Fifth Imperial Horse Guards Regiment, was a man who always paid his debts.

"Below, is it?" Clive finally said. "Then I suppose that we must find a way that will take us underground."

■ CHAPTER TWO ■

"Okay," Annabelle said. "It looks like we're on our own."

Though neither of her companions relished the thought any more than she did, there was nothing either of them could offer to put the lie to her plain statement.

"So what we've got to do now," she went on, "is figure out where we are and what the score is."

"How can there be score," Finnbogg asked, "when is no game?"

"Oh, there's a game all right. We've got the Ren and the Chaffri and Christ knows who else messing about with us. We're working on simple survival, but to them it's all just a game."

"I wouldn't mind some new gear, ma'am," Smythe said.

That brought a trace of a smile to Annabelle's lips. Throughout their adventures the sergeant had always put forth that famous stiff upper lip of the British. But strip him down to not much more than his skivvies, and all he could do was squirm.

"New duds," she said. "Coming right up. Anybody know the way to Macy's from here?" At the blank looks she received from both her companions, she gave a shrug. "Never mind. Let's see if we can't scope out the scene."

Squatting on her heels, she zipped down her jacket far enough to reach the controls of the Baalbec A-9 device that were under the skin in the center of her chest. The computerized implants on her wrist began to hum as she lowered her hand, fingers widespread. On the dirty pavement in front of her, a gridlike map constructed of faintly glowing blue lines appeared.

"City blocks, for as far as the Baalbec can input," she muttered.

Finnbogg watched her with a worshipful gaze but kept his distance. Smythe crouched down beside her. He pointed to a small pulsing spot of light.

"Is that our position?" he asked.

"You got it, Horace. Looks grim, doesn't it?"

"I'm not sure I follow you, ma'am."

"Well, think about it for a moment. Each one of those squares represents a city block—that's, like, maybe a third of a klick, give or take a few meters."

"Klick?"

"Kilometer."

Smythe returned his attention to the map. "I see."

"Right. I've got the Baalbec turned up to max, so we're getting a long-range view of maybe thirty klicks. And this city's just truckin' on off my input range."

"Finnbogg doesn't understand," their bulldoglike companion muttered.

"It's simple, Finn," Annabelle told him. "It means we're smack-dab in the middle of one hell of a big city. For all we know, it could be like this for a hundred klicks in every direction. And if it's all like what we're looking at now—then we could be in deep shit."

"No food, no water," Smythe said.

"No new clothes," Annabelle added with a teasing grin.

Smythe frowned. "This is serious, Annabelle. How can we even begin to find the others in a place this immense?"

Annabelle's smile wilted. "You got me there, Horace."

Finnbogg suddenly lifted his head, nostrils quivering. "Someone comes. . . ."

"Bloody hell," Smythe muttered.

He stood up, trying to keep himself covered while

still maintaining a defensive position. He succeeded only in entangling his cloak around himself.

Annabelle rose to her feet as well. She faced the mouth of the alleyway where Finnbogg was looking, hackles rising at the nape of his neck. Her gaze darted to her immediate left and right, trying to spot something that she could use as a makeshift weapon, but there was nothing. Before she could look further, a shadow moved at the end of the alley and a man was standing there, peering in at them.

Finnbogg growled, deep in his chest.

"Easy," Annabelle said, as she took in the stranger.

He looked like nothing so much as a burned-out wino from her own world, the kind of grizzled, half-starved street bum you could stumble across in any of the major cities. He had a pronounced stoop, unkempt hair, a few days' growth of beard, raggedy clothes that just made his frail frame seem all that much thinner.

"Whoa," the stranger said, carefully holding his hands out in front of him. They were grimed with dirt and webbed with blue veins. "Jake don't want no trouble."

"It's okay, old-timer," Annabelle said as the bum began to back away. "We're all pals here."

The bum froze when she spoke, gaze darting from her to Finnbogg.

"That's some mean-looking dog you got yourself, lady."

Annabelle didn't bother explaining just what Finnbogg was. If they were back on her homeworld, it still made sense to keep a low profile. Let the authorities get their hands on someone like Finnbogg, and Christ knew what they'd do to him. She hadn't grown up on Spielberg films without learning something. The weird and the wonderful always got the raw end of the deal.

"What do you call this place?" she asked.

"You lost, lady?"

"Not a chance. We just came off a binge, is all, Jake,

and we're kinda muddy on exactly where we ended up."

"Well, you're in the Dives, lady. Not a good place for Downsiders, but I guess you already know that. Looks like you already run into some trouble."

"Downside?" Horace asked.

Jake tapped his foot on the pavement. "Under the streets—way down below the tunnels and sewers—where the spiffy folk live."

This didn't sound much like New York or any place in her homeworld, Annabelle realized. Wonderful.

"Does the city have a name?"

Jake shrugged. "Had one, I suppose, but I don't know anybody as recollects it. You folks have any liquid refreshment left, or did you finish it all?"

"Sorry, Jake," Annabelle said. "We're all out."

"Figures. Story of my life."

"Do you know anything about a gate to the next level?" Horace asked.

Jake blinked. "Say what?"

"The next level of the Dungeon—there must be a gate somewhere on this level."

"Shit, I just live here. I don't know diddly about no dungeons or gates or levels. This here's the Dives, mister, plain and simple. Nothing pretty about it, but it's all we got. Easy to get to—just get your ass kicked up from Downside—but once you're here, you're here for keeps. 'Less you got yourself a pass to get back in. . . ."

His eyes took on a considering look as he spoke.

"No passes here," Annabelle told him, "so you can forget trying to roll us."

Jake's gaze drifted back to Finnbogg. "Hell, lady. I didn't mean no harm. We're just talking, right?"

"Just talking," Annabelle agreed. "Is there any place around here we can get some provisions—you know, clothes, food, that kinda thing?"

"Just where the hell are you folks from?"

"Not from the Dives, and not from Downside either," Annabelle said.

"So what else is there?"

"It's a long, boring story. What do you say, Jake? Can you help us out? Steer us on our way?"

"What's in it for me?"

"Our thanks," Horace said.

Jake snorted. "That ain't going to take me far, mister."

"How about we don't let Finnbogg here chew off your leg?" Annabelle asked sweetly.

Finnbogg grinned. "Chew him now—can I, can I?"

Jake did a double take that would have been amusing under any other circumstances, but right now Annabelle didn't want to lose their connection to the only native they'd run into thus far, so she didn't crack a smile. Jake had already mentioned something along the lines of the Dives being a dangerous place. They might be able to avoid trouble if he'd come through for them.

That was if he didn't just take off first.

"Betcha Finnbogg runs faster than you can," she added.

"I . . . I wasn't going nowhere, lady."

"Never thought you were. So what do you say, Jake? Will you give us a hand?"

"Sure, sure. Old Jake's just smack full of charity, you bet. I'll take you round to Casey's."

"Which is?"

He shook his head as though he thought he was talking to a moron. "Casey's, for Christ's sake. What do you think it'd—oh, yeah. I forgot. You're not from around here. It's a club, lady. Won't be much going on there this time of day, but Casey'll be there. You talk to him, and maybe, if he's in a good mood—which ain't necessarily guaranteed, you understand—maybe he'll fix you up."

"Great. Let's go."

"But the thing is, lady, it's still gonna cost you."

Finnbogg growled and took a step forward. The bum went pale, knees visibly quivering.

"Hey, I'm not talking about Jake now. Like I said,

charity's my middle name. It's Casey. He don't do nothing for nothing."

Annabelle and Horace exchanged glances. They had no money—they didn't even know what passed for currency on this level of the Dungeon—and nothing to barter.

"What kind of a club does he run?" Annabelle asked.

"You know—drinks, a little fast food, got some music in the evenings. . . ."

"Well, you can just tell him I'm auditioning for a gig," Annabelle said.

Jake gave her a once-over. "Well, I don't know nothing about music, lady, or how good you'd be at it, but you look like you got the build of a dancer."

Dancer, Annabelle thought. Right. Read stripper. Read Casey was probably a pimp, pushing his "ladies" to make a little extra on the side. Some things didn't change no matter where you went.

"Don't even think about it," she told Jake.

"I never think about things," Jake assured her quickly. "Two things I'm good at—drinking and then drinking some more. I don't want no trouble with anybody, lady—not you or Casey."

"Suits me fine, Jake. Now be a pal and let's get this show on the road. Finnbogg here's getting awfully hungry."

"We're going, we're going. Just follow old Jake and keep that—is that a dog?"

"Close enough. He's a Finnbogg."

"Thought that was his name."

"It is."

Jake looked as though he wanted to work that out, then simply shrugged and set off, Annabelle walking at his side, Horace and Finnbogg bringing up the rear. Jake kept glancing nervously over his shoulder at the latter.

"Relax," Annabelle told him.

Jake nodded. "Sure," he muttered to himself. "Relax. Right. With the teeth on that sucker I'm supposed to relax? All the hell I was looking for was a drink. Plain and simple—no frills, thank you kindly. Instead, look what I got."

"A bunch of new friends," Annabelle said with a sweet smile.

Jake just shook his head. "Christ, I could use a drink. . . ."

The descent was simple.

One merely found purchase for fingers and toes in the narrow cracks that riddled the stone face of the building—clinging to them a thousand feet above the ground—tested each before putting one's weight on it, then reached for another. Yes, Sidi thought, but when one has also been placing the whole of one's weight on such frail digits, and the descent had tortoised as long as it had, difficulty was not the problem.

Stamina was.

Occasionally a wind would rise up, buffeting them where they held to their precarious perches. All they could do then was cling to the cracks and wait it out. Only when the wind died down once more could they continue their descent again.

Above him, Tomàs kept up a steady grumble that alternated between whispered promises to the Virgin and a stream of curses in his native tongue. Sidi might have joined him in either, but he believed that cursing was merely a waste of one's breath, and he was not a religious man—at least not by Western standards. The Indian followed a belief system that was a way of life, not merely a crutch one used in times of duress. Nor did he thank a deity for what he himself had accomplished.

He had been born a Hindu; now he was something else again.

To Westerners any definition of Hinduism remained inadequate, contradictory, and incomplete. But the Hindu Way, while it appeared overtly secular, was still a religion. It comprised a complex combination of religious belief, rites, customs, and daily practices and had given birth to a bewildering number of Eastern faiths that included Buddhism, Jainism, Sikhism, and various schools of tantra and bhakti. To an outsider—particularly a Western outsider—they were all part and parcel of one great heathen belief system; to the practitioner they were the very basis of life.

Sidi was not a good Hindu.

But once he had been. It was due to his wide travels and the contact he had made with the practitioners of other faiths that he had begun to question his blind acceptance of the caste system and other long-cherished institutions of the faith in which he was brought up. He began to realize that his very questioning of that faith reflected a weakness—not in Hinduism so much as in his own ability to adhere to its tenets. Consequently, as the years had progressed, he had drifted more toward a Taoist outlook upon life.

Lao Tzu had said, "The further one goes away from himself the less he knows."

This was more to Sidi's particular understanding of the world than to the faith of his parents. Though he could recall all the teachings by which he had been raised, it seemed to him that a man must work in harmony with the world in which he found himself. Every action had a reaction—some less obvious than others, but no less profound to one who took the time to contemplate them.

Man himself was a microcosm of the larger world about him. As he did, so was it reflected in the world, the depth of his deeds' ramifications dictated by his station in the world. But the leader of a country was no more important than the lowest field-worker; it was merely that the spread of his influence was more readily felt. Neither, Sidi believed, was more important than the other.

So it was that, as he made his descent, he contemplated inner mysteries rather than conducting a conversation of complaints and pleading with a deity. An inner peace stretched within him, allowing him full control of every sense required in the descent, but wrapping him in a state of timelessness so that he came down the building's side without the same strength-eroding anxiety that ate away at his companion.

Which wasn't to say that when he finally reached the window of the story directly below the roof, he wasn't relieved.

Sidi was a human first, subject to all a human's strengths and frailties, and a Taoist second. His belief system merely allowed him to deal more calmly with the problems set before him. It didn't remove them.

As he clambered in the window, he stood for a long moment on the floor inside, apparently motionless as he eased the cramps in fingers and toes, in calf muscles and back, in every muscle. Only then, still stiff but far more comfortable, did he return to the window to help his companion inside.

"Madre de Dios," Tomàs cried as he collapsed beside the window. "Never again will I do such a thing. We are madmen both—do you hear me, Sidi? *Muy loco."*

The Indian nodded. While Tomàs sat there massaging his burning muscles, Sidi went exploring this floor of the building. Tomàs looked up hopefully at his return.

"You have found stairs, *sim*?"

Sidi shook his head.

"Then here I will die," the Portuguese announced.

"I have found some discarded cable that we might use as ropes to lower ourselves to the next floor."

"Cable?"

The Indian nodded. "It's a curious material—composed of many multicolored small fibers encased in a hard rubbery substance—but it seems strong enough to bear a man's weight."

Tomàs lifted his gaze and blew a kiss heavenward. "Truly God is merciful," he said. Then he stood up, groaning at the pain in his limbs. "Show me these cables, *amigo."*

Neville and Shriek descended from that enormous step employing the same process that they had used to reach its upper lip, only this time Neville lowered himself down Shriek's silken strand rather than allowing himself to be carried a second time. When he reached ground level, where the main body of their captors waited for them, he studied the beings with frank regard.

The damned rats truly *were* the size of a horse. As he approached the one ridden by the apparent leader of the small company, he couldn't suppress a shudder at the presence of a rodent that large—tamed or not. The white groomed fur and tinkling harnesses couldn't disguise the disconcerting fact that they were still rats. He ignored the unpleasant feeling by fixing his attention on the creature's rider. Up close the woman was even more beautiful than she had appeared from his earlier vantage point.

"Do you have a name?" she asked.

"Indeed I do, madam. I am Major Neville Folliot, currently on leave from the Royal Somerset Grenadier Guards for the purposes of exploring East Africa. My companion's name is Shriek."

"You have a most military ring to your title."

Neville shrugged. "Then let me set your mind at ease by assuring you that we are merely lost and are trespassing on your company solely by accident."

"It seemed to me that you were preparing an ambush."

"Appearances can be deceiving," Neville said, laying a hand against his heart. "Trust me when I say, we meant neither you, nor any individual of your party, the slightest harm. Hearing your approach, we merely retreated to a more advantageous position. Strangers as we are to this land, we had no way of knowing if it was friend or foe who rode toward us." He glanced about at the archers who still had their weapons trained upon Shriek and himself. "To be blunt, might I add that we are still unaware?"

The woman made a quick cutting motion with her hand, and the archers lowered their weapons. Neville noticed, however, that not one of them relaxed vigilance.

"Your story has the ring of truth to it," she said, "but let me ask you again, are you aligned with the Ren or the Chaffri?"

Shriek replied before Neville could frame a response. *We are aligned with neither, Being.*

The woman's eyebrows rose slightly as she realized that the arachnid was sentient.

"Yet their names are familiar to you—are they not?"

Shriek nodded. *We have only heard of them—from other beings on previous levels of the Dungeon. As Being Neville has already told you, we are lost. We wish only to be reunited with our companions and to journey on to the gate that will lead us down to the next level.*

That's playing one's cards close to one's vest, Neville thought, shooting his companion a sour look.

The woman said nothing for a long moment, merely regarded them both until Neville could feel himself begin to fidget.

"You," she said finally, pointing to Neville, "are obviously of a devious nature."

Neville tensed. Now we're for it, he thought. He wished desperately to see what the woman's guard was doing, but he forced himself to keep a mild look on his features and to meet her gaze directly.

"I like that in a man," the woman said.

Neville relaxed and gave her one of his winning smiles, but she had already turned her attention to his companion.

"Yet," she added, "in our present circumstances I appreciate your honesty more, Mistress . . . ah . . . Shriek, was it?"

The alien nodded. *Shriek is the name this being presently utilizes, yes.*

"We are Tuan," the woman said. "I am the Song of the Wind; my speaking name is Alyssa."

Neither the name she gave her race nor her title meant anything to either Neville or Shriek. But she could easily be a song of his heart, Neville thought.

"A name as lovely as your charms," he said.

Alyssa glanced at him. "Yes, I'm sure," she said. The trace of a wry smile touched her lips. "But be that as it may, I would prefer to address other concerns at this moment. You are the first beings we have come across in this strange land—other than vermin and the like—that are of a similar stature to us. The greater number of the rest have been giants. Our diminutive height has helped us in evading many dangers thus far, but it also hinders our attempts to converse with the other beings we have met."

There was a certain stiffness in the woman's speech patterns as she spoke the Dungeon patois that had Neville wishing he could understand her native language. The bell-like tonality when she spoke in her own tongue had been like music—and utterly suited to her beauty.

We have seen a few giants, Shriek said, remembering the monstrosity on the bridge between the first and second levels and the living-dead Lords of the Thunder in Tawn, *but most have been beings of our own size—as you are. Helpful most of them have not been, no matter what their size.*

"We were snatched from our homeland and brought to this place against our will—can I assume you are in a similar situation?"

"That's exactly our predicament," Neville said. "Torn from our loved ones and left to fend for ourselves in this hellish place."

Alyssa nodded. "Yet for what purpose? All we have been able to discover thus far is that there are two warring factions who use the Dungeon as their gaming ground—the Ren and the Chaffri—but we have been able to learn no more of them except that they exist. They might be humanoid, or they might be"—she glanced at Shriek—"of a more alien appearance, as many of the beings we have encountered here have been; but one thing is certain: we mean no more to them than the pieces on a gaming board mean to us in our homeland."

She paused as though to give either of them a chance

to comment, but Neville was still more interested in the woman's charms at that moment than he was in her dialogue, while Shriek kept her own counsel.

"Are you aware that there may well be a third set of players in this game?" Alyssa finally asked them.

Neville focused on what she'd been saying. "A third set? We don't even know who belongs to which side of the other two. And if you say there are three, then why not four? A half dozen? Or every man for himself?"

The Tuan leader slowly shook her head. "I find it difficult to decide whether you simply *are* the rake you pretend to be, or whether you have some ulterior motive to carry on in such a superficial manner."

Being Neville can be impossible when he wishes, Shriek said, *but I believe, in his heart, he means well. He appears to be one who, when confronted with a situation over which he has no control, either ignores it or makes light of it.*

"Do you trust him?" Alyssa asked.

Neville wished they wouldn't speak of him as though he weren't present, but he said nothing. He too was interested in the arachnid's response.

Shriek turned to look at him, then back at the Tuan leader. *I trust his brother more,* she said. *Being Clive has no secrets.*

"And what secrets do you think I carry?" Neville demanded.

Shriek gave a mental shrug. *Only you would know, Being Neville.*

"I protest," Neville began, but broke off as that wry smile reappeared on Alyssa's lips.

"I too sense a mystery about you, Neville Folliot," she said, "but no danger."

Lovely, Neville thought. She saw him as a harmless crank.

"Shall we join forces?" Alyssa asked.

Our first concern is to find our missing comrades, Shriek said.

"I appreciate loyalty," the Tuan leader said. "Let us compare notes. Perhaps we will be able to help each other. To find missing comrades *and* bring this struggle directly to those responsible for all our troubles."

Being Neville? Shriek asked.

What do you want? he replied so that only she could hear him. *Me to make the decision or merely to agree to yours?*

I thought that since we are companions, of equal stature—the irony in her mindspeaking was heavy—*that the decision should belong to both of us. I believe that we should see if the Tuan can help us.*

Neville regarded Alyssa again and sighed.

"I'd be delighted to join forces with so charming a company," he said, a nonchalant wave of his hand taking in all of the Tuan party, but his gaze resting meaningfully on their leader.

"You are indeed a rake," Alyssa said. "I think I will enjoy the fruit born of this meeting."

Neville lifted his eyebrows quizzically. "How so?"

"I miss companionable banter. My own people are not so comfortable treating me as a woman rather than as their priestess."

Neville and Shriek exchanged glances. Wonderful, Neville thought. To date they'd not done terribly well in their dealings with the various religious groups within the Dungeon. But it was too late to back out of the situation now. Especially considering that the Tuan had the superior numbers.

If only Alyssa wasn't so damned attractive. The way her gauzy dress clung to her . . .

He looked away and indicated the immense structures that surrounded them, each towering monstrously high.

"Is everything so large on this level?" he asked, to change the subject.

Alyssa never looked at the buildings surrounding them. Instead she winked—not coquettishly, but there was a promise in her look all the same.

"That is something," she said, "that I'm sure we will discover, given time."

This was what he wanted, wasn't it? Neville thought. To sample her charms?

Then why did he feel so nervous?

There were benefits to their larger size, Clive realized—a larger size, at least, in relation to their surroundings.

They had followed the length of one long, deserted avenue after another, making a winding course around the abandoned vehicles and rubble, until Chang Guafe brought them to a halt before a wide set of stairs that led underground.

"Ah," the cyborg said. "This will do."

"What is it?" Clive asked.

"The entranceway to an underground transportation system—a railway system, I believe, by the signage."

A railway running under the streets? Clive thought. Well, why not? With all else they had come across thus far in their travels, why should he be surprised at anything the Dungeonmasters had created?

"Of course," he said.

Guafe glanced at him. On his metallic features passed what Clive could only consider a look of amusement—if such a thing were possible—but the cyborg made no vocal comment. Clive turned back to the railway's entrance.

"Underground railways," he added. "Common as dirt, really, in any truly civilized city. Only we do have one small problem. . . ."

Together they regarded the wreckage of the two vehicles that blocked the stairwell halfway down. They appeared to be wedged tightly enough to block any egress the pair might have attempted to what lay below.

"But we have the size now to overcome such a minor difficulty," Guafe said.

"Of course," Clive said, beginning to feel like a windup mechanical toy capable of only a few phrases and actions, which it repeated over and over again.

He glanced back at Guafe, who appeared to be waiting for him to make a decision.

Take command of the situation, Clive told himself.

But he was tired of commanding. One had only to look back a few hours to see how capable he had proved himself thus far—one scrape after another, and now their party scattered God knew where and, yes, perhaps even when.

All thanks to *his* command.

But he was an officer—on leave, it was true, but an officer all the same—and he had never been one to shirk his responsibilities.

"Very well," he said, stifling a sigh. "Let's see what we can do to clear a way through."

It was hard, backbreaking labor, and even with their increased size in relation to the vehicles, it might still have proved impossible without the cyborg's superior strength. It took them the better part of an hour simply to move one of the vehicles far enough away from the other so that Guafe could peer ahead through the gap, using the faint beams thrown by his red-faceted eyes to see in the darkness.

"This appears to be the only obstruction that I can see from this vantage point," he said.

Now they realized the negative aspects of their size. Had their surroundings been of a proper scale, the pair could have made their way through the gap right then. Instead it was another hour's hard work clearing an opening large enough for them both to squeeze through.

The odd red light thrown by Guafe's eyes dimly lit the stairs that continued on past the pair of wrecked vehicles, but Clive shook his head when Guafe was ready to go on.

"I need better light than that," he said.

Back on the street he braided thick grasses together until he had made a number of makeshift torches. Three he thrust into his belt. The fourth Guafe lit for him, creating sparks by hitting his metal forearm against a stone until the dried grass caught. With torch in hand Clive led the way down once more.

The ceiling was close, but they could just walk without bending their heads. The air, the farther they descended, took on a stale quality. Clive's torch spluttered, throwing odd shadows and giving off a thick black smoke. The stairs made two turns before they opened onto a wide platform that appeared to Clive no different from any railway station in his homeland.

Except it was underground.

In a desolate city.

He walked to the edge of the platform and looked down, holding his torch above him. Sure enough, there were two paired sets of tracks, both leading off into the tunnels to his left and right.

Which direction to take?

He turned to his companion, but before he could frame the question, Guafe spoke.

"Quick! Douse your torch."

"What?"

"Can't you hear it?"

"Hear what—?" Clive began, but then he realized what it was that had Guafe worried, as he too felt the vibrations underfoot.

God help them, there was a train coming. Here, under a dead city, a train was running.

They heard its whistle then—not a steam whistle, that friendly, if somewhat lonesome, sound that Clive knew from traveling by train in the English countryside. No, it was more like a quick, short blast of a siren.

Clive ground his torch underheel and withdrew with Guafe just as the engine's headbeams appeared in the distance of the tunnel on their left.

▪ CHAPTER THREE ▪

Jake led them by a circuitous route through the dead
city, keeping to back lanes and alleys rather than the
main thoroughfares. When they did have to go out on a
street, he appeared nervous—shoulders drawn in tight,
head hunched toward his chest as though he were trying to draw his head into his shell like a turtle. Annabelle, taking stock of the general sense of decay that lay
about them, couldn't see what he was worried about.

Sure, there was a lot of rubble on the streets, and
more than one abandoned car, not to mention trucks
and buses, but there was plenty of rubble along the
route they were taking as well.

"What gives?" she asked finally.

That got her another of Jake's anxious looks.

"C'mon," she said. "I'm not going to bite you—and
neither's Finnbogg unless you screw us around—so tell
me straight. What're we skulking through the alleys
for?"

"Don't want to run into any of the gangs," Jake replied. "Most of them're sleeping off whatever the hell
they was up to last night, but you get stragglers, or
maybe some of the Baptists—John J.'s boys, you know
—and ain't nobody with half an ounce of sense wants to
run into any of them."

"Street gangs?" Annabelle asked.

Jake nodded.

"Making sure no one steps it out on their turf?"

"You got it, lady."

"These Baptists—are they a religious bunch?"

She was thinking of the Baptists back home—they

▪ 43 ▪

weren't her style, that was for sure, but they weren't connected to any street gang either.

"John J.'s like the new prophet," Jake explained. "Least he is if you listen to him. They're getting ready for the Third Coming."

"Third coming? Of Christ?"

"Yep."

"What happened to the second?"

Jake waved negligently around them. "Where the hell do you think this mess came from?"

Great, Annabelle thought. That was all they needed —another militant church. But that had always been the problem with people, didn't matter where you found them. Get a few of them together and soon enough they had themselves a religion or were worshiping something. Back home it was pop singers, movie stars, and TV evangelists—at least they ruled the heavens in Western society.

"You belong to a gang, Jake?" she asked.

"Huh! Who'd have an old fart like me? All the gangs want is the strong and the pretty." He shook his head. "What kind of a place are you from, anyway, you don't know that?"

The strong and the pretty? Annabelle thought.

"A place that's maybe not so different after all," she said. "Don't people ever get tired of this 'law of the jungle' bullshit?"

"Not so's I've ever noticed," Jake said.

"Burns my ass," Annabelle muttered.

Jake nodded. "The trick to getting by is you don't get yourself noticed. Mostly the gangs leave us street people alone, but ever so once in a while some guy like John J. gets a hard-on to convert the whole frigging world, and then you've really got to lie low."

It seemed as though he had more to say, but he went no further.

"Or what?" Smythe asked.

He'd been walking close enough to hear them and had been following their conversation.

"Or you really get to know the meaning of hard times," Jake said.

"What do you live on—you and the other street people?" Annabelle asked. "Or even the gangs, for that matter. I don't see anything—not a store, not a market stall, nothing. What do you eat? Where do you sleep? Where do you get your booze?"

"Oh we get by. Downsiders got a dump not far from here, and there's always good pickings there. They'll throw out food ain't hardly been touched. Booze we get out the back doors of the clubs—do the boss a favor and he helps you out. Me, I sweep the floors at Casey's every second night, so I get by. We sleep in any old building that ain't claimed by one of the gangs, and there's plenty of those. Plenty to go around. Ain't that many of us, you know."

"Why's that?"

"We get old, we die. Young kids that get kicked topside join the gangs—some 'cause they think it makes them special like they weren't Downside, others 'cause they figure it's their best chance to survive. But it don't matter much why they choose what they do. Being in a gang means that not many of them survive to my age. Not no more. So you get fewer and fewer street people every year." He shrugged. "That's just the way things go—nothing special about it. It's just life."

"Have you been here a long time?" Smythe asked.

"All my life. Got kicked topside when I was, oh I guess maybe nine or so, and I guess I'm about fifty-three now, so you figure it out. Didn't join no gang—that's what got me into shit Downside in the first place. I just made do. Made do, still do." He shot Annabelle a lopsided grin. "Real hard-luck story, huh?"

Annabelle glanced at him and caught the grin. "I've heard worse."

That sobered him up. "Yeah," Jake said. "Me, too. Heads up—here we go."

He paused in the mouth of the latest alley to point across the street. Astonishingly a red neon sign reading CASEY'S flickered above the door of a nondescript brownstone building that stood there. The door was open and standing just inside, surveying the street, was a tall black man with a physique right out of one of the muscle magazines Annabelle had laughed over in just about every 7-Eleven back home. He was wearing jeans, a T-shirt with the arms torn off and drawn tight across that broad chest, black boots, and shades.

"Maybe this wasn't such a good idea," she said.

If there were more like him inside—just as big and capable looking—and they happened to take a dislike to the three of them, as just about 90 percent of the Dungeon's other denizens had, they could be in big trouble.

"Too late for second thoughts," Jake said.

"That's Casey?" Annabelle asked looking over to where the black man was now waving them over.

"In the flesh."

"Well, boys," Annabelle said to her companions, "let's go check out Mr. Jones."

"Thought you said you didn't know Casey."

"I don't. It was a joke. Casey Jones was a railway man, back where I come from."

"Well round here," Jake said, "Casey Jones is something else again."

The old wino seemed to have lost all fear of Finnbogg and any of them now, Annabelle realized, and that made her bad feeling get worse.

"You coming?" Jake asked as he started out across the street.

Tomàs took charge of preparing the cable for their descent to the next story.

"*Son primo,*" he said when Sidi showed it to him. "It's made of what Annabelle calls 'plastic'—*sim?*"

"I believe so," Sidi replied.

It was a thick braid of hundreds of tiny copper wires, each wrapped in multicolored plastic, the whole encased in another layer made up of a thick black rubberized sheath. The cable was coiled around a large wooden spool, and it took the pair the better part of a half hour to wrestle it to the window. There Tomàs tied the loose end to a support beam that stood firm in the rubble of a nearby wall, using sailor's knots to make sure it remained firm.

To hoist the giant spool onto the low windowsill, they took a pair of long lengths of wood that had once been parts of the building's furnishings and used them as levers. Sweat dripping into his eyes Tomàs gave his companion a nod once they had the spool in place.

"Is there anything below?" he asked.

Sidi leaned over the casement to look down. "Nothing I can see from this height."

"Ahora bien," Tomàs said with a slight shrug that almost cost him his hold where he was bracing the spool, balanced precariously as it was on the sill.

The two of them gave it a mighty shove and stepped hastily back as it went over the casement, out the window, and down. The spool crashed against the side of the building as it dropped, the cable sending up a high-pitched whine as it unwound. Not until it was still and the cable lay taut against the casement did they look out through the window once more to study their handiwork.

The cable swung slightly back and forth below them. They could just make out its far end, some fifteen stories distant. The spool was impossible to spy from their height.

"Now this is more to my liking," Tomàs said.

Sidi nodded. "Like a ship's rigging."

"Un poco," Tomàs replied. "But enough to make our way much easier, *sim*? This time I will go first."

Sidi gave him a slight bow and waved forward. Grinning, the Portuguese hopped onto the sill where he clasped the cable between his hands.

"Do not go too fast, *amigo,*" Tomàs warned his companion.

Sidi nodded. One didn't need time in a ship's rigging to learn about rope burns.

"I will see you below," Tomàs said.

Still grinning, he began to slide down the cable,

slowly at first, but soon quickly enough for Sidi to grow nervous.

The man knew what he was doing, he told himself as Tomàs gave a happy shout from below. He swung over himself and began to swarm down, not so quickly as the Portuguese, but quickly enough so that Tomàs wouldn't be kept waiting when he reached the end of the cable.

This was, Sidi realized, the first time he'd seen Tomàs truly happy—despite the gravity of their situation. Undoubtedly because he was finally in a position where his own expertise could be brought into play.

Was that not a most human of human traits? All men and women wished to be considered of some worth— to see themselves respected in the eyes of their peers. It was a basic need that perhaps only monks could set aside.

'Let him be happy then, Sidi decided. Let Tomàs take the lead for a while. And who knew? If he truly had Folliot blood in him, it might well make the difference between success and failure for them all.

Alyssa proved to be as charming a host as any London gentlewoman, albeit her drawing room was but a small glade in a thicket of weeds—weeds that rose like trees around the small company.

Neville didn't much care for the sheer *oddness* of the immense buildings and gargantuan growths of even the commonest plant on this level of the Dungeon. The disparity between his size and that of his locale threw off his sense of perspective. Had he not had Alyssa's pleasant company, he would undoubtedly have been far more irritated than he was by the sense of insignificance with which his enormous surroundings left him.

But he did have Alyssa's company, and while she seemed overly flirtatious for a priestess, who was he to complain? Dungeon or no Dungeon, one did not look a gift horse in the mouth—especially when it arrived in such an attractive package as the leader of the Tuan.

Alyssa. Song of the Wind.

What exactly did her title mean?

As she introduced Neville and Shriek around, the litany of names—Maraja, Tuis, Fenil, Tama, Whies, and the like—all blurred in Neville's mind. The women—of which there were three all told, not including Alyssa—greeted the pair of them warmly, but the men—especially Yoors, the tall, cloudy-browed captain of Alyssa's guard—continued to regard them both with suspicion.

While the guards saw to their mounts, the ladies set out a meal that wasn't quite the fairy repast of elfin cakes and mead served in acorn cups that Neville had been half expecting, but was still welcomed by his growling stomach. Shriek politely tasted the various dishes that were set out, but she ate little.

"You have no appetite?" Alyssa asked.

I have a . . . shall we say different metabolism from your kind, Shriek replied.

"She eats flies," Neville said with a grin.

The Tuan women grimaced and hid smiles, but Neville didn't miss the flicker of—what? Disappointment, perhaps, that he saw in Alyssa's eyes.

It was a fair call, he realized. Mocking one's companions was scarcely a gentleman's behavior, whether it be at home in London or in this damned Dungeon.

"That was a bad joke and in poor taste," he said.

I'm sorry, he added privately to Shriek. *I wasn't thinking.*

You rarely do, the arachnid replied somewhat bitterly.

Neville nodded. *I deserved that.*

But if Shriek wasn't so quick to forgive, he was still rewarded by a smile from Alyssa.

"So," he said, deciding to lead the conversation onto safer ground. "Do you lead a nomadic life? I couldn't help but notice the packs your . . . ah, mounts are carrying. You seem well equipped for a mere afternoon outing."

"We call them silvers," the Tuan leader said.

"Pardon?"

"Our mounts. We call them silvers. And no, they bear no relation to the vermin that invest this city."

"I wouldn't think so," Neville said. "But to return to my question . . ."

He thought of what folktale collectors called the Trooping Fairies, for he still couldn't divorce his hosts from the magical beings that had peopled the stories of his childhood. But then what did that make Shriek and himself, when they and the Tuan were all of a size?

Perhaps, he thought with a half smile, Shriek and he had stumbled into Fairyland. Perhaps that was what the Dungeon was, and the men who disappeared for a lifetime in what was only a day in the real world had merely been trapped in the Dungeonmasters' games.

Reminded of their captors, he turned his attention back to Alyssa, who was far more pleasant to consider.

"Do you lead a wandering life?" he went on.

"Oh, no," Alyssa began. "We—"

Yoors, the captain of her guard, cut her off—politely, but firmly. "My lady, please. They are strangers. We know nothing of them."

Neville had been watching the man throughout the meal, growing progressively more annoyed with the man's all-too-obvious suspicion.

"Must we go through this again?" Neville demanded.

He stood up from where he sat with the ladies and faced the captain. Yoors's clouded brow darkened, and he put a hand to the hilt of his weapon as he rose to his feet as well.

Neville caught the movement. "Are you threatening me, sir?" he asked, his voice suddenly mild.

Neville, don't! Shriek sent to him.

You keep out of this, he told her. *This is between the good captain and myself and doesn't concern you.*

He returned his attention to the Tuan captain.

"I am warning you," Yoors said. "You are strangers, and until you prove yourselves, you will remain un-der—"

"I don't think I care for you," Neville said.

A thin, humorless smile settled on Yoors's lips. "Nor I you."

Neither of them saw Alyssa rise to her feet, and they only half heard her when she spoke. "I think this has gone quite far enough—the two of you, strutting like a pair of cockerels—"

"On the contrary, madam," Neville murmured. "We have only begun this discussion."

His sword hand came smoothly up to rest on the hilt of his saber, but before he could draw the blade, Shriek's voice resounded so loudly inside his head that he had to clasp his hands to his ears.

This is not the time!

He turned toward her. "Will you keep out of this!" he shouted.

There is danger—approaching rapidly.

That sobered Neville instantly. *Where? What?*

Before Shriek could reply, Neville felt a hand grip his arm. He was spun around and found himself face-to-face with Yoors—the Tuan's face inches from his own.

"No one turns his back on me until I—"

Neville slapped the hand from his arm. As Yoors reached for him again, Neville delivered a roundhouse blow to the man's chin that felled him on the spot.

Around him Yoors's men armed themselves. Arrows were suddenly notched to bowstrings. The ladies stepped back from the central part of the glade where they had been sitting with Neville, except for Alyssa who stood her ground and regarded him with studied worry. Neville lifted his hands—palms out.

"That was between the captain and myself," he said. "Before you act rashly, my companion"—he nodded to Shriek—"warns me that we have more pressing concerns."

This had better be good, he told her.

Some kind of dog approaches, Shriek said, broadcasting widely enough so that they all could hear.

"Are you sure?" Alyssa asked.

Reasonably. Is this bad news, Being Alyssa?

"Among the worst." She turned to her people. "Swiftly—mount up!"

Neville wondered a moment at the panic that ran through the Tuan, then he realized its source. If the approaching dog was of a similar scale to the city, then they had a very serious problem indeed.

He reached down to offer Yoors a hand up. The captain gave him a baleful glare, then took his hand. Neville pulled him quickly to his feet. In moments the Tuan were all mounted.

"Neville!" Alyssa cried, waving him over to where she bestrode her silver.

No one offered Shriek a ride, he noted, but the arachnid had already scuttled in amongst the treelike weeds. She stood hidden there, a hair spike in each hand.

Neville ran toward Alyssa. There was a crashing in the air—the sound of some huge thing pushing its way through the weeds—and a faint rumble underfoot. Neville saw Alyssa's eyes go wide and knew he was too late to escape with her.

"Go on!" he cried to her. "Ride on!"

Then he turned, saber filling his fist, to face the monstrosity that burst forth into the glade.

In the scale of the city it was no more than a small mongrel dog—part terrier, at least, though who knew what made up the rest of it. Half-starved. A feral glint in its eye. A dirty, mostly harmless thing that a man would kick away from his heels without much of a second thought.

To Neville the damned thing was at least the size of two elephants, and he knew he hadn't a chance in hell standing up against the thing armed with only his saber. It was like a mouse attacking a cat with a sewing needle for a sword.

No point in running. The monster would have him before he took two strides.

So. It was stand and fight.

The creature paused at the edge of the glade, snarling at him. It was probably puzzled, Neville realized, as to what something as small as he was doing, standing up to it.

"Come on, then!" he cried.

Oddly, Neville found himself thinking of his brother as he prepared to defend himself. I hope fate's treating you kinder than it is me, little brother, he thought.

Then the dog attacked.

Clive had his own troubles.

Hidden in the shadows that pooled deeply at the edges of the station's platform was another tunnel, much like that leading from the stairwell that they had descended, only this one maintained an even level. By the dim red light thrown by Guafe's eyes they could just see a half-dozen yards down the tunnel until it turned a corner. They had to bend their heads slightly to get inside, but there was room enough, and Clive felt that they could easily escape discovery.

Unless, of course, the riders of this underground train had this particular tunnel as their destination.

He turned to voice that concern to his companion, but then the train roared into the station. The noise of its entrance killed all hope of conversation.

Clive stared openmouthed at the machine.

It was nothing like the railways back home in England. In design it was sleek and streamlined. The engine appeared to be fueled by something other than wood or coal—in fact Clive doubted that it was a steam locomotive at all.

It pulled three passenger coaches. As soon as the train stopped, spotlights lit up on the roof of each car, flooding the station with a light so bright that Clive had to withdraw from his vantage point, rubbing at his eyes.

But he'd had time, before pulling back into the tunnel, to see the coaches unload their cargo. Men in baggy white suits with some form of glass containers enclosing their heads—How did they breathe? he wondered—and large backpacks.

"Spread out, men!" an authoritative male voice called out. "They can't be far."

He spoke in the patois of the Dungeon—strangely accented, it was true, but similar enough so that Clive and Guafe could understand what he said. The tonality of the voice had a hollow sound to it—as though it were speaking through an intercom such as Clive remembered from the lost city of Dramaran.

"That," Clive said, "is our cue to see where this tunnel leads us."

"Too late for that," the cyborg replied.

Clive gave him an odd look, but then realized that the mouth of the tunnel was filled with a number of the white-suited men. Some of them held what were obviously weapons. One pointed a device at them that was connected to a small metallic box attached to his belt. The box emitted a high-pitched clicking sound.

"Look at the size of them," one of the men said. His voice also had a hollow sound.

Size? Clive thought. But the man was right. Guafe and he were twice the size of these men.

Guafe linked his fingers with Clive, reestablishing the telepathic bond that Shriek had awoken in them all. *Do we stand and fight?* he asked.

Do you recognize the weapons they are carrying? Clive replied.

They appear to be sophisticated hand-held lasers. I would need a closer inspection of their actual specifications before committing myself to more at this point.

Deadly?

Yes—I believe we can assume so.

Perfect, Clive thought. First they had become separated from the others of their party, now they were being menaced by a band of midgets. Or perhaps—since they were underground—he should call them kobolds.

Clive held his hands out in front of him, meaning it as a peaceful gesture. The little men all scrambled back a few paces.

"We mean you no harm," Clive told them.

At that moment another of the little men arrived—one to whom the others all deferred. Obviously their leader, Clive decided. He cleared his throat to speak again, but the man ignored him, turning instead to the one with the clicking box attached to his belt.

"Readings?" he asked.

"Well into the red, sir."

The leader finally turned to look at Clive and Guafe. "You'll have to come with us," he said.

"Who are you?" Clive demanded. "What do you want with us?"

"I'll answer whatever question I see fit to," the leader said, "but only after you've been through the decam process."

"With what are we supposed to be affected?" Guafe asked.

"Radiation."

The cyborg shook his head. "Impossible. My own readings put us well within the strictest safety zone."

"Then your calibrations are off, 'borg." He looked from Guafe to Clive. "Will you come peacefully, or will you have to be sedated?"

Clive reached for his companion's hand again so that he could speak privately to Guafe through the neural web.

Sedated? he asked.

They want to put us to sleep.

Clive frowned. "We'll come peacefully," he said to the leader of the little men. *At least this way we'll have a chance to attempt a later escape,* he added to the cyborg.

Guafe gave a mental nod. *And they might have word of the others.*

I hadn't thought of that, Clive said.

"Glad you made the sensible choice," the leader of the little men told them. "Now if you two pussies would like to just stop holding hands and come out of that tunnel—nice and slowly now—we can get on with the business at hand."

Pussies? Clive asked.

Apparently some form of derogatory remark. The impression that I can gather is that he believes we are lovers.

Clive let go of his companion's hand as though he'd been gripping a hot coal.

"I'll thank you to keep your insults to yourself," he told the leader of their captors. "I'm an Englishman and a gentleman and a member of Her Majesty's Fifth Imperial Horse. I do not appreciate any insinuations as to my sexual inclinations."

"You'll thank me?" the leader asked. "How about I thank you to just shut up and do what you're told—think you can handle that?"

"We are your prisoners," Clive said stiffly. "Do we have a choice?"

The man shrugged. "First you get decammed, then we'll figure out your status, pal. Now let's go."

· CHAPTER FOUR ·

"Well, now," Casey said as Annabelle and her companions crossed the street to where he was standing. "What've we got here?"

He lounged against the doorjamb of his club's entrance and gave them a sleepy look over the tops of his shades. Real casual attitude, Annabelle thought, but she wasn't fooled for a moment. Behind that lethargic gaze the club owner was giving them a hard once-over, no ifs, ands, or buts about it.

"New blood?" he added.

Annabelle nodded. "I guess you could say so."

She started to add to that—just to get things onto a footing where they all knew exactly where they stood —but then the music spilling out through the open door behind Casey stole away her attention. It was very familiar music—at least it was to anyone like Annabelle, who was up on that San Francisco sound from the late sixties that had a revival every decade or so. Guitar, bass, keyboards, and drums, playing a clean, old-fashioned kind of pop with that touch of psychedelia that the old players had told her was impossible to duplicate unless you'd been there in those days of flower power and free love and all that hippie shit. A woman singing overtop about a pill that could make you big, a pill that could make you small . . .

"Who you got playing in there?" she asked.

Casey shrugged. "New band—just up from Downside."

"They sound just like the Airplane—way back before they became the Starship."

"Don't know about no Starship," Casey said, "but we got the Airplane here tonight—no question about it."

Of course they couldn't be the real thing, Annabelle thought. No way. But it was weird how well they mimicked the real Jefferson Airplane from her own homeworld. She could swear that was Grace Slick singing, Marty Balin backing her up on the choruses, Paul Kantner and the rest of the band. . . . She had a DAT tape of a live gig of theirs, circa 1968, and damned if this didn't sound like a tune pulled right off that tape.

Course, this was the Dungeon, wasn't it? Anything could happen, right?

But the Jefferson Airplane playing in some hellhole of a club that looked as if it was set in the South Bronx?

Well, why not, Annie B.? She thought of Wrecked Fred. If only he were here. Wouldn't he get a kick out of *this*.

Then she thought about what she was saying. If only Fred were here? Christ, the guy was back home, where they all should be. Where she *could* have been if it hadn't been for Finnbogg.

She shot the dwarf a dirty look before turning her attention back to the club owner.

Casey gave her a toothy grin. "You're here kinda early for the show. Why don't you come back when it gets dark?"

At the same time that he spoke, the band hit the line about Alice being real small, and Annabelle realized just what song it was that they were playing. "White Rabbit." Right. Alice's adventures in psychedelia. Hard on the heels of their just stepping through a looking glass to get to this level of the Dungeon.

This was just too much of a coincidence.

"They're not here to catch the show," Jake said. "Lady wants to audition for you. She and her pals are looking for some food and gear and want to pay with an act."

Casey gave the three of them another long look. His gaze lingered on Smythe holding his cloak together with a dirty fist, his bare legs coming down from under it, bare feet on the pavement; Finnbogg almost as wide as he was tall with his mouthful of big teeth, set off by a pair of enormous lower incisors; Annabelle herself, decked out in her leathers.

"We're strictly a music establishment," he said. "Maybe you should check out some of the other clubs in the Dives."

"What the hell's that supposed to mean?" Annabelle demanded.

"Just what I said. I don't see no instruments, lady, and we don't offer any other kind of gigs here. Our clientele's into music, plain and simple. Do I got to spell it out any clearer for you?"

Annabelle had to laugh. When she thought of her initial fears about running into some pimp trying to get her on his string, it all had a certain feel of justice about it. Karma. She was putting the guy down before she'd ever met him, and here he was laying a trip on her because he thought the three of them had some kind of kinky sex act going.

"You mind sharing the joke?"

Annabelle shook her head. "You had to be there," she said. In my head.

"Yeah, well I got things to do."

He started to turn, but Annabelle caught his arm.

"Look," she said. "Everything's gotten off on the wrong foot. We've hit some hard times, and we could use a little help. My friend here needs some new gear, and we could all use a meal—not to mention some directions outta this place. I'm a singer, and a damned good one—at least that's what they tell me back where I come from. Can you use an opening act?"

Casey shook his head. "Getting outta Downside's real easy. Going back down's a whole other thing."

"We're from a little farther away than this city— Downside, Topside, the Dives, whatever part of it you want to name."

"Just where is it that you're from?"

"Can we talk inside? I'd sure love to get a peek at this band. They're like history where I come from."

Casey lowered his shades. His eyes narrowed as he studied her again. "Are you talking about the US of A?"

Annabelle nodded.

That got her another toothy grin. "Well, shit—why didn't you say so in the first place?" He stood aside to make room for them in the doorway. "C'mon in."

That easy? Annabelle wondered. But she took him at his word and went on inside. Smythe and Finnbogg hesitated a heartbeat longer, then followed.

"Ain't that something," Casey said, taking up the rear with Jake. "Finally we got ourselves another American."

The cable ended halfway between levels. Tomàs climbed back up it to the windows of the previous level and sat dangling his feet over the window ledge while he waited for Sidi to reach him. The Indian arrived in short order and took a seat beside his waiting companion. Gazing down, he saw that the street was still some forty stories below them.

"Have you looked for a stairwell?" he asked.

Tomàs shook his head. "I got here just before you, *amigo.*"

They sat in silence for a few moments, studying the city—a great deal of which was still spread out below them from their perch. The taller towers were more to their rear. In front of them was an area of the city that appeared to have suffered some catastrophe, as many of the structures had fallen in on themselves to make a rolling cityscape of stunted buildings and rubble. If they looked from left to right, they could see that their building was on the edge of that area of desolation.

"They're like mountains, these buildings," Sidi said.

Tomàs nodded. *"Sim."* He pointed in front of them. "And there are their foothills."

Sidi stood. He stretched a kink out of his neck and looked into the building. He made no move to enter.

"Where to now?" he asked.

When Tomàs looked up in surprise, Sidi kept his features bland. To let the Portuguese know why he was pushing him to take command would defeat the whole purpose of the exercise.

"Where to?" Tomàs replied.

Sidi nodded. He watched as Tomàs stood beside him, his carriage straighter, a more assured look in his eye than he'd had at any other point during their journeyings through the Dungeon.

"We look for a stairwell," Tomàs said. "Or more cable —*sim*?"

Sidi smiled. *"Sim,"* he said.

It was darker inside this level of the building than it had been above. Although the sun remained invisible behind the gray sludge of clouds outside, the day was lengthening. Light leaked steadily from the sky, deepening the shadows inside.

"We could use a torch," Tomàs said.

Sidi nodded. "Or Chang Guafe's eyes."

They moved away from the window, deeper into the building, then both men froze. Something was moving in the darkness ahead of them.

In a situation such as this discretion was the greater part of valor. Neville firmly believed that. It was only plain common sense that a man retreat from certain failure if he could. On the other hand, the elder Folliot was no coward. With his back up against a wall and no place to run, he could be as fierce as any lioness defending her litter.

So as the feral dog charged him—surely the monster weighed in at three tons—he held his ground until the last possible moment. Not until the monstrous jaws were almost upon him did he dart to one side, slashing with his saber.

The creature's teeth snapped on air. A shrill, ear-piercing yelp arose as the saber cut across its nose. The dog cut away, shaking its head. Blood sprayed.

Neville gave a quick glance to where the mounted Tuan watched from just within the shelter of the tree-like woods surrounding the glade.

Too far for him to make the attempt to reach them.

The dog's hackles rose, and a rumbling growl came from deep in its chest—loud enough to be mistaken for thunder. Neville circled slowly, feeling like a mouse-sized matador in a normal-sized bullring, all advantage lying with his gargantuan enemy.

It wants but one thing, Neville thought with black humor. For dinner this evening, not beef Wellington, but Folliot Wellington. Served fresh. Utilizing only the finest ingredients, of course.

The dog paced his every movement, drawing closer with each step. Blood still dripped from the wound on its nose, but it paid no more attention to the injury. All its awareness was focused on the insect-sized creature that had stung him.

"I don't suppose you could do me the favour of bleeding to death?" Neville asked the creature in a mild voice.

The dog charged by way of reply.

Uncertain as to its intelligence Neville wasn't about to experiment at this moment by repeating his earlier trick. This time he charged as well, a bellow rising up from deep in his own chest, saber swinging. Paltry though the noise was, and for all the small target he made, the dog was thrown off by his attack.

It changed its mind halfway through its charge and tried to duck away.

Well, wasn't it said that mice frightened elephants? Neville thought.

Instead of backing off himself, he continued his own attack, getting close enough to cut one hind leg as the monstrous dog scurried aside. It yelped again—and then again.

The second cry surprised Neville until he saw that Shriek had come to his aid. Three of her hair spikes sprouted from the creature's muzzle. Given Shriek's command of biochemistry, Neville didn't doubt that she had adjusted the spikes to carry their maximum poisonous effect—but with the animal's great size, they did no harm. Yet they were enough to disconcert the dog some more. Then the Tuan guard came riding up

at Alyssa's command, circling the creature on their
silvers like some bizarre absurdist's portrayal of elfin
bedouin.

They fired arrows from the saddle until the creature's head literally bristled with shafts. It yelped at the
prick of each tiny shaft, shaking its head to and fro,
snapping at the elfin riders. But now one shot took the
creature in the eye—it would have to be from Yoors's
bow, Neville noted sourly—blinding it on that side.

Howling, the enormous terrier fled off through the
weeds.

"That's done it!" Neville cried, brandishing his saber
above his head. "We've got it on the run now."

Alyssa pranced her silver near him.

"Quickly!" she cried. "To mount."

"But we've chased it off," Neville said. "What's the
sudden hurry?"

Before the priestess could reply, a series of howls
rose up from every side.

"Because," Alyssa added to the sound of the pack,
"these dogs never hunt alone."

Of course not, Neville thought. Of course bloody not.

He sheathed his saber. Taking a running jump toward her mount, he leapfrogged onto its back. A moment later he had his arms around the priestess, the
firm pressure of her back against his chest. This close to
her his nostrils filled with the scent of apple blossoms
and roses that hung about her. Strands of silvery hair
tickled his cheek.

If only, Neville thought, he could relish her proximity without the nag of more pressing worries, such as
simple survival. If they did survive, he'd allow himself
that luxury. Until then . . .

Mistress Shriek, he called out on the neural mind-
web he shared with the arachnid. *Can you keep up
under your own locomotion?*

Have no fears for me, Being Neville, she replied.
There was a moment's pause before the alien added,
But I thank you for your concern.

The howls grew louder. No—they were simply closer.

Alyssa kicked her heels against her silver's flanks, and the whole company was off, darting through the gigantic forest of weeds like so many shifting shadows.

Inside the train coach there was no sense of motion. Nor could Clive hear a sound except for those that he or his captors made as they shifted in their seats. The interior of the coach had only two long benches along either wall by way of furnishings. Clive and Guafe sat against one wall, their captors across from them. Illumination was provided by overhead lights encased in long glass banks. The windows had been opaqued so that nothing outside the coach could be seen.

The little men kept their distance. Their unfamiliar weapons remained trained on both Clive and his companion, but they refused to converse, for all Clive's attempts to draw them out. When he looked at Guafe, the cyborg appeared to have shut down his systems, leaving Clive with only his own thoughts for company on the journey.

It was pointless to speculate on their captors' motives, he soon realized. The principal difficulty in attempting to second-guess any being he met in the Dungeon, no matter what level, had been brought home to him long ago. Each group of beings had such alien mental processes—no matter how close their resemblance to people of his own world—that any conjecture was futile. All that tied each diverse element of them together was the Dungeon itself . . . and the underlying thread of a plot that appeared to exist solely to confound his family.

It was at that moment that he realized that each group of their original party to have gone through the looking glass had in its number one member of the Folliot family—that was, if Annabelle's suspicions of Tomàs's origins were indeed correct.

But surely they had chosen who would go with whom on their own?

It had seemed so, but now Clive felt that it was not merely an unhappy coincidence. Coincidence, as such, did not appear to exist in the Dungeon. Once again he perceived the hand of the Dungeonmasters at work. How they had manipulated the choices, he couldn't begin to guess, but work it they must have.

How did the others fare? Had they arrived together in one place, or were they now scattered in four separate parties, in God alone knew what difficulties of their own?

Considering their ill-fated trials to date, it was no doubt the latter.

He wished that the neural web in which Shriek had initiated them could operate without the need for physical contact. He didn't need such contact to communicate mentally with Shriek. He had tried to reach her numerous times since arriving through the looking glass to this world—as he had been able to do on the previous level—but there was simply no reply. It was as though the bond between him and the arachnid had never existed.

Or worse—as though something had happened to the others. Something worse than the fix he and Guafe were in at the moment. If he could just reach out to touch the arachnid's mind, or Annabelle's—if he could at least know that they were safe—it would make his own captivity that much easier to bear. But as it was, he had to consider not only how to extract Guafe and himself from their present predicament, but also how to gather the rest of them together once more.

The task—from his present perspective—appeared hopeless. No doubt whenever they arrived at their destination, they would be confronting yet another replica of his brother Neville. Or of his father. Clive ground his teeth together. If only it could be the Dungeonmasters themselves. If he could be allowed but a few moments alone with them, a good sword in hand, he'd have the damned truth out or he'd cut out their—

The leader of what Clive had named—in his own

mind—kobolds entered the coach at that moment, breaking off what had begun of a very pleasant fantasy.

"Well, sweethearts," the leader said. "End of the line."

Beside Clive, Guafe became functional once more. He stood up, the red facets of his eyes glittering. Clive rose to stand beside him.

"Who are you people?" he asked the leader. "What do you want with us?"

"We're real people—not freaks."

Clive glared at him. "We are not—"

"Just shut up and do what you're told, and we'll all get along fine—okay?"

Clive took a step toward him but immediately stayed his advance when the kobolds brought their weapons up. The shift from casual guarding positions to those of a more threatening nature was swift as thought. Clive stood stiff and straight, hands clenched at his side.

"Attaboy," the leader said. "Just come along nice and easy."

They were led from the coach onto another platform, but this one bore no resemblance to the deserted station where they'd first boarded the underground train. The area was lit with blindingly bright lights set in the ceilings. The surface of the platform was so polished it gleamed. More of the little men were waiting for them—all in the white suits with the glass bubbles on their heads.

From the platform they were taken down a long corridor that eventually brought them into a small square chamber.

"Strip," the leader told them.

"I protest," Clive began, but a weapon aimed at his face quickly stilled him.

"Just strip."

Clive turned to his companion, but Guafe was already removing his clothes. Face hot under the kobolds' stares—especially that of the leader who stood watching with a smirk on his lips—Clive followed suit. When they were both stripped down, the kobolds collected their clothing and retreated back into the corridor. A door slid out of the wall, locking Clive and Guafe in the chamber.

"God in heaven," Clive muttered. "What kind of men are these?"

Guafe merely shrugged. He took a seat on the floor, back against the wall, and shut down his systems again.

"Thank you for your companionship," Clive told him.

The cyborg gave no response.

Clive prowled the confines of the small chamber, starting back in alarm when a cloud of gas began to issue from the ceiling. In moments he grew drowsy and had to sit down himself. His head began to spin once he was seated. He put it between his legs and tried to breathe as shallowly as possible, but the gas was already in his lungs, coursing through his blood system.

What an ignoble fate, he thought. He hoped the others had managed to escape the kobolds' clutches—though knowing the Dungeon even as little as he did, they could well be in worse straits.

He tried again to stretch the neural web that he shared with Shriek and the others, calling out to them. As his consciousness began to slip away, he thought he could hear someone returning his mental cry.

Clive. Clive . . . ? Can you hear me, Clive . . . ?

Just as the darkness took him, he realized that the voice was very much like that of his old friend, George du Maurier.

· CHAPTER FIVE ·

The band looked just like the old vids that Annabelle
had seen of them—except they were onstage, front and
center and big as life, not squeezed down onto a vid
screen, the image flickering with imperfections. Slick
and company had begun another song—one Annabelle
didn't recognize—but that psychedelic sound remained, augmented with visuals now because there
was a screen in back of the band on which colored
patterns kaleidoscoped liquidly in time to the music.
And the band, just cooking with that old-time music . . .

"Jesus," Annabelle said softly. "Talk about a time
warp."

Smythe nodded beside her. "Warped, indeed. It's
ghastly."

"You're jiving me—right, Horace?"

Her however-many-times great-grandfather's companion just blinked at her.

"You *like* this . . . noise?" he asked finally.

Annabelle shook her head, dismissing him. Instead
she drank in the sounds that came from the stage. Her
fingers twitched, looking for the neck of her Les Paul
as she watched the band play. It was long moments
before she could pull her attention away to take in the
rest of the club.

It wasn't much different from a hundred others she'd
played in New York, LA, London, or any place in between. It was dark, the walls covered with old band
posters. Small round tables, three or four chairs to each,
were scattered across the floor. There was a dance floor

in front of the stage. A bar along one wall with a door
leading back into the kitchen. Familiar territory for
Annabelle. She didn't realize just how much she'd
missed it until she was standing here, letting it all wash
over her again, firing up her blood.

But then her gaze fell on a woman sitting near the
stage—a pretty white woman, blond and slender in a
simple flower-print dress, nursing a mulatto child at
her breast.

"That's my old lady Linda," Casey said, coming up
beside her. "And our daughter Cassandra."

Annabelle hardly heard him. The pride in his voice
never registered. All she could do, looking at the
mother and child, was think of what she'd lost.

Amanda, her own daughter.

Who'd be thinking that her mom was never coming
back by now.

Amanda.

Whom the Dungeonmasters had cloned into a kind
of vampiric creature and set upon her.

Amanda.

Who was going to grow up without a mother or a
father now.

Amanda.

Her vision filmed over with tears. Forgotten was the
band and its marvelously archaic music. Forgotten was
the club, Finnbogg, and Smythe standing near her,
Casey still talking to her. All she could think about was
this frigging Dungeon and what it was doing to her.
Because of the band onstage, no doubt, the lyrics of
another old song came to her. Something about the
games people played.

Why was it all happening to her? What did the Dungeonmasters want with her or any of her family? What
was so goddamned important about the Folliots anyway?

"You okay?"

She blinked, turned slowly to see—through a film of
tears—Casey regarding her with an odd look on his
features. She shook her head.

"No, I'm not okay. I'm being fucked over no matter which way I turn—think that'd make you feel okay?"

Casey took a step back from her, hands held out in front of him. "Take it easy, lady. You're the one that's come to me looking for—"

Annabelle reached out to one of his hands with a feather-soft touch, fingers fluttering for a moment on the dark skin, before she dropped her hand to her side. She sniffed and wiped her eyes on the shoulder of her jacket with a quick motion of her head.

"I'm sorry," she said. "I'm just . . . seeing your wife there with her kid . . . it reminded me of everything I've lost. . . ."

The band had stopped playing. One by one they shut off their amps and the PA system and drifted off the stage. Most went out the door that led to the kitchen. The one that looked like Kantner took a seat at the bar.

"C'mon," Casey said. "Have a seat. I'll get you something to drink."

Annabelle let herself be led to a table and sat down. Finnbogg and Smythe joined her while Casey went to the bar. There he served Kantner a beer, before returning to the table with a tray laden with four frosty brown-bottled beers, moisture beading on their sides. He handed one to each of them, hesitating over Finnbogg until the dwarf reached out and took the proffered bottle. His wife—now that the baby had finished suckling—lowered her blouse over the one bared breast and joined them, jiggling the baby against her shoulder.

"You want to tell me about it?" Casey asked.

Annabelle looked at him. He looked different up close, with his shades off. His features were warm with the obvious affection he had for his own little girl as he took Cassandra from her mother to hold her for a while. Not so much like some tough punk as just a hard guy with a lot of heart. She'd known a lot of men just like him—back in her other life. Roadies. Bodyguards they'd used from time to time. Or just the plain every

THE HIDDEN CITY ■ 71

day joes that she used to meet back when her band still played the club and college circuit.

So while she didn't know Casey from Adam, she did know a lot of guys who wore a one-dimensional image like a flag, like a biker did his colors, though unlike most bikers the ones she'd liked seemed to carry something softer in their hearts—hidden away where it couldn't get so easily tromped on. She could easily see herself spilling out all her hurts to him. Sitting here in a club so like the kinds of places where she used to hang out that she felt homesick, with a real genuine woman at the table—not some exotic alien, just plain folks.

But could she trust these feelings? The frigging Dungeonmasters seemed to know just what strings to pull to get the reaction they wanted. Was she just letting herself in for more hurts? She couldn't forget the too-obvious coincidence of the Airplane playing that big hit of theirs, about Alice and all that Wonderland shit, just as they got here through a mirror of their own.

She looked at her companions, first Smythe, then Finnbogg. The three of them needed some help—no question about it. She sighed, then cleared her throat.

"Like I said," she began, "we're not from around here. . . ."

Casey nodded. "You heading on, or do you plan to go native?" he asked, looking at her from around the nodding head of his infant daughter.

His wife put a hand on his arm. "Let her tell it in her own way, Case."

After another brief hesitation Annabelle did just that.

Sidi and Tomàs backed slowly to the window until it was directly behind them and they could go no farther. From the darkness in front of them the sound of movement continued as whatever hid in the shadows drew nearer. Sidi looked about the floor at their feet, but there was nothing lying about that they could use as a weapon.

"*Madre de Dios,*" Tomàs murmured.

Sidi looked up to see that a tall skeletal creature had stepped forward from the darkness. It was at least two feet taller than either of them, a humanoid shape that appeared to be literally just skin covering bones. It had an extra joint in each of its four limbs, which made it appear to be standing slightly askew when it stopped its forward motion. Its vestigial nose and ears gave its oval head a pronounced almondlike shape. Its eyes were tiny and black, reflecting back the light from the window with a bright glitter that reminded Sidi of Shriek's multifaceted eyes.

Tomàs leaned closer to him. "What is it?" he asked softly.

Sidi shrugged. It appeared nonthreatening, but this was the Dungeon, so that meant little.

"Can you speak?" he asked the creature in the patois of the Dungeon.

It lifted one hand to chest level, and Sidi saw that while it had only three fingers, they too each had an extra joint. Its opposable thumb had only two joints. One long finger tapped its skeletal chest.

"Brezhoo," it said.

Sidi cocked an eyebrow. "Yes?"

Was it the creature's name, or a description of what it was? Perhaps, as with Finnbogg, it was both.

"Brezhoo," it repeated.

Sidi and Tomàs exchanged glances, then the Portuguese touched his own chest.

"We are men," he said. "I am Tomàs. My *amigo*'s name is Sidi." He offered it a quick smile.

"Mehn," the creature repeated bobbing its head. When it copied Tomàs's smile, its lips drew back to reveal rows of sharp teeth with two long, pronounced fangs in the front.

Tomàs swallowed thickly. "Yes," he said. "Men."

"Tayste ghood—mehn?"

Before either of them could react, that strangely jointed arm whipped out. Its fingers caught the Portuguese by the front of his shirt and hauled him in close. Sidi immediately launched himself at the creature, but the other arm lashed out with blinding speed and sent him stumbling into the shadows until he tripped on some obstruction hidden by the darkness.

He fell to the ground but recovered quickly. When he turned, it was to see his companion still struggling in the creature's grip. But no matter how desperately Tomàs battered at the creature with his fists, the long fangs were lowering steadily toward his throat.

With a wordless cry Sidi launched himself at the creature again. Sensing his attack, it sidestepped lightly, this time striking the Indian with enough force to knock him out the window.

The Tuan's silvers ran with a far smoother gait than Neville was accustomed to in a mount—due no doubt, he realized, to their relation to the rodents of his own world. They didn't gallop so much as scurry through the forest of tree-high weeds, but at a speed that would have left a good English horse winded in no time at all. Unfortunately the pursuing pack of gigantic hounds was making better progress still.

With his arms firmly wrapped about Alyssa's slender waist, he leaned over her shoulder to speak.

"I don't suppose you have any fairy spells at your command?" he asked. "Some wand or similarly useful device that you could wave about and make the damned beasts disappear?"

"We're not witches," she replied.

"No. No. Of course not."

But they still appeared—to him, at least—for all the world like the fairies from the old folktales that nannies delighted in telling to their charges back home in England. How could he not see them so? They were delicate-boned and silver-haired, the women beautiful beyond compare, the men handsome, their mounts enchanted. Surely Oberon and his court would have appeared so? There was really no difference that he could perceive. Except, of course, for their size.

They weren't the diminutive creatures of those tales

—at least not in relation to his own size. When one considered this oversized world, however . . .

A new thought occurred to Neville that brought a sinking feeling to his stomach.

What if this world *was* normal-sized and it was just they who had been reduced? The Tuan, Shriek, and himself. He had yet to discover how the Tuan had arrived in the Dungeon; but stepping through a looking glass, as he and Shriek had, in a manner that only Reverend Dodgson could have invented for his heroine . . .

Hadn't she, at some point in Dodgson's narrative, been reduced in size as well?

When one considered the resemblances between the two worlds . . . the underground Wonderland as Dodgson had described it was a place almost as absurd as the Dungeon—if not quite so perilous. Still, it had talking rabbits with pocket watches, packs of cards that came to life, and all manner of preposterous creatures and situations. It would be so like the Dungeonmasters to place his party in such a situation.

Could he—Lord help him—now look forward to encounters with hookah-smoking caterpillars, disembodied cat's grins, and the like?

And what of the others—Clive, Smythe, and all? Were they wandering about this ruined city as well, mouse-sized and in similar dire straits?

Better not to think on it, he told himself. Better to concentrate on the situation at hand, for the monstrous dogs were steadily gaining on them, and if something wasn't done about them, and done quickly, it wouldn't matter how absurd the Dungeon became, for he wouldn't be here to see any of it.

He chanced another glance back to see that the foremost of the dogs was advancing far too rapidly. What small lead they had gained on the pack was quickly being swallowed by the extended gait of the huge animals' broader step. The agility of the silvers as they bore their riders through this forest of vastly oversized vegetation gave them little advantage when the dogs could simply plow through it. To the pack this was simply a field of weeds—not the forest it was to Neville's company.

"Duck your head!" Alyssa cried suddenly.

Neville looked forward and bent quickly, his chest pressed against her back. They were approaching a curb where the buckling pavement of the street met the sidewalk. There was a small rectangular crack in the lip of the curb, set in the gutter near a sewer grate. The riders ahead of them entered it, two at a time. The silver bearing Alyssa and himself darted in after them, taking them into the safety of its darkness. Shriek followed, hard on their heels.

Once inside Alyssa brought her mount to a halt, and the whole company turned to face the narrow entranceway. Moments later the light was blocked as the first enormous dog's head pressed close, snarling at them, but the entrance was too small to permit it to come in after them. It dug at the pavement all the same, scrabbling to get near them.

In the close confines of their hiding place, the sounds of its growling boomed uncomfortably loud. Shriek tossed a hair spike directly at the monstrous beast's nose, which caused it to retreat, but another dog immediately took its place.

Alyssa turned away to look at her guards.

"Is there an exit?" she asked Yoors.

The captain shook his head. One of his men had already gone as far into the darkness as he could, but the way was blocked with rubble and ancient refuse. There was no telling how deep the blockage went.

Alyssa sighed. "Then we wait."

Neville dismounted and lifted her down. "Wait?" he asked. He thought of the dogs from his own world and how difficult it was, unless they were very well trained, to heel them once they had a scent. "But hounds such as these—"

"Will be tenacious," she said with a nod. "I know."

Neville surveyed what there was to see of their refuge, little that there was of it. There was a dankness in the air. The ceilings were low. But at least it was large enough so that their quarters would not be too crowded.

The dogs had given up their attempts to enter. Stepping close to the opening, Neville saw that they lay outside in a half circle, gazes locked on the narrow entryway. Growls greeted his appearance. When one enormous beast rose to its feet, Neville ducked quickly back inside.

"It could be a long wait," he said.

When Clive became aware of his surroundings once more, he realized that they'd been transported from what the kobolds' leader had called the decam chamber to yet another unfamiliar room. Both he and Guafe were no longer nude. They wore white gowns that came down to their knees—garments that appeared to have been hastily stitched together to fit their larger size. The room's walls were paler than the bright glare of the decam room—easier on the eyes. Pallets had been made for them on the floor by the simple expedient of dragging together a number of smaller mattresses, large pieces of some man-made material serving as sheets.

There were no other furnishings in the room. No windows, no sign of a door, although one side of the room was completely taken up by a mirror. Of their captors there was not a sign.

Chang Guafe lay motionless on his pallet, all systems shut down once more. Clive reached over and put his hand on the cyborg's shoulder.

Chang? he asked.

The red-faceted eyes flickered open immediately.

Are you well? Clive added.

The cyborg sat up. For a long moment he was motionless, attention apparently turned inward as he took stock of his body's present condition.

Nothing appears to have been tampered with, he said finally. *And you?*

Well enough. Confused, but well.

Guafe looked toward the mirrored wall, then faced his companion again. *We are being observed.*

As Clive started to look, the cyborg sent a quick warning into the Englishman's mind.

No, he said, continuing to use the neural web that connected their minds when they were in physical contact. *Do not look. They are behind the mirror, watching us.*

Behind the mirror? Clive thought. How was that possible? But then he remembered how they'd arrived on this level of the Dungeon.

Is it another gateway? he asked.

Something far simpler, Guafe replied. *A two-way mirror. It allows them to observe us, while remaining unseen themselves.*

But to what purpose?

Guafe gave a mental shrug. *I expect it is because we are something unexpected—beings that do not fit into their normal scheme of what should and should not be. I assume they are observing us to see what action we will take, if any. If we remain docile, they will have to come to us.*

I find the waiting hard—not knowing what to expect.

Exactly, Guafe replied.

Clive waited for his companion to continue, then realized that there was nothing to add. Their captors wished to keep them on an uneven keel—it was as simple as that.

I had a strange experience, Clive said after a few moments, *just as I lost consciousness earlier.*

What was that?

I tried to reach Shriek or one of the others through the neural web.

You had some success?

Not exactly. It wasn't until I began to lose consciousness that I received a response. But that response was from none of our companions. I—this will seem far-fetched, Chang—but I heard the voice of a man from

*my homeworld calling to me. That of my friend,
George du Maurier.*

What did he say to you?

Clive shook his head. *He was merely calling out to
me. I lost consciousness before I could respond.*

Interesting, the cyborg said.

*But how was it possible? I must have imagined it, for
other than mindspeaking with Shriek, we've never
been able to speak to each* other *without physical contact, let alone reach out beyond the Dungeon. Only
Shriek had that ability, and even she has never been
able to communicate beyond the Dungeon's borders.*

*I believe it has to do with the decontamination pro-
cess we underwent,* Guafe explained. *They ran some
very complex tests on our neural cortexes. Something in
the process must have allowed you to project your
thoughts to your friend and then receive his.*

What does it mean? Clive asked. *This confuses me.
Those of us taken from my world have arrived here
from many different times. Are they all one single time
line, or are there many different ones—some where I
return to England, others where I have never left in the
first place? And if that's true, then is the time line that I
know the real one?*

And where did that leave Annabelle? he wondered.
As a figment of a possible future? Perhaps as another
construct of the damned Dungeonmasters?

God, he hated how they had brought him to a state
where he must question every loyalty, every truth.

Not necessarily, Guafe said. *If the Dungeonmasters
can pluck us from any number of worlds and times, it
stands to reason then that communication between all
those various places and times would continue to exist.*

Clive gave a mental nod in agreement. No matter
how preposterous such things would be considering
the physics of his own world, it sounded logical enough
for the Dungeon. He thought again of that voice he'd
heard—he was as sure it had been du Maurier's as he
could be of anything—and then another concern arose
in him, for he remembered something else that he'd

sensed, just as that unconsciousness had swept over him.

He'd had the feeling that a hidden memory was trying to surface in his mind—something important, something forgotten, something disturbingly lost. Reaching for it was like knowing a word but being unable to grasp it while in the middle of a conversation. The more he tried to recall that memory now, the further it slipped away from him.

I'd give a great deal for some answers, he said.

As though on cue a door slid open in one of the walls closest to the mirror. The leader of the kobolds stood there with two men. None of them wore their bulky suits or the glass bubbles over their heads any longer, but the two men accompanying the leader still carried their weapons, both of which were trained on Clive and Guafe.

"The Speakers are ready to question you now," the leader said. Before Clive could frame a word, the leader held up his hand. "Yup, and they just might answer some questions too, if you're real lucky. So up and at 'em, now. Look sharp. Nobody's going to hurt you unless you start making trouble first."

A sharp anger rose in Clive at the amusement he saw in the leader's eyes, but he kept his own counsel. Letting go Guafe's shoulder and so breaking their neural contact, he rose stiffly to his feet.

You and I, he thought, looking at the leader. *We will have our day yet—don't ever doubt it.*

But for now he let himself be led, docile, down yet another long white corridor.

· CHAPTER SIX ·

There was a long silence as, another round of beers later, Annabelle finished up her story. That silence stretched around the table until Casey finally nodded his head.

"We've been there," he said. "Linda and me—we met up a couple of levels back and made it this far before we realized she was carrying Cassandra. Figured it was time to stop then. Got settled in here and" —he shrugged—"just never went any farther. Kinda hard to keep on going when you've got a kid in tow. I mean, the Dives ain't no great shakes, but the weirdness you know—especially in this place—sure beats the weirdness you might be heading into."

"But why?" Smythe asked. "What can they possibly want with so many different kinds of peoples?"

Linda pushed her hair back from her face and took Cassandra from her father. She lifted her blouse to nurse the baby again, and Smythe averted his gaze. Annabelle and Linda exchanged smiles.

"I got kicked out of a mall back home," Annabelle said, "for nursing Amanda in a public place. It gets so bizarre. The theaters've got posters up with guys ripping each other's hearts out, every 7-Eleven's got skin mags sitting right beside the candy bars, but something natural—something positive—like nursing your kid . . . well, that's just obscene."

Linda nodded. "I've been thinking about what you found out in the baron's library on the last level," she said, bringing the conversation back to the matter at hand.

"You mean Tomàs being related to the Folliots?"

"Yes. Did you ever read much Jung—you know, racial subconsciousness and all that?"

Smythe and Finnbogg just looked blank, but Annabelle nodded.

"I know the basic theory," she said.

"Well, for us all to share a racial subconsciousness," Linda went on, "there's got to be some connection between us all—right?"

"I suppose."

"No, think about it for a moment. If you compare the world's population in the late sixties—Casey's and my time," she added before Annabelle could correct her. "Compare it to the world's population a thousand years before that—we're growing by leaps and bounds. You take interracial couplings—and they've been going on for as long as there've been people. I mean it can be as simple as an Arab marrying a Greek, okay? Well, the gene pool has got to include a bit from just about everybody that ever existed. We have to ignore some cultures—certain Australian aborigines, for example, who have never married outside of their cultures. Or Inuit —those kinds of peoples. But other than that, maybe we really *are* all brothers and sisters under the skin."

Annabelle nodded. "By the nineties—in our world— genetic archaeology's pretty well traced all of humanity back to a common ancestress who lived somewhere in ancient central Africa."

"Which proves my point."

"The Age of Aquarius," Annabelle said with a smile.

"Could be it's not so farfetched," Linda said.

"Then what about the aliens?" Smythe asked. "Beings like Shriek, or our friend Finnbogg here?"

Linda turned her gaze to the dwarf.

"And this," Casey said, "is where our theory gets its first hole."

"Maybe," Annabelle said, "and maybe not. Depends on whether you believe the tabloids or not."

"Tabloids?" Smythe asked.

"After your time," Annabelle told him. "They're like

newspapers, except they carry just the juciest and most farfetched stories. 'Biker Nuns Kidnap Pope' or 'Man Gives Birth to Collie Pups'—that kinda thing."

"Just a load of crap," Casey said.

Annabelle grinned at the expression on Smythe's face.

"But that kind of thing is impossible," the Englishman said.

"Sure it is. Just like all the reports of UFOs and aliens taking people away to study them are. But what if they're not? What if cataloged with all the crap are some truths, but we just don't have any way of telling one from the other? I can't tell you how many times I've seen articles about people who were supposed to have been taken away by flying saucers, studied like lab animals, and then returned. There's guys that've made a living writing books about this kind of thing.

"So what if some of that was real? UFO reports go back for as far as there is written history—maybe further back if you take the oral stories about fairies and stuff like that as just the only way those people back then could talk about extraterrestrials."

"So you're saying the gene pool could cover the whole universe?" Linda asked.

Annabelle shrugged. "I don't know. I always thought all this 'the aliens have landed' stuff was crap, myself. But maybe it isn't. If there *is* something special about the Folliots that gets them dumped into this Dungeon, then maybe that's why we've got Finn and the rest of them in here with us."

For a long moment no one spoke. Then Smythe said, "Because they're related?"

"You got it, Horace."

"But then why am I in here?"

"You were with Clive when he got snatched."

"And what about us?" Linda asked.

Annabelle shrugged. "If Finnbogg can be related to the Folliots, then there's nothing stopping you from being related as well."

"Interesting theory," Casey said.

"But you're not buying it?"

"Didn't say that. Just said it was interesting. Course, you gotta remember that there's going to be a certain reproductive incompatibility between species. Seems to me if the Ren and the Chaffri are into filling the place up, then there just aren't going to be enough Folliots around to do it. Not enough pure ones—because it seems, with all the trouble they're going through with your great-grandfather and great-uncle, that they want the pure ones."

"I'm holding onto my theory," Annabelle said. "At least until a better one comes along."

Casey shrugged. "The way I see it, it doesn't make much difference anyway. We're still stuck here."

"Then you'd better think about it some," Annabelle said. "Because if it *is* on the level, then that means holing up here in the Dives isn't going to make a whole lot of difference in the long run. The Dungeonmasters'll be after you sooner or later to bring you back into the game."

"Unless this is our part in the game," Casey said.

"What do you mean?"

"Sitting here with you. Giving you a moment to catch your breath before you go on. Providing some new gear and provisions—and directions?" he added. "I mean, you are going on?"

Annabelle gave him a long, hard look and wished he hadn't said that. She was just starting to relax a little bit, but now he had to go screw it all up. She looked away, around the club. Kantner had left the bar now, joining the rest of the band backstage, probably. Jake, the old wino who'd brought them here, was sleeping with his head on a table just a few yards away. Otherwise they had the place to themselves.

Nice place for an ambush, Annabelle thought, but then realized that with the way things were going, if this was an ambush, it was a mental one. Of course, that wouldn't make it any less dangerous.

Not here.

Not in the Dungeon.

"We don't have any other choice," Annabelle said.

Linda shook her head. "There's always choice."

Annabelle grinned. "Can't see a world without free will, can you?"

Linda shook her head.

"Well, welcome to the Dungeon," Annabelle told her. "Because the only free will you'll find here is what the Dungeonmasters'll give you."

It was pure instinct that saved Sidi as he went hurtling out the window. Without stopping to think, his hands reached out for the cable that his subconscious mind, at least, knew was there. By the time his conscious mind remembered the cable, he was already holding onto it, the force of his body's impetus swinging him away from the building.

Tao, he thought. Every action has a reaction.

Then the cable was swinging back toward the building. The window loomed up in front of him. He tucked in his legs, rode the cable to the end of its short arc, and launched himself at the creature again.

This time he succeeded in dislodging its grip on Tomàs. The Portuguese fell in a bundle of limp limbs as the creature was knocked back into the shadows from which it had first issued.

Sidi rode the creature, making sure it took the brunt of their fall when they landed. Something cracked under him as they hit the floor. The sound was like the snapping of a dry bone. Sidi didn't take time to investigate the damage he'd inflicted on the creature. He scrambled back into the lighted area by the window, rising in a defensive posture over his fallen companion.

When the creature came stalking forth from the shadows once more, one forelimb hanging limply at its side, Sidi took a step forward, putting himself between it and Tomàs. Behind him the Portuguese coughed, trying to catch his breath. The dry hacking sound was loud in the stillness. In front of him the creature's eye gleamed with pain and anger.

"Hurtz," it said.

It took another step forward, but before Sidi could mount an offensive against it, a small shaft sprouted in the creature's forehead. It gave an odd squawking sound, its eyes widening with surprise, then fell stiffly to the ground.

Sidi turned slowly. Behind Tomàs, who was now sitting up, Sidi saw perched on the windowsill a small being that he could only describe as a feral child.

The newcomer was no more than four feet tall and dressed in worn leather trousers and a tunic of sewn-together rodent pelts. His feet were bare. His features were worn to the bone, hair a rat's nest of brown curls, eyes like a mongoose's, flashing and alert. In his hands was a small bow, notched with a second shaft, the point of the arrow aimed directly at Sidi.

The Indian stood perfectly still. "We owe you our lives," he said.

The newcomer grinned, showing a mouthful of human teeth that were stained yellow and brown.

"Got that g'ant good," he said.

He didn't lower the bow.

Sidi nodded. "Is that what it was?" he asked. "A g'ant? The creature called itself a brezhoo."

"That's what they call 'emselves. We call 'em g'ants 'cos that's what they're looking like—all g'ant and spid'ry."

Tomàs had recovered enough to take in the newcomer as well. *"Christo,"* he muttered. "Now what?"

"This . . . ah, being . . . has just rescued us," Sidi said. He didn't take his gaze from the feral child.

"I'm Poot," the newcomer said. "Frenchy calls us EPs, but we all got names just like real people do."

"EPs?" Sidi asked.

"Les enfants perdus," Poot said.

"The lost children," Sidi repeated, translating the newcomer's terrible French to the Dungeon's patois. It suited the child.

"Are there many of you?" Sidi asked.

"Thousands," Poot assured him.

"And can we be friends?"

The child shrugged. "What for? Don't trust nobody over ten—that's what Frenchy says. 'Cept for him. You gotta trust him, or he'll sew your ears to your shoulders. Said he would, for sure, and Gren says she maybe saw him do it once."

"We've only been in the Dungeon for a few months," Sidi said. "How old does that make us?"

Poot appeared to consider this for a long moment, then he slowly lowered his bow. "Not even a year, I guess. I dunno. Frenchy'd know. Let's go ask him."

As he turned to look out the window, Sidi and Tomàs exchanged glances.

"What is going on here, *amigo*?" Tomàs asked.

"You coming?" Poot asked before Sidi could reply.

"Coming where?" Sidi asked.

Poot pointed out the window to where a rope ladder hung beside the cable they had used to descend from the roof of the building. The two men joined the boy at the window and looked up.

"*Asno,*" Tomàs said. "What is it?"

"A balloon," Sidi replied. "A hot-air balloon."

Looking down at them from over the rim of its basket were the faces of three more feral children, not one of them older than Poot. Their faces seemed very white in the fading light—like the heads of three small ghosts, peering down at them.

"If God had meant us to fly . . ." Tomàs began, but he broke off as Poot gave him a suspicious look.

"You're not coming?"

"*Ahora bien,*" Tomàs told him. "Of course we will come. We only need our heads examined, eh?" he added to Sidi as he climbed back onto the windowsill. He began to ascend the ladder then, mutterings of *"Muy loco"* drifting down as he went.

"Your friend talks funny," Poot said to Sidi as the Indian joined him on the windowsill.

Sidi shrugged. He was more worried about what would happen when they met this Frenchy that the boy had spoken of. They might be able to trick Poot into thinking they were under ten, but a grown man would be another thing altogether. Especially one who could command an air vehicle such as this for his charges to ride about in.

Then he was on the swaying ladder himself, climbing up. As soon as Poot stepped onto it as well, one of the children in the basket threw off their moorings, and the balloon began to drift away from the building, Sidi and the boy swinging on the ladder below it.

Neville had never been one to wait patiently for anything or anyone. In a world of doers and those done to, he preferred to count himself amongst the former, for all the Dungeonmasters' attempts to fit him squarely in amongst the latter.

It was true that the company was pleasant—if one discounted the scowling Captain Yoors and his fellow guards—but the situation itself irked the elder Folliot to no end. Bad enough to be trapped by a pack of common dogs, but in such a place? The dampness had gotten into his clothes, making them stick uncomfortably to his skin. The air was foul, as though something had died and then rotted in here.

He found himself pacing back and forth in front of the entranceway, until Alyssa finally asked him to please sit still for at least two minutes running as he was driving her mad. That was all Neville needed.

Grunting some unintelligible reply, he made his way to the back of their hiding place to investigate the blockage.

"I've smelled composts that had a better odor," one of the Tuan guards said, joining him there.

Neville studied him for a moment, his mind replaying the moment of introduction, until he had a name.

"You're Fenil?" he asked.

The guard nodded.

"You don't mind talking to the enemy?"

A slight frown touched Fenil's features. "What do you mean?"

"Your captain doesn't think much of me."

Fenil smiled then. "Yoors doesn't think much of anyone unless he can trace his bloodlines back to the High Forest. It's our lady who commands this company, and as she has accepted you, then I will do the same."

Unless I betray that trust, Neville thought, completing the guard's unspoken thought.

What are you playing at now, Being Neville? Shriek asked.

Neville glanced at where the arachnid was resting near the doorway so that she could keep watch on the pack outside.

Nothing untoward, Neville replied. *That I promise you, madam watchdog.*

A mental sigh carried from Shriek to him, but she spoke no more.

Neville turned back to study what he could of the blockage. It was composed of tightly packed refuse— rags, rotting material, and Lord alone knew what. He gave a piece of tightly wadded cloth an experimental pull. It came away easily, but a noxious odor quickly arose as the material was moved through the still, dank air. Behind him the silvers shifted nervously in their harnesses.

"There's no telling how deeply it's blocked," Fenil said.

Neville nodded. "So one of your fellows mentioned earlier. But there's a simple, if not pleasing, way to find out—don't you think?"

Fenil wrinkled his nose but nodded. "I can't abide waiting either," he said.

They set to it then. At first they were careful to touch the unpleasant material only with their hands, but soon they became inured to the stench and fell to it without consideration as to how much of the foul slop they got on themselves.

Their companions kept well away from them as the stink pervaded the whole of their hiding place. They kept as close to the cleaner air that came from the entranceway as they could without arousing the dogs. But Shriek came to join them, and then another of the guards, one named Thulen, and soon they began to make better progress still.

It was when Alyssa herself came to join the workers that Yoors finally arose.

"My lady," he said. "Now you go too far."

"Propriety means nothing in a situation such as this," she replied. "Would you have them labor on our behalf and do nothing to help?"

Gladly, his eyes said, but he shook his head and called to the remainder of the guards to join him. But Neville and the others had already worked their way seven or eight feet in, and a part of the blockage gave way to fall on the opposite side of where they were working just as the guards approached.

"Too late, old chum," Neville told Yoors. "We're through."

"Torches," Alyssa said.

Guards brought them out from their saddlebags as Neville and his companions continued to widen the hole. By the time the torches were lit and brought forth, the opening was large enough for a man to step through.

Covered with slime and stinking like a pair of sewer rats, Neville and Fenil grinned at each other.

"Do the honors," Fenil said, handing Neville a torch.

The Englishman winked at Alyssa as he took the light.

"Gladly," he said.

Thrusting it through the hole ahead of himself, he stepped through to the other side.

The Speakers were a pair of small dapper men and an overweight woman, all three dressed in loose-fitting robes the color of a robin's egg. Their hair—even the woman's—was cropped close to their scalps. Their features held little expression and seemed all of a kind, even taking into account the woman's broader face. One of the men wore a pair of spectacles.

They sat behind a long steel-framed desk with a glass

top and looked up as Clive and Guafe were brought in. They made no greeting.

The man with the spectacles returned his attention to a small stack of paper on the glass surface of the desk in front of him. The other two merely regarded the prisoners with what Clive could only describe as boredom.

The two guards and their leader directed Clive and Guafe to a pair of makeshift chairs—roughly sized to their larger stature—that had been placed directly across from the desk. Beside them stood another man and woman and a small trolley on which sat an array of technical equipment. Clive regarded the gear with suspicion before turning his attention to the Speakers.

"I think we've been patient for quite long enou—" he began, but the guard leader tapped him on the shoulder with the butt of his weapon before he could finish.

"Be good," he said, "and maybe you'll get a chance to say your piece."

Clive clenched his fists but kept silent. Beside him the female technician was studying Guafe.

"I'm afraid the evaluators can't be trusted in regard to this one," she said to the Speakers. "We'd have to take him apart to find out just where the flesh leaves off and the cybernetics begin. And then we'd still have to recalibrate the evaluators."

The man without the spectacles nodded. "We'd like them in one piece for the present," he said. "Hook up the other."

"We can judge some of the validity of what the cyborg has to say from this one's reactions," the male technician said as he approached Clive. "But we won't guarantee any of it a hundred percent."

He pulled a wire with a suction cup attached to its end from the belly of the largest machine and lifted it toward Clive's brow. Clive shrunk back until he felt the muzzle of one of the guards' weapons touch his back. Then he froze.

"It's merely an advanced form of a truth detector,"

Guafe said. "I believe it works on a neural level—isn't that correct?"

The technician appeared surprised at the cyborg's knowledge, but he nodded. "It's completely harmless."

Harmless or not, Clive wasn't happy as the electrodes were attached to each temple, his wrists, and his ankles, with three more placed on his chest.

"Can we get on with this?" the woman Speaker asked.

The man with the spectacles nodded. "Let's just give the evaluator a quick test." He looked directly at Clive. "How many of us are sitting at this table?"

"This is nonsense," Clive said.

The muzzle of the guard's weapon jabbed his kidney.

"Three," he said then.

The machine hummed on the trolley beside him, and Clive suddenly felt an odd buzzing sensation run up and down his spine. It spread out to touch his every nerve end, but one part of it remained centered at the base of his spine. A warmth sat there; not unpleasant, but not natural either.

It was the machine that was causing this, Clive thought. This evaluator. But while that might be the origin of what he felt, he couldn't shake the apprehension that the device was waking something more than merely an evaluation of how truly he replied.

"What is the color of our robes?" the Speaker went on.

"Blue."

"Are you a native of this world—please answer in the affirmative."

"I am not a—"

"A simple yes, if you please."

Again the jab in his kidney.

"Yes," Clive said.

"Thank you," the Speaker said. "Do you have enough data, Chary?" he added to the female technician.

She nodded. "There appears a slight anomaly—a ghosting in his neural pattern that the program can't explain—but with that taken into account, we shouldn't have any difficulty in obtaining a reading."

Before anyone else could speak, Clive leaned forward. "Could someone please explain"—he ignored the sudden jab in his kidney as the guard tried to stop him from speaking—"just exactly what it is that you want from us?"

"We are *not* here to satisfy your curiosity," the Speaker without the spectacles replied.

"Oh, give the man a break, Hoyd," the female Speaker interrupted.

Speaker Hoyd frowned, but the third Speaker nodded. "Go ahead, Lena," he said.

"It's really quite simple," Speaker Lena said. "We are trying to find out if you really are Clive Folliot, or merely a clone grown from one of his cells."

"A clone!" Clive cried.

The machine hummed at his side as he spoke. The curious buzz followed the traceries of his neural system.

Speaker Lena ignored his outburst and went on. "The Dungeon's been up to its ears in Folliots of every size, shape, and description lately—some with true blood, most not even vaguely related but who take the name for their own, all the same."

"I *am* Clive Folliot, madam," Clive said. "Make no mistake about that."

Again the machine's hum. Again the accompanying sensation in his nervous system.

"He's telling the truth," the male technician said.

"Check your data infeeds," Speaker Hoyd said, "because whoever he is, he can't be Clive Folliot. What we need to ascertain is what he hopes to accomplish by this charade and most importantly *how* he has acquired a body that contains all the necessary traces for him to have grown up in the England of the true Folliot's time. He even has the real Folliot's scars—all correctly aged!"

"That's because I *am* Clive Folliot!" Clive shouted.

The machine hummed beside him. The accompanying buzz was accentuated—it was sharp this time, awaking a slight pain between his temples and behind his eyes.

"The evaluator is not malfunctioning," the technician stated firmly.

"How's it possible?" the Speaker with the spectacles asked.

"The Chaffri will stop at nothing to best us, Kian," Speaker Hoyd said.

"But his size . . ."

"My size?" Clive asked. "There's nothing wrong with my size—it's you who are diminutive."

The evaluator made a crackling noise, and Clive began to shake.

"Oh no," Speaker Kian said. "I can assure you of this much, whoever you are—the real Clive Folliot and we are all of one size. Not giants such as you and your companion."

"Freaks," the guard leader muttered softly behind him.

The mirror, Clive thought. It was something to do with the mirror. Just as Dodgson's Alice had shifted in size in her Wonderland . . .

He couldn't continue the thought. The machine beside him shorted out, and his back arched as blue fire ran through his nerve ends. He would have fallen forward, but the female technician caught the bulk of his weight and, with the help of a guard, pushed him back into his chair. His eyes rolled backward, and he lost all awareness of the questioning room.

He saw instead a uniform grayness. A strobing blue light flickered behind his eyes—reminding him of that lost memory that he could not quite grasp. It burned in a lost, dark place in his mind, almost present, but frustratingly just out of reach. Then his attention was snared by other matters as, slowly, a portion of the grayness in front of him cleared—a section in the shape of an oval mirror. And then it seemed he was looking into a Victorian sitting room—directly into the astonished features of his friend, George du Maurier.

"Clive?" he heard du Maurier say. "Good Lord, man. What are you doing in my mirror?"

"Mirror?" Clive replied. "What are you doing in my dream?"

Before du Maurier could reply, the grayness took Clive away again.

▪ CHAPTER SEVEN ▪

Twilight had come and gone while they talked. Darkness held the streets now. With the coming of night the bar began to fill up with the oddest collection of people Annabelle had run across since her time in the khalif's prison, way back on the Dungeon's first level. Linda had left for the apartment she and Casey had in back, taking her daughter with her. She offered the place to Annabelle and the others to rest up, but Annabelle shook her head.

"I want to check out the scene," she said.

No, be honest, she told herself. What you really want is to hear some good ol' rock 'n' roll.

Casey took up his position behind the bar—but not before providing Smythe with some new gear. The trousers and shirt were old and patched, the shoes a little tight—but the canvas would stretch, Casey assured him.

"And it sure beats walking around bare-assed under that cloak—don'tcha think?" Annabelle had added.

So now they sat near the stage, watching the club's regular patrons drift in. Almost all were human; fashion was what set them apart. There was everything from full-body tattoos and shaved pates to bewildering arrays of multicolored rags and the most amazing peacock hairstyles that would have put to shame the old punks from the eighties in Annabelle's homeworld.

It was only on closer—if circumspect, after staring got her some fierce scowls—inspection that Annabelle began to notice physical differences. Noseless beings with odd, flat faces. A beard that proved to be hundreds of thread-thin tentacles. A woman with three breasts, running in a row down the center of her chest. What looked like a beer-bellied tattooed biker who proved to have instead a marsupial pouch from which a small head poked as soon as he was served.

There were two waitresses who were kept on their feet in a constant rush from bar to tables for the first hour as the club filled up. Then things finally settled down, and the moment Annabelle had been waiting for came as the Airplane took the stage again.

For a good half hour Annabelle was taken away from all her troubles. She didn't think about the Dungeon, about their missing companions, about anything but the music. Smythe left to take up Linda's offer as soon as the first song ended, but Finnbogg stayed with her, singing along on every chorus whether he could pick out the words or not. It wasn't until the band ended their first set with "White Rabbit" that Annabelle came down from her high.

The three men who suddenly sat down at her table didn't help.

All three wore leather vests to show off their muscular chests and arms. Greasy black hair was tied back in ponytails. One—the obvious leader—went so far as to be wearing a pair of shades. He grinned at Annabelle, showing a gold-capped front tooth.

The band had left the stage as soon as the song ended, and the club filled now with crowd noise as its patrons stretched their legs and began to talk with each other.

"You're new," Gold-tooth said to her.

"Don't think so," Annabelle said tiredly. "I feel all grown up."

That gave Gold-tooth and his friends a chance to give her a long once-over, smirking the whole time. A quiet growl rumbled deep in Finnbogg's chest.

"I meant, new around here," Gold-tooth said. "I like to check out the new blood, y'understand. See what they're made of. Whatcha got there?"

He pointed to where the Baalbec A-9 merged with the flesh of her forearm.

There was no way this could end pretty, Annabelle thought. Here and there throughout the crowd she could spot other men wearing the same black vests, their chests bare. Some kind of gang—no question about it—which was not going to make things easy, even with Finnbogg at her side.

She was just trying to figure how far she should let this go when Casey suddenly appeared beside their table to glower down at Gold-tooth.

"Don't push it, John J.," he said.

Great, Annabelle thought, remembering what Jake had told her about the Baptists and their leader. It had to be the Prophet himself. This she really needed.

"Easy," John J. replied. "You look after secular matters, brother, and leave the people's spiritual welfare to me."

Casey shook his head. "I told you—you and your boys are welcome here any time you want—but no preaching. Save it for the streets."

"It's cold out there on the streets," John J. replied. "Real cold. A hard, tough world. Shame if you had to relocate on a street corner, what with being a new daddy and all."

"That does it," Casey said.

He started to reach for John J., but the Prophet put his hands up placatingly. "Hey, hey, Casey—be cool. You got a lot of friends in this here club right now, but we've got some numbers here too. You want this place coming down around your ears?"

Annabelle was completely bored with all the macho posturing going on—both from John J. and her own rescuer. All she'd wanted was to listen to some good music for a couple of hours before she had to hit the battle lines again. Was that really too much to ask?

"Listen up," she said.

They both turned to look at her.

"I appreciate the concern, Casey, but I don't want to bring trouble down on this place."

"See?" John J. said. "Lady likes my company."

"As for you," she told him, "whatever you're selling —I don't want it, so why don't you go bother somebody else?"

"I'm here to look out for your soul, lady."

Annabelle shook her head. "My soul's in great shape, so take your business somewhere else. This table's reserved."

She could see him flexing his muscles, wiring himself up for a challenge.

"Oh yeah? Or else what?"

She saw Casey shaking his head. Right. Don't antagonize him. I'd love to take this outside, Annabelle thought, but you can only play 'em as they come.

"I'm trying to be real nice about this," Annabelle said. "Why don't you do us both a favor and find somebody else to hit on?"

He moved so fast that she never saw it coming, never had a chance to activate her Baalbec. He just reached out across the table and half pulled her back across it, using a handful of her jacket's lapels to hold her by. Drinks fell off the table. Casey started to move in to help her, but two other Baptists rose to block his way.

John J. was just grinning in her face—that gold tooth flashing—when Finnbogg lunged across the table, breaking John J.'s grip on Annabelle. Off balance, she fell to the floor. By the time she got up, it was to see Finnbogg pinned to the floor by a couple of Baptists, John J. holding the edge of a long, wicked blade against the dwarf's throat.

Where the hell was he hiding that? Annabelle wondered.

"The Lord's talking to me!" John J. cried, raising his voice so that it carried throughout the club. "Hell, yes. He's talking and I'm listening. And you know what he's telling me, brothers and sisters? He's telling me it's time for this little dog-boy lying here at my feet to meet his maker."

Oh shit, Annabelle thought.

John J. chose that moment to look right at her. "Can I get a big amen from you all on that?"

The balloon drifted slowly over the ruined city. The tall buildings reared darkly about them as though the balloon were nothing more than a seed pod floating in some immense forest. But when was there ever a forest this large? Sidi wondered. When was there ever a city this large?

Only in the Dungeon . . .

With the fall of night they could see pinpricks of light below them. Some were from open fires—but others appeared to be of an electric origin, which puzzled Sidi. He'd already seen on previous levels what sort of complicated equipment was needed to furnish even the simplest current. If such devices existed below, then it would seem the city was not nearly so deserted as it had first appeared.

That brought a smile to his lips as he took in their youthful companions. No, it wasn't so deserted at all—was it?

"Watcha smiling for?" Poot wanted to know.

"I'm just happy that we've escaped danger and are with friends," Sidi replied.

"EPs make real good friends," Poot assured them.

"They look kinda old," the female of the remaining EPs noted dubiously.

She'd been introduced to them as Nacky. The other two were Agog and Merrybe.

"Not even a year old—either of 'em," Poot told her.

Nacky scratched at the tangle mat of her hair and shrugged. "Dunno. . . ."

"Frenchy'll know, you betcha," Merrybe said.

"Maybe," Nacky said. "Maybe Frenchy'll box us good, bringing home just a couple of Topsiders and no good loot."

Simple they might be, Sidi thought, but that didn't make them simpletons.

"You got any good loot?" Agog wanted to know.

Poot nodded happily. "Yeah, give Frenchy some loot, and he'll be happy. Maybe make you EPs, too."

"Loot?" Sidi asked.

"Treasure," Tomàs explained.

He had been standing at the rim of the basket, looking down at the dark streets passing below. He turned now and leaned with his back against the rim to look at the feral children.

"Eh, *mi niños*? Is it treasure that your Frenchy collects? Gold and silver and sparkling gems?"

Nacky shook her head. "What good's that?"

"It can buy you whatever you wish."

"Buy?"

The faces of the children creased as they pondered the word.

"What do you call loot?" Sidi asked them.

"Toys," Poot said promptly.

Agog nodded. "With working parts—Frenchy likes them best."

"Like this," Nacky said, and she pulled a small pistol from the pocket of her jacket and waved it in front of them.

"Be careful where you point that thing," Tomàs said.

Nacky just laughed. She aimed the muzzle straight at him and pulled the trigger.

"Bang!" all the children shouted together.

They laughed uproariously at how Tomàs jumped. The Portuguese gave Sidi a pained look.

"Madre de Dios," he said. "They are *loco.*"

"They are children," Sidi said. "As we are," he added quickly when Nacky frowned at him. "We are all children, and children like games." He stuck his hand in his pocket. "What have I got in my pocket?"

"Your hand!" Merrybe cried.

"Grub!"

"Loot!"

"A dead mouse," Poot said.

While the children continued to guess, Sidi shook his head each time they were wrong. Caught up in the game, no one paid any attention to where the balloon was drifting until it bumped into the side of a building. Tomàs, still leaning on the rim, grabbed at the rigging to keep himself from falling over.

"We're home!" Poot cried.

"Home, home, home!"

Agog leaped up onto the rim where he balanced precariously for a long moment before jumping from the basket to the ledge of the nearest window. Merrybe threw him a rope, and in moments the balloon was firmly moored to the building. He and Poot joined Agog on the ledge, quickly followed by Tomàs.

"What *did* you have in your pocket?" Nacky wanted to know before they joined the others.

Sidi took from his pocket a small round pebble pocked with bits of quartz. "A lucky stone," he said. "Here. You can keep it."

Nacky's eyes widened. "For true?"

When Sidi nodded, she grinned and stowed it carefully away in an inner pocket of her jacket.

"I never saw a stone that good before," she said.

"C'mon, c'mon!" Poot cried from the window ledge.

"Hang onto your shirt!" Nacky shouted back. She gave Sidi another big grin, obviously having decided that he could be a friend. "Let's go see Frenchy."

Ah, yes, Sidi thought as he followed her across to the ledge. Frenchy.

He doubted the EPs' leader would be won over by anything so simple as a kind word or a lucky stone.

"I hope you have something in mind, *amigo*," Tomàs said as the EPs led them deeper into the building.

Sidi only wished he did.

Tomàs nodded at the look on the Indian's face. "I didn't think so," he said.

Already his shoulders were sagging, the momentary sense of self-worth that had awoken while descending the tower was quickly wearing away.

"Don't worry," Nacky told them. "Frenchy likes all us EPs. You'll see."

We will see, Sidi thought. True enough. But will we like what we see? Or more to the point—will Frenchy?

Then they were led down a last corridor into a broad room and the time for wondering was gone.

The room was enormous. Torches thrust into brackets in the walls cast a flickering light over a scene out of a madhouse. There were children everywhere—all of them dressed in rags and tatters. Their hair was long and matted, or cut short into uneven tufts. Their faces were all thin, their eyes both childlike and feral. But strangest of all was the figure propped up on cushions at the far side of the room who could only be Frenchy.

He was not a man—that much was plain. He reminded Sidi more of some gigantic caterpillar or slug, given somewhat human features and two slender forearms. On his bald pate was a red fez. His only other garment was a yellow-and-green vest, pulled tight over his bulbous chest. In one of those impossibly slender hands was the mouthpiece of a hookah pipe. As he drew in the smoke, the water in the pipe bubbled. He let a slow stream of smoke out through the broad nostrils set dead center in his face. There was no nose to go with them.

His eyes were tiny, almost lost in the folds of fat that blurred his features. His mouth was a wide slit that ran literally from ear to ear. The head was as big as a normal man's torso; his body's bulk many times that again. All over the cushions, and scattered on the floor around them, were heaps and piles of small mechanical devices in various stages of repair.

His loot, Sidi realized.

"Brought you some new EPs, Frenchy," Poot said proudly.

The creature's tiny eyes studied Sidi and Tomàs while he inhaled another lungful of smoke from the hookah.

"Did you now, *mon petit* Poot," he said finally.

His voice was surprisingly thin and high-pitched, coming as it did from such an immense body. How did he move? Sidi couldn't help wondering.

"Found 'em, we did—up in an old tower," Poot said, grinning happily.

"But these are too old to be EPs," Frenchy said.

Poot's grin faded. He took a couple of steps away from Sidi and Tomàs, as did Agog and Merrybe. Nacky hesitated at Sidi's side, before sidling away as well.

"Didn't know," Poot said. "They said they were only a year old."

"Actually," Sidi spoke up, "what I said was that we had only been in the Dungeon for a few months. I'm afraid the boy misunderstood me."

Frenchy nodded slowly. "You're not Topsiders either," he said.

Sidi noted that Nacky and the others visibly relaxed at that.

"No," he said. "We're from another world entirely."

The sluglike face remained impassive. More smoke was inhaled, then exhaled in a series of smoke rings that made a number of the EPs clap their hands with delight.

"*Alors,*" Frenchy said finally. "Tell me about it."

Once Neville and his companions made their way past the blockage, they realized that they had found an entranceway to the city's storm-sewer systems. For a company that was proportional to the size of the city, it would have been cramped quarters at best—and impossible to traverse with mounts. But to their diminutive company the rounded passages were enormous and presented no problems whatsoever.

There were other hazards to their small size, however.

The flickering lights of their torches sent odd shadows scurrying in all directions. The tunnel walls were slimy to the touch, the footing slippery—even for the clawed toes of the silvers. Lying on the bottom arc of the immense concrete pipes was an endless series of large pools that they had to take care to circumvent. The still surface of the water gave off odors more noxious than that of the blockage they'd had to remove to enter the tunnels in the first place, while the basins were deep enough in places to easily drown a man and his mount. The cesspools had been left behind since the last storm waters entered the tunnel, which left them all with a sobering thought.

"Pray it doesn't rain," Neville said to Alyssa as they rode along at the fore of the company.

She nodded. "And that we don't meet up with the feral cousins of our mounts that haunt these tunnels."

"So you know your way about in here?"

"No. Do you?"

"Not likely," Neville said. "We arrived on this level of the Dungeon only moments before meeting you."

They rode on in silence for a while after that until they came to a pool that spread so wide across the tunnel that they couldn't circle it without falling in.

"Now what?" Yoors asked, riding up.

Shriek? Neville called to the arachnid. *Can you lay webbing along one side of the wall that we can use as handholds?*

I believe so, Being Neville.

Can I help?

A mental chuckle was her only reply as she moved to where the edge of the pool met the steeper wall.

"My companion will lay down a web that we can crawl along," Neville said to Alyssa.

"What of the silvers?" Yoors asked.

"They'll have to swim."

"In that foul muck?"

Neville shrugged. "It's that or you carry them."

In the end the silvers swam through the pool while the company slowly edged their way along the steep wall, using the web spun from Shriek's spinnerets to cling to. They reached the far side without mishap, though the silvers were befouled and gave off a smell strong enough to make them all choke. The unpleasantness was compounded when the beasts shook themselves dry.

"How far do you think we've come?" Fenil asked as he worked on the coat of his mount, trying to clean away the worst of the muck.

"By our reckoning," Neville said, "in consideration of our size, I mean—perhaps half a league."

Not far, Shriek said.

"No Tuan has ever been very far into the labyrinth of tunnels that lies beneath the city," Alyssa said. "We've done a little exploration of them about our base camp, but we run into continual dead ends."

Neville nodded. That was his fear as well—that they'd come up against a blockage too tightly and too deeply packed to allow them through. He let her comment about a base camp pass for the nonce. It hadn't surprised him, as he'd already surmised that the Tuan had come to the Dungeon in a much larger company than the few of them he saw represented here.

"Dead ends, is it?" he said. "Then it's best we find a way out as quickly as possible."

"Or a way down."

"My lady," Yoors protested. "You speak too much."

Both Neville and Shriek ignored the captain to give Alyssa considering looks.

What do you mean by that, Being Alyssa? Shriek asked.

"The entrances to the next level—they're supposed to lie in an enormous living city that lies under this dead one."

Neville looked at the ground underfoot. "Another city?"

"Where the principal players in this Dungeon dwell: the Ren and the Chaffri. Half belongs to the one—half to the other."

Shriek nodded slowly. *You said earlier, Being Alyssa, about there being a third set of players . . . ?*

"So we've been led to believe."

"And are they in this city as well?" Neville asked.

"No. The way to them is through a gate to the next level of the Dungeon."

"And as the gates lie in the city . . ." Neville began.

Alyssa completed his sentence. "Then we should be looking for a way down, not up. Exactly."

* * *

When Clive regained consciousness, he found himself in yet another chamber. Unlike any of the rooms he had seen so far, this one was pleasantly furnished, albeit to a being half his size. Brocaded velvet drapes hung on either side of a large window that overlooked a brightly lit plaza where the people of this underground city went about their business under the simulated sunlight of man-made lighting. There was the oversize bed upon which he lay, ankles dangling over the end, a table and chair near the window, paintings of scenes from his own England on the walls, a dresser on the far side of the room with a mirror above it.

Remembering his hallucination in the questioning room when he'd thought he'd seen du Maurier speaking to him again, Clive studiously avoided looking into the mirror.

The diminutive size of the furnishings gave him an odd sense of misappropriation—as though he'd been left to sleep in a child's playhouse. That sensation was accentuated when the small door opened. Speaker Lena and a guard entered, both of them still only half his own height.

"How are you feeling?" Speaker Lena asked.

Clive sat up—moving gingerly when the bed creaked under the shifting of his weight.

"Where am I? Where is Chang?"

"You are in one of our guest rooms—one that a certain Speaker had been known to use for his private parties, which is why the bed is closer to what would be comfortable for your size than you might find in some of the other rooms. Your companion is waiting for us in the dining hall. Do you feel up to joining him?"

Clive had that uncomfortable feeling of having missed something important.

"Why are you suddenly being so friendly?" he asked suspiciously.

Speaker Lena shrugged. She turned to the guard. "You may go now," she told him. When the guard had closed the door behind him, she sat down on the end of the bed.

"You feel safe in my presence?" Clive asked.

"Oh, yes. I only had Guard Ourn come with me in case you woke in a state of disorientation and tried to attack me. There's no need for him to be here now."

"How do you know I won't attack you?"

"Because—with the evidence laid irrefutably before us—there can be no doubt that you are the true Clive Folliot. And the true Clive Folliot is a reasonable man, and a gentleman. I believe you'll hear us out first."

"And . . . and my size?" Clive asked.

"We realize now that the Chaffri must have been responsible for altering it. We have our own technicians working on a solution at this very moment."

"I am feeling confused, madam. Why should my being who I am alter your feelings toward me?"

"Because we want to be your friends, Clive Folliot. Because only you can help us in our struggle against the Chaffri."

"And why would I do that?"

"Because you will be helping yourself." Speaker Lena stood then. "We had a seamstress take your size while you slept. Using your decontaminated clothing as a model, she has sewn you a new wardrobe."

Clive glanced at where she pointed to see the clothing set out on a chest that lay at the end of the bed.

"We thought you would be more comfortable in your own familiar style than in the fashion of our city."

"Thank you," Clive said absently.

"You're very welcome. I'll wait for you outside. I'm afraid you'll have to bend a bit to get through the doorway, but the door's unlocked."

Clive nodded. When she left, he got carefully out of the bed. Sitting on his haunches in front of the dresser, he peered into the mirror.

"George?" he said softly. "Are you there?"

There was no reply.

Of course there would be no reply, Clive thought. Had he gone mad? Twice now he thought he'd received a communication from his old friend—and one of those times he had actually seen Du Maurier—but both events had occurred during moments of extreme stress. They were hallucinations, plain and simple. They were what he *wanted*, not what was.

He had confronted so much madness in this Dungeon that he longed with all his heart to touch something of his old life—just to feel that there was a real world beyond this house of Bedlam. Naturally he would imagine George to be the one he could reach—George being the only one of his friends fascinated with paranormal phenomena. Who else to reach for? But what he wanted and what he received, in this place, were never the same. If he wished to communicate with George again, he must first win free of the Dungeon.

It was that simple.

But if he could reach out to Du Maurier . . . pass a message on to his lover Annabella so that she would know he had not deserted her . . .

Clive frowned. That nagging sense of his missing something returned again. There was something about Annabella and du Maurier. . . .

But no sooner did he reach for the memory, than it was gone once more. Clive turned from the mirror to dress, irritated with himself for wanting the impossible to be real. It was time to deal with the present situation. Attempting to salvage some kind of sense from this latest morass of confusion that the Dungeonmasters had placed him in—that would require all of his concentration.

But it was a hard thing to do to put the past aside. Hallucination or not, seeing Du Maurier, hearing his voice again no matter that none of it had been real . . .

Enough, Clive told himself. Dressed in his new clothes, hair combed with his fingers, he bent low and stepped out the door into the hall where Speaker Lena was waiting for him.

CHAPTER EIGHT

Neither Annabelle nor Casey was in a position to do a thing to help Finnbogg. Annabelle was still off balance, just rising from where she'd fallen, one hand gripping the edge of the table that lay on its side beside her. Casey was held back from interfering by a pair of the Baptists. That left Finnbogg on his own. With the Prophet's knife at his throat.

"I didn't hear nobody tell me amen," John J. said. "Are y'all heathens?"

There were Baptists scattered throughout the crowd —enough so that if it came down to a fight, the sides were pretty evenly matched. A lot of people stood to get hurt, not to mention the fact that the club would get trashed.

"C'mon," Annabelle tried.

She straightened one of her legs, then drew it up under herself to give herself something to push off with. Big gang or not, there was no way she was going to let Finn die without giving it her best shot.

"He never did nothing to you," she said.

"I don't want your dog-boy's blood," the Prophet told her earnestly. "It's the Lord wants it. Guess He doesn't like to hear some smart-mouthed slit giving one of His people a hard time—you hear what I'm saying."

"Is that all?" Annabelle asked. She lifted her hand to her bodice as she spoke and activated her Baalbec A-9. "Hell, let's you and me go have some fun. Just leave my friend alone."

John J. shook his head. "Kinda late for that. It's not

just me that's pissed now, y'see. You got the Lord wanting His righteous cut."

"Whatever," Annabelle said.

Because as soon as that knife was away from Finn's throat, John J. was going to find out just how close the Baalbec would let him—never mind his Lord—get to her.

But the Prophet never did get to find out.

"Is there some kind of problem here?" a new voice asked.

John J. looked up into the muzzle of a nickel-plated .44 automatic held in the steady hand of Jack Casady, the Airplane's bass player.

"Butt out, pal," the Prophet told him. "This isn't your business."

Casady shrugged, but the .44 never wavered in his hand. "Seems to me that when a guy's got a knife to the throat of someone in my audience, that makes it my business. Let the kid go."

"It's not a kid," John J. said. "It's not even human."

"More human than you, maybe," Casady replied.

"You're buying into more trouble than you can handle, pal."

Casady laughed. "You think this is trouble? Try calming down a club full of whacked-out Angels sometime."

"Angels?" John J. asked.

Annabelle knew what he was going to say even before Casady spoke. Angels, all right, though they were anything but.

"Hell's Angels," Casady said.

The Prophet's eyes narrowed as he looked up above his glasses at the bass player. "Siding with Satan," he said. "That's blasphemy."

Casady shook his head. "I didn't say I rode with 'em; I just said I've had to deal with them in my time. But you want to talk about taking the Lord's name in vain, you ever stopped and had a real hard look at what you're trying to put across as His word?"

By now others in the band had wandered over to see what was going on.

"Trouble?" Kantner asked.

"Nah," Casady told him. "Guy's just having a little fun. Now he's going to put the knife away and let the kid up—right, friend?"

Ever since the Airplane's bass player had drawn down on the Prophet, there'd been a shift of mood in the room. Annabelle didn't doubt it was a hard life in the Dives. A gig like this one tonight was one of the few chances they had to let go and forget those bad times— just as she'd been trying to. Right about now those who didn't wear the Baptists' colors were sick of screwing around.

"Let's have some more music!" somebody called out.

"Yeah!"

"Everybody's waiting, friend," Casady told the Prophet.

For one long moment Annabelle was sure that John J. was going to cut Finn's throat anyway—just out of sheer perversity. But then he pushed Finn's head away and rose smoothly to his feet, the knife disappearing back into its sheath in his boot.

Casady's automatic tracked the whole movement. Finally freed, Finn turned, a deep growl coming up from his chest until Annabelle thumbed off her Baalbec and caught him by the shoulder.

"Never mind him, Finn."

Under her hand his muscles trembled.

"Why don't you take a little hike around the block," Casady told the Prophet, "just to cool off? And take your boys with you. We're here to have some fun to-night—nobody wants any trouble."

John J. stabbed the air in Casady's general direction. "You're dead meat. You, the girl, and the dog-boy there. The good Lord forgives, but I don't."

Casady laughed again. "Hey, I'm on contract," he said. "I don't live, so I can't die. When my time comes, I'll just fade away."

"Not before I get a piece of you," the Prophet muttered.

But having already been forced to back down once,

he knew it was too late to try to regain the upper hand. Before, when half the crowd was still undecided and nobody really wanted trouble, the Baptists would have had no problem—taking out half the hardasses before anyone really knew what was going down. But now, with everyone primed and ready to dance on Baptist heads, all the Prophet could do was retreat.

But there was going to be a later—and it was going to come real soon. That promise lay in the Prophet's eyes as he backed away through the crowd. Casady waited until John J. was out the door, then winked at Annabelle and headed for the stage, where the rest of the band was getting ready to start the next set.

"What did he mean by that?" Annabelle asked Casey.

"We've got to get you out of here," Casey said. "And fast. If John J. rounds up enough men and comes back looking for you, there'll be all hell to—"

"What did Casady mean about not being alive?" Annabelle demanded.

Casey blinked and looked over at the band. "I got 'em off a batch of GBCs that were boosted from Downside. Friend of mine who got them for me knew the kind of sounds I'm into—my own time in the good ol' US of A."

"And what does that mean?"

"What does what mean?"

"GBCs."

"Genetic blueprint cards—like these."

He pulled what looked like a pack of credit cards from his pocket and showed them to her. Familiar faces rolled by. Hendrix. The Stones. Moby Grape. Lothar and the Hand People. Joplin.

"What are you telling me?" Annabelle asked.

"Look, we've really got to get you out of here," Casey said.

She grabbed his arm as he started to turn away. The band struck up a new song, and she had to shout over the music to be heard.

"What the hell are those things?"

"I told you—they're GBCs. Each of them holds the genetic blueprint for the person pictured on them. That's what they use for entertainment Downside, except once the gig's over, they usually boot the kids back into their cards. Me, I figure if they're good enough to play for me, they can do what they want when the gig's done. Only problem is, it's like Casady says: if they don't get to plug into some sounds on a regular basis, they fade away. They get real hazy until you can almost see through them, then"—he snapped his fingers—"they're gone like they never existed."

"There's people in those cards? Real people?"

Casey shrugged. "I don't know how it works. They're just like real people, but they fade if you don't keep 'em busy."

"You've grown clones of all those musicians?" Annabelle asked, pointing at the GBCs that were still in Casey's hand.

"They're not clones—they're replicas. You'd see the difference straightaway if you saw the real McCoy standing side by side with one of them."

"How do you grow them?"

Casey shook his head. "I told you, they're not clones. You need a projection box. Then all you do is stick the card in, flick a switch, and you got yourself some entertainment."

"That's obscene."

"Maybe the way they use 'em Downside—where you're going—is obscene, but I treat 'em good. Treat 'em like people. Why the hell do you think they stepped in and helped out like they did?"

Annabelle looked up at the band onstage. Casady caught her gaze and nodded to her. She smiled weakly, then looked away.

"I feel sick," she said.

Finnbogg touched her arm, concern plain in his features. "Don't be sick, Annie."

"Yeah," Casey said. "Save it for Downside. This kinda shit's tame to what you're going to find when you get down there."

"Yeah, but—"

"Now are you coming? Or would you rather have another waltz with John J.?"

Annabelle took a last look at the band, then nodded. "I'm coming."

"Well, let's fetch Horace and get you the hell outta here."

Sidi regarded the flat features of the EPs' caterpillar-like leader and thought, tell him about how they had come to be here? Frenchy appeared to accept without question that they were from another world than the Dungeon, but how could anyone be expected to believe all that he and his companions had been through since they had first arrived? There were times he had difficulty believing it all himself.

And there was simply so much to relate.

"Where do I begin?" he said.

Frenchy blew another series of smoke rings to the delight of his entourage of *enfants perdus*. His tiny eyes glinted behind the smoke.

"How did you arrive in the Dungeon?" he asked. "Where did you come from? Tell me all. Time is one thing of which we have no lack, *mes amis*—not in this place."

Sidi glanced at Tomàs, who merely shrugged as though to say, you tell it. So the Indian did just that.

Not long into the story most of the children drifted away to amuse themselves rather than listen to Sidi's dry description of the events that had befallen him and his companions over the past months. But Poot and Nacky stayed, as did a few of the other children, and Frenchy himself proved to be an attentive listener.

"You were old and now you are young," he said when Sidi described his time spent in the Chamber of the Venerated Ones. *"C'est merveilleux."*

"Perhaps," Sidi replied. "But it wasn't an experience I'd care to repeat."

"I understand," Frenchy said. "Perhaps better than you might imagine. But please. Go on."

Sidi continued the story then. Frenchy made no more interruptions until Sidi described how Baron Samedi had destroyed the clone banks on the previous level.

"You are certain?" the EPs' leader asked sharply. He lifted himself slightly, rolls of flesh jiggling like gelatin with the movement, and leaned closer. "It was all destroyed?"

There was something in the tone of his voice that Sidi couldn't quite put his finger on—an intensity that belied the nonchalant attitude he had presented to the travelers since they'd first arrived. Sidi and Tomàs exchanged nervous glances.

"Answer me!" Frenchy cried.

All around the room the various EPs froze where they stood to turn nervous faces toward their leader. Beside Sidi, Nacky and Poot were visibly shivering.

"Yes," Sidi said. "So far as we could tell, it was all destroyed."

Frenchy pinned him with a long, considering glance, then slowly settled the vast bulk of his body back onto the pillows. The various EPs relaxed once more. Frenchy turned his gaze skyward.

"*Sacré mains,*" he said softly. "Perhaps God will answer prayers even in this *damné* place."

"You are familiar with that level of the Dungeon?" Sidi asked.

Frenchy touched his bulbous chest with one slender finger. "How do you think I came to be like this? I too was drawn into this Dungeon through no choice of my own. I made my way through the levels until I was taken on the previous level and . . . experimented upon."

"We were told that those were clones growing in those vats," Sidi said.

Frenchy nodded. "But it amused my captors to manipulate the source bodies as well. What I have seen in that place . . . it was *monstrueux.*"

"You were not always as you are now?" Sidi asked carefully.

"I was born in Paris, *mes amis,* in the year of the revolution—1789. My name was Georges Corbeil. I was still a boy when I was first captured, but I never had a chance to become a man. Instead I was made into this creature you see before you now. The boy I was still lives within this grotesque body, but I am the only one to remember him now."

"Christo," Tomàs breathed.

"And so you gather around you children," Sidi said, "who will not remind you of the monsters disguised as men and women who did this to you."

Frenchy nodded. *"Mes enfants perdus."*

"May we call you Georges?" Sidi asked.

"Georges Corbeil is dead," Frenchy said bitterly. "The only name I have now is the one my cellmates gave me before it was my turn to be taken to those *laboratoires damnés* where this was done to me. You have my eternal gratitude for helping to wreak my vengeance upon those monsters."

There was a long moment of silence during which it seemed no one even breathed. Sidi and Tomàs thought of that room with its hellish vats. Imagining a similar fate befalling themselves, they could only shudder.

"I am very sorry for you," Tomàs said sincerely.

Frenchy shrugged. "It was a long time ago. I do not let it trouble me now."

No, no, Sidi thought. You don't let it trouble you at all.

"Please," Frenchy went on. "Continue with your story. After you destroyed the vats, eh? What befell you then?"

The rest was simple to tell.

"From reports they have brought me," Frenchy said when Sidi was finally done, "I believe that my children have seen some of your companions. But tell me—were you not all of similar proportions?"

"What do you mean?" Sidi asked.

"The children have told me of two groups of new-comers to the Dives. One of these could well be your mechanical being and his companion, but the children tell me that these two are twice the height of a normal man."

"Do they exaggerate?" Sidi asked.

That got him an elbow in the ribs from Nacky, who was still sitting beside him.

"Not if they know what is good for them," Frenchy replied. "Perhaps the Dungeonmasters experimented on them?"

"That would not be possible," Tomàs said. "We all went through the mirror at almost the same time."

"Then these must be clones of your friends—clones grown twice their size. The children tell me that they went below."

Sidi nodded. "What of the other group the children saw?"

"That one had a woman leading them."

Annabelle! Sidi thought. She was still alive. His heart skipped a beat, as it did whenever he thought of her.

"And she had with her?" he asked.

"A broad dwarfish being with the features of a dog, and a hairless man wearing little more than a cloak."

That would be Finnbogg and Horace. Sidi turned to Tomàs, and they shared a grin. At least three of their companions were safe.

"Can your children take us to them?" Tomàs asked.

Frenchy nodded. "But I would not advise it, *mes amis.* They have gone to a dangerous area in the Dives. Tonight the voice of the streets tells me that the Baptists are angry and gather in strength in the very area where your friends were last seen. You would do better to wait until the excitement has died down."

Sidi didn't know who or what Frenchy meant by the Baptists, but he did know that if there was trouble brewing near to where their friends were, then the odds were better than good that Annabelle and the others would be in the middle of that misfortune. That was simply how it seemed to work in the Dungeon.

"We have to join them as soon as possible," Sidi said.

"*Alors,*" Frenchy said. "I am indebted to you, so I will help you as best I can. I will have one of my children take you near to where your friends were last seen, but I cannot risk more of them than that."

"I'll take them," Nacky said. "I'll take them right into Casey's. I ain't scared."

"And what, *ma petite,* if you do not find it so easy to return? If the Baptists catch you, they will not be kind. They will keep you from me and your brothers and sisters, and then you will grow old. Would you like to risk that?"

Nacky simply shrugged. "I ain't scared," she repeated. "I kicked a Baptist once—right in his knee—and took off fast. He never even tried to catch me."

"We don't want to risk your children," Sidi said, "but we will need a guide."

"Malheureusement," Frenchy said, "this body of mine, *c'est immobile.* It will have to be one of the children."

"I'm really not scared even a bit," Nacky assured them.

"Me neither," Poot added.

"I was never scared, ever," another of the EPs, whose name they didn't know, piped up.

Tomàs smiled. "One guide will be enough, I think."

"Perhaps it will be one too many," Frenchy said. "You don't know these Baptists, *mes amis.* They are very strong and tonight—I have been told—they are very unhappy. If they were to catch you or your friends . . ."

"But they are our friends," Tomàs said.

Sidi nodded. "If there is a chance that they are in danger, how could we not go to help them?"

Frenchy nodded wearily. *"C'est vrai.* In a place such as this we have only our friends. Go then—with my blessing. Nacky will guide you, since she seems so eager to go."

"I've got a lucky stone," Nacky said, "so everything'll just work out better 'n good."

Sidi and Tomàs rose to their feet. Nacky started to tug on Sidi's hand, but he held back long enough to give Frenchy a short bow.

"It's been an honor to meet you," he said.

"If you survive, bring your friends to speak with me," Frenchy replied. "I can show you a way below."

"Below?"

"Into Downside. If you wish to go on to the next level, you must go among the Chaffri and the Ren to do so."

There would be time to worry about that later.

"We will try to return to see you," Sidi said. Then he gave in to Nacky's insistent cries of "C'mon, c'mon," and her tugging on his arm.

"Adiós," Tomàs said. He tapped a forefinger against his temple in a quick salute before he hurried off to join Sidi.

Frenchy nodded to himself as they left. *"Oui. Adieu et bon chance, mes amis,* but I fear I won't be seeing you again."

Tomàs and Sidi heard that, but then a crowd of laughing children were clustered around them to see them off, and if Frenchy had anything more to say, they didn't get to hear it.

"What do you think these Baptists are?" Tomàs asked Sidi as Nacky led them into a stairwell.

"They're bad and ugly," Nacky called back over her shoulder.

Of course, Sidi thought. They were a danger of the Dungeon, so what else could they be? But he thought of the tragic figure they had just left behind them, of Shriek and Finnbogg and others he had met who didn't fit into a certain consideration of what was beautiful, and realized that he was doing Frenchy, and many another victim of the Dungeonmasters, or perhaps just victims of simple fate, an injustice.

It was those who wore ugliness in their hearts—of them one must take care.

Impossible as Neville might have thought it, he and his companions eventually grew used to the noxious stench that pervaded the sewer system. It was worse when their mounts had to disturb the still pools, but

only nominally so, and they soon became inured to that
as well.

More disturbing was the increasing appearance of
heaps of rubble where parts of the ceiling had fallen in.
Though each time the debris proved passable, they
could not help but worry that the next time their route
would be well and truly blocked, and they would need
to turn back.

They kept track of the hours by the lifetimes of their
torches. As a torch lasted approximately twenty minutes, Neville reckoned that they had been in the sewer
system for almost two hours when they finally rested
on a low platform that the silvers reached by means of a
sudden, heart-stopping scrabble up a face of loose
stone.

Of them all Shriek appeared the least discomfited by
both their surroundings and the rough terrain.

*My olfactory senses do not have the same reference
points as do yours, Being Neville,* she explained when
Neville complained to her about it, *so I am not as
troubled with the smell. And my physique is better
suited to navigating our route than are either yours or
the Tuan. Our positions were reversed on some of the
other levels.*

And she had offered no complaint then, Neville
thought. But of course Shriek, being who she was, left
that unspoken.

I'm merely frustrated, he told her. *Rationally, I'm
happy that it goes so easily for you.*

What Neville had come to recognize as a smile
passed briefly over the arachnid's features. *But physi-
cally, it is not so easy to be logical,* she finished for him.

Exactly.

He leaned back against the side of Alyssa's mount,
which lay stretched out on the platform, eyes closed,
breathing even. Alyssa sat a few feet away from him.

"I think you and Shriek have brought us luck," she
said, turning to look at him.

"How so?"

"We've never come this far before in any of the tunnels."

Neville laughed. "Thank the dogs then—not us."

Alyssa shook her head. "How do you keep your spirits so cheerful? My own people make no pretense of how little they're enjoying this place."

She nodded to her companions who, all except for Fenil, lounged against their own mounts, dour looks on their faces. Fenil leaned over the edge of the platform, torch held out above his head, trying to spy what he could of the road still to come.

Neville shrugged. "I could make a joke and say I've seen worse."

"But . . . ?"

"It's no joke, but I have seen worse. At least here no one's trying to loosen my head from my neck. These tunnels are as charming as swimming in a privy, but we are still free. We do what we do by our own inclination. And . . ." He laughed again, but this time there was a sardonic note to his humor.

"And?" Alyssa prompted him again.

"Each step we take brings us closer to the bastards who have put us into this situation in the first place."

Alyssa said nothing for a long moment, only staring off into the darkness, then she slowly nodded. "I too have words I wish to share with the Dungeonmasters." She turned to look at Neville. "How long has your party been trapped in here?"

When Neville shrugged, Shriek said, *It varies. I have been here for a few of what Neville terms years; for Neville it has been a year or so. One of our companions claims a residency of ten thousand years.*

Neville smiled, thinking of Finnbogg and his preposterous tales. But it was true that each one had some kernel of truth hidden in it.

"I believe it," Alyssa said. "In this place I will believe anything. In my homeland we have tales of the Weeping Desert—where souls go who have not served the Great Wind with all the heart, strength, and loyalty that they might have. They are sent to the Weeping

Desert—there to suffer until the Great Wind's Second Moon returns. This Dungeon has appeared too much like the Weeping Desert, at times, for my liking."

Neville began to describe the last level they had passed through, which had been so much like the hell of his own homeland's religion.

"We saw no such place," Alyssa said. "Neither the place of fires, nor the barony, nor the medicine tent with its evil twins."

"Not twins," Neville said. "One of our companions—the cyborg Guafe—explained it to us. The Dungeon-masters can grow exact replicas of us from the smallest particle of our body. He called them clones. But they are not like twins that have grown together in the same womb."

"How can you be so sure?" Alyssa asked.

"Because one of our missing companions is not only my brother, but my twin as well. And as Shriek will vouch for me, I'm sure, we bear little resemblance to each other, save for that physical family resemblance that any siblings might share."

"But these vats . . ."

Neville nodded. "I agree. It's an evil process."

But blame not the creatures themselves, Shriek added. *Rather, blame those who created them.*

"I'd sooner kiss the butt of the Night Troll," Yoors said, speaking for the first time, "than forgive such monsters."

Neville smiled to himself. He had been certain that the captain hadn't been dozing as he'd pretended but listening to the whole of their conversation.

"They killed his brother, Shian," Alyssa explained.

Yoors shook his head. "They didn't kill him—they butchered him. Butchered him like some animal while we were forced to flee without giving him his final rites."

If one looks deep enough, Shriek said in her mild voice, *we can see a reason for every being's temperament.*

When no one replied, Neville realized that she had narrowed her neural broadcast so that only he could hear what she said. He nodded, understanding what she meant.

I'll try to be easier on him, he told her.

He could feel her smile in his mind. *There is hope for you yet, Being Neville.*

Alyssa was unaware of the conversation that had gone on between the two. "It was in that damned desert," she was saying, "the one that finally led us to this level."

"You saw no looking glass? None of what I described?"

Alyssa shook her head. "Only what seemed to be an endless waste. And there were creatures in it—dry, scaly monsters that thrived in the desolation. Shian was killed by one just as we reached the entranceway to the gate. . . ."

"I'm sorry, Yoors," Neville said. "For everything."

The captain gave him a hard look before turning away.

Neville glanced at the arachnid. *I'm trying, Madam Shriek, but he's not helping. What does he want?*

Perhaps a chance to come to grips with his loss? she replied.

"What made it worse," Alyssa said, "was that we were so close to escaping. All we needed were another few moments and—"

Fenil hissed suddenly. He drew back from the edge of the platform. Yoors was immediately on his feet, quickly followed by the others.

"What is it?" the captain asked.

"Something is approaching," Fenil replied. "Something very large."

"Perhaps more than one something," Yoors said as he reached the edge of the platform and peered off into the darkness.

Lovely, Neville thought. Trust the Dungeonmasters to make certain that there was never a dull moment.

* * *

Like the room in which Clive had woken the hallway where Speaker Lena waited for him would not have been out of place in any good London gentleman's home. Its very familiarity reawakened Clive's homesickness once again.

East or West, Home is Best.

Clive had always thought of that little homily as a middle-class ideal, but now, after months in the Dungeon . . . What he wouldn't give to be home once more. His present surroundings merely accentuated that yearning.

The hallway was carpeted underfoot in a deep burgundy. The walls held sconces converted to electrical lighting and portraits of muttonchopped gentlemen and charming ladies in scenes that reminded Clive of his friend Du Maurier's work for *Once A Week* and *Punch.* Side tables with decorative urns and statuary could be found every ten feet or so, and the ceiling, while uncomfortably close because of Clive's current size, was delicately arched.

Clive felt like some lumbering beast as he followed Speaker Lena down the hall, their footfalls masked by the deep pile of the carpeting.

"This building is the Speakers' Hall," Speaker Lena explained as they walked. "It lies across the city from where you were first brought in. This particular wing is dedicated to English Victoriana—the patterns and expressions of your own particular era."

"Why?" Clive asked.

Speaker Lena paused to look at him. "I'm sorry?"

"Why is this wing dedicated to my era?"

She smiled. "Because there are many among us who have taken a great liking to your particular period." She began to walk on again. "Your time was one of glorious advances in the arts—a flowering of science and creative expression."

Clive thought of all the progress the world had come to know in the century after his own—of all that his great-granddaughter had described to him during their months together. From all he'd seen of this city so far, its inhabitants were easily as technologically advanced.

"I would think you would see us a primitive people," he said.

"In some ways—yes, of course. But the spirit of your time was so open to that which was new. . . ."

Clive blinked. Open to that which was new? He considered the society of his time, the Church of England, social mores, class structure. . . . When he compared their likes to how men and women could live together, as he'd come to understand through his relationship with the lost members of his company, he knew that there was a great deal that could be changed in English society—and all for the better.

It was still home, to be sure, and he longed for it, but if ever he could return, he would be a far different man than he had been before he had put England's shores behind him.

"I believe you have an idealized impression of my time," he said.

Speaker Lena shrugged. "Probably."

"And have you been there?" Clive asked.

He had been wondering for some time if the beings that inhabited the Dungeon ever crossed over to the worlds from which the Dungeonmasters kidnapped their unwilling game pieces. And then there was the consideration that anyone he met in this place might actually *be* one of the Dungeonmasters. So he meant to question and learn all he could; to be friendly but to keep his own counsel; and above all to look for the chance to escape so that he could get back to the true business at hand—reuniting with his companions and defeating the Dungeonmasters.

"Well?" he prompted the Speaker when she didn't answer him at once. "Have you?"

Speaker Lena smiled. "Of course—but I'll never actually live there, so what harm does idealizing do?"

There was harm in the spread of any lie, Clive thought, even when its basis merely lay in ignorance or thoughtlessness, but he was hard put to explain exactly why—even to himself. Until he could, he saw no point in contesting the point with his present companion.

"What of the Hall's other wings?" he asked instead.

"I was going to tell you to prepare yourself," Speaker Lena replied as they approached a door at the end of the hallway.

The door was enormous—solid wood panels with brass gilding and knobs. On either side of it stood tall vases, brimming over with bouquets of fresh roses. The blossoms seemed tiny to Clive. Unreal.

"Prepare myself for what?" he asked.

"Each wing has a different decorative theme. We are a people who delight in the acquisition of cultures, wholeheartedly embracing whichever appeals the most to us—at least until another, more attractive one comes along. The houses and apartments in the city might have a room dedicated to, say, the Sak of ancient Heline—a race of beings who would spend their formative years in a cocoon, before emerging as brilliantly tattooed insectoids—side by side with another given over to the Ming Dynasty of your own world's China, or the sand-faring Lem, the artifacts of whose entire culture are based solely on spheres."

"And beyond this door?" Clive asked.

"Lies the Hub of the Speakers' Hall, which corresponds roughly to Central Plaza—the inner core of the city, which is given over to our own culture."

She opened the door as she spoke, and Clive found himself looking at whiteness. Walls, floor, ceiling, the clothing of the people—it was all blank. Ciphers. Everything was utilitarian. There were no statues, no paintings on the walls. Angles were precise with an utter lack of decorative appeal.

He turned to give his companion a puzzled look. "But . . ."

Speaker Lena nodded sadly. "We are a chameleon people," she said. "We have no culture of our own—only what we borrow from others."

"But I don't even see that."

"It's not considered good form to wear one's obsessions in public."

"I see," Clive said.

But he didn't. How could a race of people exist without a culture of their own? Surely it was impossible. At some point in their history they *had* to have had fashions and fads that they could call their own. Didn't they?

"Come," Speaker Lena said.

She led him out into the Hub, which proved to be an enormous room inside which could have easily fit a half dozen of the Great Exhibition's famous Glass Palace. Here their shoes clacked on the floor, and Clive was very much aware of the attention he drew. From the looks upon the faces of those he passed, he saw that they viewed him in much the same manner as had the leader of the guard who had first captured him and Guafe in the underground railway station.

He could almost hear the guard captain's voice hissing, "Freak," in his ear as he watched their gazes slide from his own. The rising grumble of their voices as they spoke of him followed unpleasantly in his wake. Their antagonism, coupled with his recent thoughts of du Maurier, brought an odd memory to mind—that of the time he'd met the tragic Mary Wollstonecraft Shelley not long before her death in fifty-one.

After meeting the poet's wife he had searched out and read her novel of the Modern Prometheus with great interest, even going on to take in the London stage production of the book.

There had been a pathos about the monster that had deeply moved Clive—more so in the novel than in its adaptation to the stage. He had found himself thinking, in the weeks that followed his first reading of the novel, of just how the monster had felt, trying to imagine himself in a similar position.

Now he knew.

He wasn't the same hideous monster—at least not to his own gaze, nor from the image he had seen looking back at him from the mirror earlier today—but to these people he was a freak of nature all the same. How else could they perceive him as he towered above them, twice as tall as the tallest in their number?

"Perhaps we should have taken another route," Speaker Lena said softly at his side.

Clive bent lower to hear her. "Why's that?"

"Because I have the uncomfortable feeling that things are about to become very ugly," Speaker Lena replied. "Quickly! Make for that far door."

But it was already too late. Though they still kept their distance, the crowd was thickening, and their epithets were no longer muttered under their breath but hurled at Clive in loud voices instead.

Things were becoming ugly indeed, Clive realized as one of the crowd threw the core of a piece of fruit at him.

▪ CHAPTER NINE ▪

Horace was waiting for them by the door that led back into Casey's apartment. He had a crowbar, the only weapon he could find on such short notice, in his hand. Linda stood beside him, a worried expression on her face.

"Thanks for the thought," Annabelle told Smythe, "but the crisis is over." She glanced at Casey. "Isn't it?"

He nodded. "If we get you out of here right away. Back on the floor John J. might've let his boys cut loose if Casady hadn't got the drop on him. We let him stew a while, and he could get up enough hardasses to make a run at the club. But if he knows you're gone, things'll cool down. No matter what John J. says, his Baptists like to have themselves a drink and some good music once in a while, and this club's the best there is in the Dives. They won't wreck it."

"What about you and Linda?"

"I'm telling you, Annabelle. We'll make do. You're the one that's got to get outta here. Pronto."

"And Casady?"

"He's a GBC replica. What's John J. going to do to him?"

Behind them in the club the Airplane were still cooking on the stage, a raunchy rock 'n' roll number with Slick's cool voice soaring overtop. Replicas, Annabelle thought. Jesus.

"I guess the thing that bothers me the most," she said, "is that they know what they are and it doesn't seem to bother them a bit. I mean, what kind of a life is that?"

Casey shrugged. "The only kind of life they'll ever know."

That woke an echo in Annabelle's mind. She chased it down until she came up with the song: "Tobacco Road," on *Takes Off*. Right. A little too apropos for her present mood.

"I know it doesn't seem right," Linda said. "We felt the same way you did until we got this latest batch of cards and talked to them. The originals are still out there in the real world, doing what they do best. The replicas really are happy just playing their tunes."

"Those originals aren't all out there anymore," Annabelle said.

Casey gave her a hard look. "What's that supposed to mean?"

"People die—musicians just the same as everybody else. Hendrix, Morrison, Joplin, Lennon . . . they're all gone now. All that's left is their music—at least that's all we ever thought was left. But I come here and find that the Dungeonmasters have managed to steal a piece of their souls, or whatever the hell it is that they do to get 'em into those cards, and you've got their ghosts up playing on a two-bit stage." She shook her head. "I always thought rock 'n' roll heaven was going to be different, you know?"

"Hendrix . . . Joplin . . . they're dead?"

Annabelle nodded. "You don't want to hear the whole roll call—believe me."

"Morrison too?" Linda asked. "And Lennon?"

"I always thought they'd get the band together and start playing again," Casey said.

Linda nodded. "Who else is gone?"

"Like I said: you don't want to get me going," Annabelle said. "You've gotta understand, I'm from the ass-end of the twentieth century—the big one-nine-nine-nine. I recognize the faces on those cards you've got 'cause my mom turned me onto all that old music. But I don't think any of those people are even players anymore. Kids don't want to get their rock 'n' roll from some grayhead, old enough to be their grandfather."

"Man," Casey said. "I'd never want 'em to stop playing."

Annabelle shrugged. "Well, you got a point. A lot of the old guard's still going strong. Course, what keeps those bands on stage and cutting CDs is that the fans who grew up listening to 'em are now investment bankers and brokers and the like, and they can afford the pricy concert tickets and shit." She shook her head. "I remember seeing a poster for Garcia and the Dead playing a concert in Wembley just before I got dumped into this place."

"You'd never want the Dead to stop playing."

Annabelle gave him a sad smile. "Guess that's what keeps them grateful, right? But it don't do much for those who are really gone. . . ."

Casey straightened up. "Okay. That's a bummer, but we don't have time for any of this. I'd love to sit down and talk about the Fillmore and all, but we've got to get you out of here, or you won't even get the chance to have a replica on one of these cards."

"What makes you think I'd want . . ."

Annabelle's voice trailed off as the thought struck home. What was she saying, she didn't want to have a part of herself in one of those cards? Knowing the Dungeonmasters, they already had pieces of her playing gigs all over the frigging Dungeon.

"I really think I'm going to be sick," she said.

"You don't have time for that kind of shit," Casey told her.

Linda pressed a small sack of provisions into Finnbogg's arms.

"Take care of yourselves," she said.

"Thank you, madam," Smythe said. "And you, Mr. Jones."

"Now listen up," Casey said as he led them to where the club's back door opened into an alleyway. He gave them quick, concise directions on how to find safe passage to Downside.

"Once you're heading down through the tunnels, just keep the paint splashes on your left—they're about shoulder level," he finished up. "You should do okay. Linda threw a couple of flashlights in your pack that've got enough juice in 'em to take you all the way down. Just don't go wandering, 'cause I don't know how long they'll last after that."

"How do you know about this passage?" Smythe asked.

Casey grinned. "It's a smuggler's route, and you, folks, are looking at one of the prime movers of Chaffri goods in the Dives. Don't worry. I'm not steering you wrong."

Smythe nodded. "Anything else we should know about the passage?"

"Just stick to my directions, and you'll do fine. You shouldn't run into any of the Chaffri's zeros, but you've still got to keep your eyes open. They've got more snares down there than you can shake a—"

"Zeros?" Annabelle asked.

"They're a kind of simulacrum—all fiber and plastic and metal, but they've got human brains housed inside, wired up to computerized motor units." He took in the looks on Annabelle and Smythe's faces. "I told you there was weirder shit than the GBCs down there."

"Can you give us any weapons?" Smythe asked. "Even just a saber?"

Casey shook his head. "That's prime goods up here, and something the smugglers don't run up to us real often. They're too hard to boost from the Chaffri. I mean you figure it—if you were the Chaffri, you might let toys and shit get into our hands, but weapons? That's just buying trouble."

They had reached the back door now.

"Hang loose a minute," Casey said.

He eased the door open and slipped outside, returning in a few moments.

"I don't know. It feels quiet—maybe too quiet for a night in the Dives."

"We can't stay," Annabelle said.

She gave Linda a kiss on her cheek and accepted a

hug from Casey before leading her small company out the door.

"Give 'em hell," Casey said before he closed the door.

"You bet, sailor," Annabelle told him.

The club door closed with a soft snick, then they heard the bolt being engaged as it was locked. Annabelle looked at her companions.

"Okay, kids," she said. "Time to boogie."

"Amen," a quiet voice from behind her added.

They turned to see the alleyway filling with Baptists, John J. in the fore. By the time they looked back the way they'd been heading, it too was blocked by gang members.

"Time to say bye-bye, sweet world," the Prophet told them, "because the Good Lord's best shepherd is looking to harvest your souls. And the real sad thing—least it's sad from your point of view—is that there ain't no GBCer here to save your asses now."

Nacky kept up a constant chatter as she led Sidi and Tomàs from the tower of *les enfants perdus* and out into the night-cloaked streets of the ruined city. When they finally reached the ground floor of that first building and stepped out onto the cracked and buckling pavement, Tomàs stamped a foot on the ground and grinned at his companion.

"Por último," he said. "No more desperate climbs or swinging like monkeys from a rope, *sim*?"

Sidi smiled back at him. He too felt relieved to finally be on the ground once more.

"I would think," he said, "that as accustomed as you are to a ship's rigging, you would have been more comfortable in the heights."

"There is a *grande diferencia* between the two," Tomàs replied. "Trust me."

Sidi looked up the clifflike face of the building behind them. It seemed to rise as tall as the heights of the Himalayas in the darkness.

"A very big difference," he agreed.

"C'mon," Nacky said impatiently, tugging on Sidi's arm again. "Lots of way to go still."

"Then lead on," Sidi told her.

She kept steadily to a quicker pace than either of the men would have assumed a child could. Mostly they went by main boulevards, skirting the heaps of rubble, pushing through waist-high fields of weeds that grew right out of the pavement. But from time to time they would spy a fire ahead, and then Nacky would lead them by circuitous routes through alleyways and deserted buildings.

"Whose fires are those?" Sidi asked her as they by-passed yet another.

He could dimly make out figures gathered around the fire, warming their hands to the flames, lounging on the ground, sharing bottles of what he assumed was alcohol.

Nacky shrugged. "Rubbies or gangs. At this time of night it don't matter which. They're 'll trouble."

"Rubbies?" Tomàs asked.

"Bums," she explained. "They've got no home like Frenchy made for us, and they're too old to belong to a gang."

"Ah," Tomàs said. "Beggars. Yet who do they beg from?"

"They just make do, like we all do, 'cept they don't make do as well."

They skirted the fire, entering the ruin of a building that was merely support beams standing like dead tree limbs over the building's original foundation. A mountain of fallen stone showed where its walls had fallen—so long ago now that the sharp edges of the stones were rounded by vegetation.

Two more back alleys through increasingly better-weathered buildings brought them out onto a main thoroughfare once more. Ahead of them they could now see another fire, but there was something different about this one. A few blocks closer and they could see that it was an enormous burning cross.

"Oh, this is bad," Nacky said.

She hid behind a mound of fallen stones, pulling at her companions' sleeves until they crouched down with her.

"What is it?" Sidi asked.

Nacky pointed to the cross. "That's the Baptists," she said.

Sidi could count close to fifty men gathered around the fire. They wore only trousers and vests, their bare skin gleaming in the light cast from the burning arms of the cross. There was something at the base of the fire that had their attention. Because of his angle of sight, Sidi couldn't make out what it was that interested them so.

"Can we go around them?" Tomàs asked.

Nacky shook her head. "See that sign?"

Now that it was pointed out, both men could see the neon CASEY'S that hung on the wall of the building behind the gang.

"That's the club where your friends went," Nacky explained.

"Isn't there a rear entrance?"

"Oh, sure. But look."

Once more Sidi studied the open ground where the Baptists were gathered, and this time he saw what he'd missed before. There were gang members standing on guard the length and breadth of the area. He started to turn to Tomàs, but then the Portuguese's hand touched his arm, fingers tightening.

A shift in the crowd had made enough of an opening for Sidi to catch the familiar crest of Annabelle's short-cropped hair. A moment later he spied Finnbogg's bulk, then the crowd shifted again, and the two were lost from sight.

"We won't need to go to the club anymore," he told Nacky.

"You don't want to help your friends now?"

Sidi nodded toward the burning cross. "The Baptists have our friends."

"Better say bye-bye to them," Nacky said. "Better

say it from here and real quietly, 'cause you can't do
nothing else now."

Sidi turned to look at Tomàs.

"Asno," the Portuguese muttered unhappily. "What
can we do now?"

Sidi's hands clenched into fists as he stared out at the
Baptists once more. The flickering of the flames on the
burning arms of the cross sent shadows skittering
across the gathered men and out to where the darkness
pooled deeper by the buildings. The constant motion
of the Baptists and the red tinge of the light gave the
scene a hellish quality all too reminiscent of the fire
fields they had passed through on the previous level.

Barely passed through.

"I don't know," he said. "There are so many of
them. . . ."

"We must do *something,*" Tomàs said.

Sidi nodded. Yes, of course. They would do something. Those were their friends out there. And Annabelle . . . They had to do something more than
crouch here and watch.

Only what?

There was no need of their own torches to cast light
on the two immense beings that were coming down
the tunnel toward them, for they gave off a pale luminescence that appeared to originate from their own
skin. Taking in their height, their enormous bulk, Neville realized that he had not in fact had even an inkling
as to how Swift's hero had felt when he first reached
Brobdingnag.

The buildings above, huge in scale to his own size,
the feral dogs . . . neither could have prepared him
for the helplessness he now felt regarding the two beings that presently approached them.

They were scaled to the size of the city, and, had
Neville been in proportion himself, would have stood a
head shorter than he. But what they lacked in height
they more than made up for in bulk. They were bal-
loonish creatures—round heads attached to round bod-

ies without the benefit of visible necks. Their legs were squat, their arms insect thin.

And they were as alike as two peas in a pod.

Twins.

Enormous, grotesque twins.

"What have we . . ." one began.

". . . got here?" the other finished.

"Little . . ."

". . . people."

"Small as . . ."

". . . mice."

Their voices boomed in the confines of the tunnel. More disconcerting was the way the one finished the other's sentences, as though they shared one mind. Their enormous faces bent down to look at Neville's party, eyes like saucers, smiling like a pair of bedlam inmates, their grins stretching from ear to ear.

"But we've . . ."

". . . seen their like before."

"Haven't . . ."

". . . we just?"

"Dip them in . . ."

". . . chocolate, wrap them in . . ."

". . . pastry, and won't they taste . . ."

". . . just fine?"

The two fat faces turned to each other, happy as a pair of bedlamites. If it was possible, their grins had widened. Two large hands rose, fat fingers reaching toward Yoors and Fenil.

While the rest of their party could only gape at the pair, Shriek quickly tugged free a handful of her hair spikes. Quick as an adder's strike she threw them. By the time the first pair of spiked missiles struck—one in a left eye, the other in a right—there were four more spikes already in flight.

The monsters roared. Clasping at their eyes, the remaining spikes punctured their fat hands. They reared to their full height, bellowing with pain. The sound rumbled like thunder and was answered by alarming groans from the walls and ceiling of the tunnel.

Fly! Shriek cried to her companions.

In moments the Tuan were mounted—Neville sharing Alyssa's silver once more—and the quick beasts skittered down the face of loose stone that led up the platform where they had been resting. The well-trained animals responded to their riders' commands and darted between the legs of the giants, who lumbered about, shouting with pain.

"Kill them . . ."

". . . all!"

"Mash them, smash them . . ."

". . . flat as cow turds!"

The giants stamped about, trying to stop the fleeing Tuan. They roared and howled, batting at the air as though to ward off a cloud of stinging gnats. But these gnats were Shriek's hair spikes, which she continued to toss with great effect at the pair until the roof over the platform began to give way and she had to make her own escape.

She ran at the heels of the rearmost Tuan and was only a few feet behind them when a great foot came down and squashed both rider and mount flat. Blood and less easily defined matter sprayed over the arachnid and the floor of the tunnel all about her. She lost her footing and fell, gaze turned upward to see another foot coming down at her.

She rolled desperately aside, but she was so close to the descending foot that she felt a rush of air as it hit the ground. She cast off with a thread from her spinnerets, snagging the rough cloth of the monster's trousers. When he lifted his foot again, she rode up with him, casting out another thread as his foot came down once more.

This one snagged the tunnel wall so that, when she let the first loose, she swung out and away from under the feet of the two monsters. Each blind in one eye, they could still see enough to realize that all save one of their prey was escaping.

"Catch . . ."

". . . them!"

Shriek! Neville cried, looking back over his shoulder. Clouds of rock dust hid her from his sight.

Coming . . . Being . . . Neville . . . Shriek managed to reply as she swung herself to the floor.

As soon as she touched ground, she was off and running, the monsters hard on her heels. All around them the tunnels grumbled and groaned. Dirt and bits of stone cascaded down in blinding showers. The ground shook under the monsters' tread. The tremors threw off her sense of equilibrium, making it difficult for her to keep her balance.

Shriek! Neville cried again.

He looked back, trying to spot her amid the falling debris.

He saw only a fog of powdered stone.

Shriek! he cried again, desperately now.

For all his attraction to Alyssa, for all that the Tuan seemed more his kind than the alien, it was at that moment that Neville understood that a bond had grown up not only between Shriek and himself, but between all the members of their original party. He realized that he'd rather die with his companions than seek safety on his own or with comparative strangers.

The intensity of the bond surprised him, but he put further conjecture along those lines behind him. There was no time for it just now.

He loosened his grip from Alyssa's waist.

"Neville . . . ?" Alyssa began to ask.

But Neville's attention lay only on their backtrail.

Shriek! he tried one last time.

Still no reply.

He was about to leap off Alyssa's mount then, to go back and help the arachnid, when he saw her burst through a cloud of dirt, her body wreathed in gray dust. She seemed shaken, moving not so quickly as she was normally able.

But she was alive.

She raced to catch up. When the dust briefly cleared again, Neville saw one of the giants fast approaching as

well. A moment later, and the other was in view as
well.

Just when Clive was certain that the unpleasantness
in the Hub was about to develop into a full-scale riot,
the door that Speaker Lena was steering him toward
opened, and a number of guards stepped through, led
by the captain who had first captured him in the underground station.

The crowd shuffled uneasily at their appearance.
When the guards brought their weapons up to firing
positions, they immediately began to disperse. In moments Clive and the Speaker were alone with the
guards in the center of the immense chamber. Around
them the Ren went about their business as though
nothing untoward had ever occurred.

"A fortunate arrival, Cavet," Speaker Lena said.

The guards' captain shrugged. "We've already been
through the same thing with our other"—he paused
significantly—"guest. Not that I can see why you'd
bother."

"Cavet . . ." Speaker Lena warned.

"I know, I know. But look at the size of him. He's like
something that grew on the underside of a Chaffri
breeding tank, and the 'borg—you can't tell me he isn't
a Chaffri construct."

"That will be quite enough. It's no fault of our guests
that the Chaffri did this to them."

"Yeah. Right."

All I would need to do, Clive thought, would be to
just bring my fist down on the top of his tiny head.
Perhaps there were benefits to this size. Though, of
course, with those guards and their weapons . . . He
didn't doubt that it wouldn't take much for the weapons to be trained on him rather than to protect him as
they were now.

"It seems I'm not well liked here," he remarked to
the Speaker. "It makes me wonder, yet again, why I
would want to help you."

He kept his tone mild, but the Speaker didn't miss the flash of anger in his eyes.

"An unfortunate accident," she began.

Clive shook his head. "I don't think so. What strikes me as particularly odd, however, is how a people so enamored with alien cultures can dislike aliens as much as they do."

"It's not that they perceive you as alien," Speaker Lena said. "It's that they see you as an ally of the Chaffri."

"At this moment," Clive replied, giving the captain Cavet a hard stare, "I am an ally of neither your enemies, nor you."

Now the anger was reflected in the Speaker's eyes, but it wasn't directed toward Clive.

"Guards," she said, "you will answer directly to me now."

"Speaker," Cavet began.

"You, Captain Cavet, are hereby relieved of duty and under house arrest. You will turn in your weapon and remain at your apartment until a board of inquiry has been convened to judge your actions—actions, I would like to add, that are in direct contravention of your orders. Clive Folliot and his companion are our honored guests." Her gaze raked the remainder of the guard. "You would all do well to remember that."

The men shifted uneasily, not one of them willing to meet her gaze.

"Cavet," she said. "Your weapon."

For one moment Clive was sure the man would refuse, perhaps even use the weapon on the Speaker or himself—guest or no guest—but then slowly he handed it to one of his men. Turning abruptly, he stalked off.

Speaker Lena pointed to one of the guard. "You will go with Cavet to see that he does indeed return to his apartment, and will remain on guard at his door until you are relieved. The rest of you will accompany us."

Respectfully guards held the doors open for them both, following once the Speaker and Clive had entered. This hallway had a completely machinelike appearance. If Annabelle had been with them, she would have described the decor as having the appearance of the innards of a computer. Circuitry and wiring rambled in a bewildering pattern across floors, walls, and ceiling. Banks of tiny red light flashed in confusing patterns. To Clive it was reminiscent of what he'd spied of Guafe's inner workings the times when the cyborg opened one of his bodily panels to make some adjustment or other.

He imagined a cyborg yet larger still than either he or Guafe, a simulacrum as large as a city, and they were walking about inside it. . . .

The idea brought a queasy feeling to his stomach. To allay it, he turned again to his companion.

"I don't think your people's animosity has anything to do with who I am or am not allied with," Clive said as they set off down the corridor.

"No, truly—"

"They see me as a monster," Clive interrupted. "I've seen the look before—it's not easily forgotten."

He didn't add that it had been on his own features when he was first confronted with Shriek or some of the other more alien beings he had previously encountered in the Dungeon. He was not proud of those reactions—not now, when he realized how true those same alien beings had proved to be, time and again.

He thought again of Mrs. Shelley's novel, and that monstrous creation of the doctor that wreaked such havoc in its pages. The monster hadn't been evil of itself—rather, it had been driven to its evil actions by the wrongs committed to it. Considering his own feelings when confronted by the crowd in the Hub, he saw how easily such a point of view could be acquired.

"A monster," he repeated.

He turned to look at the Speaker. When she wouldn't meet his gaze, he nodded to himself.

"My people are enamored with alien cultures," she said finally. "Unfortunately, they hate the aliens themselves for having those cultures where they have none."

"And you?" Clive asked. "Do you hate as well?"

Speaker Lena glanced briefly at him, then pointed to the walls. "This was patterned after a cyborg race—related, perhaps, to your companion Guafe—who created a culture of their own in a derelict space station near the planet of Elex. Elex itself was devastated by a nuclear holocaust two centuries ago, as you count time. . . ."

Clive shut her explanation off and thought instead of his missing companions. He prayed that they were in more fortunate circumstances than he and Chang had found themselves, though he doubted that would be the case.

They were all mad—Ren and Chaffri and whoever else was in charge of this Dungeon. He didn't want to help them. Not for a moment.

All he wanted was to bring them to their knees for what they had done to him, to his family and friends, and then be done with them all. For that he needed to be patient a while longer.

But patience was a virtue that he found harder and harder to embrace with each moment he spent in the Dungeon.

■ CHAPTER TEN ■

Annabelle didn't even have time to activate her Baal-bec before the Baptists were upon her. In moments she was knocked to the ground, her arms pinned. Coarse ropes were unwound from Baptists' waists to tie her hands together behind her back, then she was dragged to her feet.

Weaponless as he was, Smythe hadn't had a chance either. Only Finnbogg put up a decent struggle, taking out a half dozen of the bare-chested Baptists before he too was overwhelmed. When they finally tied him, it was with enough ropes to hold a half-dozen men, but still the dwarf bristled and snarled at them.

"Don't hear you mouthing off much now," John J. said. "All I see is a slit who's going to learn her place—like the Good Lord made her to. Don't matter how much you hate me, 'cause it ain't going to change a thing."

Annabelle glared at him. He'd removed his shades since leaving the club to reveal the eyes of a fanatic. The Bible-thumpers back home could be fanatics as well, but at least most of them were pretty conservative. You'd never catch a real Southern Baptist in the getups of the Prophet's followers, running in street gangs like LA homeboys, looking brain dead instead of religiously inspired.

These Baptists seemed more secular than born-again, for all the Prophet's rhetoric. They were just a bunch of bad-news crazies. Capable of just about anything.

Where did the Dungeonmasters dig these guys up?

Probably didn't, she realized. It was the Dungeon that did this to them.

So should she feel some empathy for John J. and his merry men?

Not bloody likely.

Because whatever John J. had planned for them, Annabelle didn't doubt that it'd be more along the lines of the Inquisition than a Bible meeting. It was hard to feel empathy for somebody who was about to go pogoing on your bones.

John J. peered more closely at her, laughter dancing in his eyes at her impotent fury.

"Heaven has no room for hatred," he told her.

"Do tell. Then how're you getting in?"

He laughed. "I've been there and back again, slit. I'm John the Baptist, born again."

"Yeah? So what's the *J* stand for? Jerk?"

Real bright, Annie B., she told herself as he cuffed her across the face. It was an openhanded blow, but it struck her hard enough to knock her to her knees and make her ears ring.

Finnbogg growled fiercely, deep in his chest, but the Prophet simply ignored the dwarf. He grabbed Annabelle by the lapels of her jacket and hauled her back to her feet.

"Look," he said.

He steered her toward the end of the alley. Other Baptists brought Smythe and a snarling Finnbogg along.

"Do you see where your mockery of the Lord brings you?" John J. asked.

Annabelle stared at the cross the gang had erected directly opposite the club's entranceway. There were dozens more Baptists gathered around it, many of them holding aloft torches that made shadows flicker on the cross. The smell of gasoline was strong in the air.

As they stepped from the alley, the Prophet gave a signal. A Baptist touched his torch to the cross, and the gas-soaked wood burst into flame; then the three captives were brought close enough to feel the heat blistering at their skin.

"Do you have any faith at all?" John J. asked her. He used an orator's voice now to speak above the crackle of the flames.

"Because if you do, you're about to become a martyr to it, slit. When the Baptists call you to prayer, y'see, you either pray, or you burn in hell. Now I know that sometimes the odd mistake gets made, so just to make sure that you don't get accidentally shuffled out of purgatory, I'd like to make sure you get a taste of the flames as you're heading on your way."

Annabelle couldn't believe this was happening to them. After all they'd come through on the previous levels of the Dungeon, to be burned at the stake by this bunch of losers seemed the most unfair fate of all.

She swallowed dryly. Well, she'd be damned if she'd give them any satisfaction.

"Real . . . thoughtful of you," she said.

The Prophet shook his head admiringly. "Unrepentant to the end—I like that in a martyr. Tell me— do you hear voices at all? Have you seen visions?"

"Screw you," Annabelle told him, and spat in his face.

That earned her another cuff.

"Okay," John J. said. "Fun's over. Throw 'em in, boys, starting with the slit."

Finnbogg howled and strained at his bonds. With so much attention suddenly trained upon the dwarf, Smythe chose that moment to act. He'd remained so passive that the Baptists had thought him thoroughly cowed. He had played the part of an utter coward, trembling and shaking, his entire carriage that of a smaller man, fearful of his own shadow, never mind the Baptists.

As Finnbogg struggled mádly in his bonds, actually snapping a few of the ropes, Smythe moved suddenly, breaking the grips of the two men restraining him. Before they could recover, he threw himself at Annabelle, butting his head at her chest.

The blow broke her free of the hands that had been holding her captive and sent her stumbling toward the flames before any of the Baptists could carry out John J.'s order. With the heat of the fire right in her face, Annabelle backpedaled furiously. She ducked the grasping arms of the Prophet's followers, getting far enough away from the burning cross so that the Baptists' leader was between her and the flames.

Cursing, John J. grabbed at her himself.

"Sidi," Tomàs cried in a harsh whisper. "We can't let them die."

The Indian nodded. "We will work our way closer."

"But the guards . . ."

"Let me deal with the guards."

Sidi rose from their hiding place. Crouching low, he moved forward across the cracked pavement like a ghost. The nearest Baptist guard, attention on the action near the burning cross, never had a chance.

Not against what Sidi was.

When he first began to question the more orthodox Hindu beliefs in which he'd been raised, Sidi had briefly become involved with a sect of Phansigars and trained with them until he realized that life as one of Kali's Thugees was not what he was looking for either. But he had appreciated the skill of using one's body to its fullest—of the combination of meditation and physical training that made both mind and body, and hence one's spirit, strong.

So he looked to other belief systems that combined the two. When he finally embraced Taoism, he trained in one of their esoteric martial arts schools until he was adept, not only with the sacred weapons, but in *muto* as well—the art of fighting without weapons, where one used everything, and nothing, to bring about victory in combat.

When he was so close he could have reached out and touched the guard, Sidi rose suddenly to his feet. The heel of his hand struck the guard across the throat, breaking his windpipe. As the guard fell, the Indian grasped his hair, jerking the man's head back and snapping his neck. Slowly he lowered the corpse to the ground and checked the man for weapons, coming up with a knife that had a ten-inch blade, edge honed sharp as a razor. Thrusting the knife into his sash, he moved still closer to the burning cross, keeping to the shadows just beyond the light thrown by the flames.

A second and then a third guard fell to his silent attacks. He collected their weapons as well, passing one to Tomàs as the Portuguese and Nacky joined him. They were now close enough to the cross to see that the Baptists had captured three of their missing companions—Annabelle, Smythe, and Finnbogg.

"What now?" Tomàs breathed in Sidi's ear.

What now? Sidi weighed the odds, but no matter what plan of action he considered, there were simply too many of the Baptists for them to deal with. With only the knives he had taken from the men he'd killed, they might as well still be weaponless. Yet to leave their friends . . . that was unthinkable.

They needed to divide the Baptists' forces. If they could create a diversion . . .

He turned to Tomàs, a plan beginning to form in his mind. But just then Finnbogg went mad. Bound as he was, the dwarf fought his captors all the same. The ropes that bound him were snapping free, and the Baptists fell upon him with fist and toe. Sidi watched as Smythe used his own guards' momentary loss of attention to butt Annabelle in the chest with his head, knocking her toward the flames. Annabelle spun away from the fire, but then the leader of the Baptists reached for her.

There was no time to create a diversion, Sidi realized. There was time now only to act.

Without a word to his companions he drew his two stolen knives from his sash and charged into the melee, cutting at the Baptists with a blade in each hand.

If Neville and his party didn't have quite so many enemies to deal with, the two that they did have more than made up for their lack in numbers by the sheer bulk of their size.

Hurt as the giant twins were, all their mad humor had left them. They appeared now to be a pair of mobile mountains—two great heaps of flesh with but one objective, and that was to eliminate their tormentors. But while their humor had vanished, their madness had not, for they were singing as they pounded their way through the tunnels.

"Here we go . . ."

". . . round the . . ."

". . . mulberry bush . . ."

The children's song took on a hellish quality, for they sang in time to their monstrous tread, their voices high and shrieking, the volume making the tunnels rattle and Neville's ears ache. Whenever they came to the final line of the refrain, they shouted it in unison—

"ALL! FALL! DOWN!"

—stamping their feet in time.

And indeed, sections of the tunnels did fall down, in ever larger clouds of debris.

Shriek ran alongside the silver that bore Neville and Alyssa. She had caught hold of the hind bow of its saddle, but while the silver helped her keep up, what with two riders and the arachnid leaning on it more and more, the poor beast was falling well behind those of the other Tuan.

And the giants were rapidly catching up.

Shriek, Neville told her. *You must let go.*

The arachnid's weariness was apparent in the tone of her reply. *Yes, Being Neville. There is no reason that we should all three of us die.*

Neville gripped her hand before she could let go of the saddle. *I don't mean that!* he told her. *You have to get ahead of us, if you can. Far enough ahead of those monsters to stretch your web across the tunnel so that we can go under it, but it will trip them.*

A fine plan—but I have not the strength.

Then find it, Neville told her, his voice ringing harshly in her mind, *or lie down and die now.*

Shriek's head snapped up. For all her alien features Neville could read the rage in her eyes. He lifted his hand from where it had gripped hers.

Go on, he said. *After all you've been through—give it all up to the likes of them.*

He nodded to their rear where the giants followed, still singing their mad children's song.

". . . mulberry bush . . ."

". . . mulberry bush . . ."

"ALL! FALL! DOWN!"

The ground quivered underfoot as though shaken by an earthquake.

Shriek glanced back. *Damn . . . you . . . Being Neville. . . .*

She let go and darted ahead. Where she found the necessary strength, Neville couldn't even guess, unless it was fueled by her anger at him—and that was exactly why he'd spoken as he had. He just hoped that they would survive so that he could explain it to her.

But Shriek had already guessed it for herself. Her new strength came not from the anger that she'd initially felt, but from another source entirely. She had secreted a concentrated dose of what worked as adrenaline in her alien physiology into one of her hair spikes, then injected it into herself. It gave her the necessary stamina—but it was a highly dangerous action, for it could easily burn out her nervous system as well.

But for now she was running as she had never run before, gaining on the other Tuan, then passing them. When she was well ahead of even the foremost of the Tuan, with the sound of the giants' pursuit considerably lessened, she flung herself at a wall, spinnerets creating silk at many times their normal rate.

She attached the thread to that wall, leapt across the tunnel to the other, pulling the thread high and taut just before the first of the Tuan rode under it. Back she went again, then across once more. By the time she'd attached the third thread to the wall, she could no longer move.

All she could give, she had given.

She collapsed against the wall, her body's reserves of strength drained and used up. She wasn't sure if three threads would be enough, but it was all she could do. She let her mind go blank.

Clouds of stone dust covered her at the approach of the giants. Neville and Alyssa passed her, not needing to duck under the thread as she'd fastened them high enough to let them get easily by. Neither of them saw either the thread, or Shriek, where she lay with her limbs splayed out.

". . . mulberry bush . . ."

". . . mulberry bush . . ."

The giants came, with their shrieking voices and thundering tread. The foot of the first snagged on the thread. It pulled, stretched, far, and farther, almost to its breaking point. . . .

But it held.

And the first giant went sprawling out the length of the tunnel. His twin saw the danger, but he was moving too quickly to stop himself. The resulting impact when they both hit, first one, then the other, brought half the roof down on top of them.

Neville and Alyssa had pulled up as they saw the giant falling.

"All fall down," Neville said with a hard smile.

They braced themselves for the crash, but nothing could have prepared them for its violence. They were both thrown from the back of their silver, Neville cushioning the Tuan as best he could.

The ground shook with long, tumultuous tremors. Parts of the tunnel collapsed all around them. The air filled with dust, so thick they choked and were blinded. When the dust finally began to clear, they could see the two giants, one on top of the other. The bottom one had cracked open his head when he fell. The one on top had a length of sharp rock embedded in the back of his skull.

Dead, the pair of them. And half-buried in a make-shift cairn that was more than either of them deserved, Neville thought.

He rose shakily to his feet and helped Alyssa to stand. The other Tuan returned, Fenil catching Alyssa's frightened silver and calming it as they all regarded the dead monsters.

"We've Shriek to thank for our rescue," Neville said, "both when the giants first attacked, and now for their death."

Alyssa nodded. She turned to look for Shriek amongst her company but couldn't find her.

"Where is she?" the Tuan leader asked.

Fenil pointed toward the giants and the rubble that almost covered them. "The last I saw of her was back there—when she was setting the trip wire for the giants. . . ."

Neville gazed bleakly at the mess.

Shriek, he called. *Shriek!*

There was no reply.

Shriek!

He reached out with his mind but could not find that familiar neural web by which he knew the arachnid's mind.

"If she was caught under that," Alyssa began.

She didn't finish, but Neville knew what she left unspoken. If Shriek had been caught under that rubble, she was dead now. There was no possible way she could have survived.

But he refused to believe it.

By the light of their torches it was hard to see if the tunnel was completely blocked now or not. But it didn't matter. He'd dig through it, if he had to. He started back toward the bodies of the giants and began to climb the rubble.

After a moment Fenil, then Alyssa, climbed up behind him.

Guafe was easy to spy in the dining hall when Clive and Speaker Lena finally arrived. He was on the far side of the room, his metalplated head and eyes rising above the crowd. For though he sat on his haunches, he

still reared taller than either of the two techs who
shared the table with him.

To Clive the hall had the appearance of a large restaurant, but one entirely devoid of even the simplest
decor. There were perhaps half a hundred tables, at
which sat various of the Ren, each of them dressed
alike, the food colorless and bland in appearance, their
plates and cutlery all identical, giving the entire place
an antiseptic air. It seemed more like the laboratories
Clive had seen on previous levels than a place in which
to have a meal.

All conversation halted as he and the Speaker
stepped through the door, but here, unlike the Hub,
the Ren merely returned to their meals after a long,
curious gaze at the second giant in their midst. Their
scrutiny brought a flush to Clive's cheek, and he forced
himself not to fidget under their gazes, matching their
curiosity with a calm disregard. He was only partially
successful.

The Speaker led Clive to the table where the others
were waiting for them.

"Are you hungry?" she asked Clive.

She indicated an area on the far side of the room
where various Ren were filling trays with foodstuffs
displayed under glass coverings. It all had the same
unappetizing appearance.

Clive shook his head. "Only for answers."

The techs sitting with Guafe were the same pair that
had seen to the equipment when the Speakers were
initially questioning Clive and Guafe. The female was
named Chary, Clive remembered. The male was now
introduced to him as Howell. It was the male who
addressed their immediate problem.

"We've isolated the discrepancy," he told the
Speaker, "between our records of the subjects and
their actual physical appearance."

"And?"

"It has to do with the mirror the Chaffri used to send
them to this level."

"I see."

"Well, I don't," Clive said.

He felt irritable and awkward crouching by the table. It made him feel as though he were visiting children in their playhouse, all the furnishings scaled down to half his size. The surreptitious glances he was continually given by the Ren at the other tables only heightened his discomfort.

"It appears," Guafe explained, "that the device used to bring us here—the mirror we stepped through—was in fact a teleportation mechanism that utilizes a form of molecular disruption to transfer physical objects over great distances. It's because it hadn't been coded to our particular party that we ended up arriving in different places—and, in our case, a different size."

"The others have been found, then?" Clive asked eagerly.

Chary shook her head. "But we're working on it. What we can do now is put you through a properly coded teleporter and return you to your normal size."

"By sending us where?"

Chary laughed. "It won't be necessary to send you anywhere. The whole procedure can be done in one of our labs."

"There'll be no danger," Howell added.

Well, that would be half their problems solved, Clive thought. But he wondered—could they trust the Ren not to teleport them into some new, worse danger while supposedly "helping" them through this problem?

He wished he could take Guafe aside to discuss it with him, but there didn't appear to be much opportunity for privacy in the Ren city. More troubling was how comfortable the cyborg appeared with their captors. It was true that these two were mechanics, and so able to answer the questions thrown up by Guafe's insatiable curiosity; but all the same they appeared to be getting along too well for Clive's liking.

Because he remembered . . .

Try to put it from his mind though he did, he couldn't forget that chessboard he'd seen, before stepping through the mirror, and the two traitorous playing pieces.

Guafe and Sidi Bombay.

If they *were* working with the Dungeonmasters . . .

Clive shook his head. It had to have been just another trick of the Dungeonmasters—just something else to throw him off his stride—of that he was sure.

Wasn't he?

"If it'll make you feel any better," Chary told him, "I'll step through with you—just to prove that there's no danger."

Was his face that easy to read?

Clive sighed and nodded stiffly. "That would do much to set my mind at ease."

"Your other questions—" Speaker Lena began.

"Can wait, I think," Guafe broke in. "Don't you think, Clive? I for one would prefer to conduct any further conversation on a more equal footing."

To stop being a freak in the eyes of the Ren, to stop feeling that his smallest movement would create the same disaster as a bull let loose in a lady's sitting room? Much as Clive wanted answers to all the troubling questions, he could not agree more.

"First this teleportation device," he said, "but then" —he glanced meaningfully at the Speaker—"some answers."

Speaker Lena nodded. "We will help you in any way we can, Clive. Though you still don't trust us, I assure you—we share the same foes. The danger they represent is enormous. They must be stopped, but neither of us can do it on our own. We need your help, as you need ours. And time is running out for all of us."

▪ CHAPTER ELEVEN ▪

As the Prophet grabbed her, Annabelle realized just what it was that Horace had been up to. He'd activated the controls of the Baalbec A-9 in her bodice—the controls she couldn't reach herself because her hands were tied behind her back.

With the protective device operative, the leader of the Baptists was bounced away as soon as he laid a hand on her. He was flung backward, knocking over a can of gasoline as he was driven straight into the burning cross. The spilled gasoline ignited with a thundering whoosh.

Wide-eyed, Annabelle saw the Prophet go up in flames.

He howled—a raw, wailing cry that didn't seem human. Staggering from the fire, he was a flaming pyre in human form. He came straight for Annabelle, arms outspread.

She backed away. No matter how much she'd wished him dead, she hadn't wanted this. No one deserved to die like this.

Watching their leader burn, the Baptists were all frozen for a long moment—long enough for Finnbogg to snap the last of his bonds in a sudden frenzy of desperate strength. John J. lurched forward, two, three more steps, then collapsed, the howl of his pain fading to a whining shriek. Then dying completely.

They all stared at the black thing lying there in the light of the flames. It was difficult to believe that it had once been human. The raw smell of burnt meat filled the air. Then the full understanding of just what had happened to their leader settled among the Baptists.

The momentary tableau dissolved into an out-and-out melee.

The Baptists fell upon their captives, but their attack came a little late. Adrenaline pumping through her, Annabelle watched the world fall apart for the gang members.

Finnbogg was on them like a werewolf from one of the old Hammer flicks that Chrissie Nunn—the keyboard player from her lost band—used to watch over and over again. He was all tooth and fang—a literal killing machine that the disoriented Baptists found impossible to contain this time.

One of the gang members came at her, a long, wicked blade in his fist, but her Baalbec flung him back against his companions. Two more attacked Smythe. Annabelle ran toward him—Baptists flung away on either side of her as they tried to grab her—but knew she was going to be too late. The knives were slashing out. Horace was going to die. . . .

But then a familiar figure was there, a knife in either hand, cutting down the Baptists, taking time to slice through Smythe's bonds before he spun away to where the gang members were thickest.

Sidi!

Annabelle couldn't believe it. The frigging cavalry had arrived.

She saw Tomàs as well, in the crowd, holding his own against the Baptists as he fought his way to her side. He started to reach out toward her wrists to cut her free.

"Don't!" she cried. "The Baalbec!"

The Portuguese hesitated, then nodded, turning to help Smythe, who was waging an unequal battle with another pair of Baptists.

They were going to do it, Annabelle thought. Jesus, they were really going to take the bastards down.

She looked for the others of their party—Clive and Shriek and the rest—but saw only a small, feral-looking child. A Baptist came at her, and the girl kicked him in

the groin. When he doubled over, she hit him on the
back of the head with the length of pipe she was carrying, laughing delightedly as though this were only a
game.

Where was everybody else? Annabelle wondered.

She'd have to worry about that later, she realized, as
another Baptist threw himself at her only to be flung
away by the Baalbec for his trouble. Annabelle grinned
at the stunned look on the man's face, but the grin
faltered when she realized that the Baptists were re-
covering from their initial disorientation. They had
backed away to form a half circle that enclosed the six
of them—Smythe and Tomàs; Sidi, Finnbogg, the feral
child, and herself.

Behind them was the cross. Behind it the front of a
building, its windows set too high in its walls for them
to get through, the doorway blocked.

"Okay, mothers," the foremost of the Baptists
shouted. "You had your fun. But you don't kill a
Prophet and live to brag about it. No way. No *way!*"

By the light of the burning cross Annabelle realized
that the man actually had tears in his eyes.

"You got to pay," he went on. "You got to *pay!*"

The Baptists roared in unison—a loud, wordless cry
that held all their anger and despair. They lifted fists in
the air, and the night air bristled with knives, clubs,
and makeshift weapons.

"Oh, Jesus," Annabelle muttered.

She moved to the front of her small group.

"Don't, Annabelle," Sidi said.

She gave him a quick, small smile. "At least they
can't touch me," she said. "I'm going to buy you some
time—so get moving. Just take one of those alleys on
either side of the building and get out of here!"

Her companions merely ranged themselves at her
side.

"We'll chew them to pieces," Finnbogg growled.

"Yeah, right. With the odds still four to one we're
really going to make a statement." She glanced at

Smythe. "Horace, you've got some sense—get everybody out of here."

Smythe merely shook his head. "We're in this together."

The Baptists were still working themselves up to attack. Any moment now, Annabelle thought, and it's going to be game over.

"Sidi?"

"I've just found you again and you expect me to leave?"

Annabelle sighed.

"This is your friend?" the feral child asked the Indian.

Sidi nodded.

"How come no one cuts her loose?"

Before Annabelle could explain about the Baalbec, the Baptists' cries rose to a sudden crescendo.

"Heads up," Annabelle said, "here they come."

And come they would have, if the big boom of a handgun hadn't cracked across the Baptists' cries. All gazes turned to the source of the sound.

"Hole-lee," Annabelle said.

It was a real cavalry.

Ranged in a long, ragged line in front of Casey's were the members of the Airplane and a half-dozen other bands. Casey himself stood in the center, with the old wino Jake on one side of him and Jack Casady on the other. It was Casady who'd fired the gun. Here and there Annabelle spotted other handguns in the hands of some of the musicians.

One of the Baptists took a step toward the club, and a long-haired man that Annabelle vaguely recognized as belonging to some late sixties, early seventies band, leveled his weapon and fired, dropping the Baptist in his tracks.

What did Casey do? Annabelle wondered. Call up the whole pack of GBCers he had? And where had they got the weapons? Better still, why hadn't they given her group any?

That was easy to answer, she realized. Her group was

going on and might be able to pick up gear wherever they went, but Casey and his people were stuck here and needed whatever they had just to survive.

"Okay," Casey cried. "It ends here."

Beside him Casady waved his .44 automatic, the silver weapon glinting in the firelight. "Anybody have a problem with that?" he asked.

The remaining Baptists muttered, but none of them seemed ready to take it any further.

"Now you boys are going to wait right out here with us," Casey went on, "while our friends head on their way. Where they're going, they won't be back, so this thing's over—everybody agree?"

Finally one of the Baptists spoke up. "Yeah? And what about the Prophet?"

Standing beside Jake, a bare-chested man in leather pants and long dark hair smiled grimly. "Well, that's what you get when you play with fire."

Annabelle blinked when she recognized the man. Jim Morrison. Her mother was forever playing his albums.

"It's got to end right here and now," Casey said. "One way or another."

The man who'd shot the Baptist a few moments ago patted his handgun meaningfully.

"Okay." The Baptist who'd been doing all the talking put his knife away in its boot sheath.

Casey and Jack Casady came across to where Annabelle and the others were standing, circling around the Baptists.

"You saved our asses," Annabelle said, looking at Casady. "Again."

Casady laughed. "Like I told the man inside, you got to take care of your people, and seeing how Casey tells me you're a player too, well, hell. We're supposed to let them get away with this kind of thing?"

"Well, thanks."

"You remember the way I told you to go?" Casey asked.

Annabelle nodded. "Just let me get these ropes off."

Sidi went to cut her free, but Tomàs caught him by the arm.

"Remember her device, *amigo*," he said.

"Just give me a sec' here," Annabelle said.

She went over to where the remains of a street sign stood poking up out of a thicket of weeds. Leaning over, she pressed the Baalbec's control against the end of the sign, shutting the device off.

"Okay," she said. She turned around and offered up her hands. "Who's going to do the honors?"

When Sidi had cut her free, she took the time to give him a hug before rubbing at her chafed wrists.

"I hate to push," Casey said, "but you've got to get moving. We're holding them now, but just looking at you long enough's going to make them think, what the hell. The next thing you know, they'll have a go at us anyway."

"You'll be all right?" Smythe asked him.

"No problem—trust me. Just get going before the shit hits the fan again."

"I'll go with you a ways," Casady said.

Annabelle glanced at Casey's pocket where she knew he kept the GBCs that had called up the various musicians in the first place.

"I thought . . ." she began.

"That's right," Casady said. "If we don't play, we just fade away." He smiled. "But it's no big deal. We just end up back in the cards, so many digitized bits of data, until we get called up again."

"But . . ."

"It bothers people around us way more than it bothers a GBCer. Now, c'mon. Let's go before Casey pops a vein."

He led off. With a final wave to Casey and a nervous look at the Baptist, Annabelle and the others followed. Once they were out of sight of the gang members and the burning cross, she and Sidi filled each other in on what had happened since they'd each stepped through the mirror.

"You haven't seen anything of the rest of them?" she asked.

"Nothing of Clive?" Smythe asked almost at the same time.

Sidi shook his head.

Annabelle looked back the way they'd come. "Christ, I hope they landed in a safer place than we did."

There was enough room at the top of the heap of fallen stone that covered the giants for Neville and his two companions to squeeze through. By the light of their torches they searched for Shriek. When they finally found her, lying where she'd fallen, limbs splayed loosely about her and covered in stone dust, Neville feared the worst.

He scrambled up to where she lay, blinking away the sudden dampness that blurred his sight.

Shriek?

He searched for her mind, but there was still no reply. The neural web joining the two of them was gone as though it had never existed.

"Damn them," Neville said. His voice had a strangled sound to it. "Damn the Dungeonmasters, and damn their bloody games."

Alyssa stood beside him, looking down at Shriek's body, and laid her hand on his shoulder. "Is she dead?"

Neville nodded.

"Are you sure?" Fenil asked.

Dangerous lights flickered in Neville's eyes as he looked up at the Tuan. "What's *that* supposed to mean?"

Alyssa's fingers tightened on his shoulder. "We are all friends here, Neville."

Fenil nodded. "Her body—it's so different from ours. . . . I was wondering if perhaps, when her kind is hurt, they withdraw into themselves to make their healing easier."

Neville thought then of his travels in India and Africa, of the fakirs and shaman he had met and the things they could do with their bodies. Some could slow down their bodies' metabolisms to such an extent that they appeared dead—even to the closest scrutiny.

He looked back down at Shriek again.

Is that it? he asked. *Have you taken yourself away to heal?*

When he thought of the effort it must have taken for her to get as far ahead of their party as she had to set the trip wire, of the terrible toll it must have taken . . .

But she lay stiff and silent. Unresponsive.

Perhaps he wasn't focusing his mind properly. He recalled the exact order of events when Shriek had first opened the neural web between them—and remembered something of importance. It had begun with physical contact. Her chitinous skin touching his in a hand grasp.

He laid a hand on either side of her head and bent over her until his forehead rested against her own. Closing his eyes, he sought the web again.

Shriek . . . ?

There was still no response. But now, far off in the darkness behind his closed lids—a darkness that was a mental realm, rather than a physical one, he quickly realized—he thought he saw a glimmer of movement. A spark that flickered in the endless dark, teasing and distant.

He narrowed the focus of his searching thoughts and sent them deeper into the darkness, pursuing that flickering spark. It fled away from him, so that he never drew any closer to it, no matter how quickly he pursued it.

But he refused to give in. He kept at it, forcing his thoughts to follow the spark. He lost all sense of his body where it crouched in the tunnel above hers. When the last sense of contact with his physical form slipped away, he suddenly gained on the spark.

His thoughts, fueled by that success, increased their speed until he was upon the spark, hard on its heels, then close enough to touch. He grabbed at it, and the darkness melted away in a flare of blinding light that stunned him.

He had the abrupt sense of vertigo—as though he were falling for miles through the heart of a star. Try though he did to stop his plummeting descent, the fall had all the unyielding grip of gravity running its course. When it finally ended, it was through no effort of his own, but because he had come to the end of his passage.

The blinding light dimmed to normal lighting. He found himself occupying the semblance of a body—his own body—standing on an alien landscape. The sky was a deep orange all about him, the land a place of flat gray expanses, dotted with odd purple-and-blue growths. And in front of him, creating a massive silk web between two upright black stones that had all the look of the ancient stoneworks in Neville's own England, was Shriek.

For long moments Neville could make no sound. His throat was constricted and dry. The alien quality of the landscape left him with a sense of both estrangement and an odd reverence. It was as though to speak here would be as disrespectful as carousing would be in a cathedral.

But finally he spoke all the same.

". . . Shriek . . . ?"

At first he thought the arachnid hadn't heard him. She continued to weave her giant web, spinnerets producing the silk, her limbs drawing it forth and setting each strand in place with an assuredness that was both aesthetic and mechanical, all at once. It was only when he was about to call her name again that she finally halted her work and turned to regard him.

There was an odd look on her features—almost, Neville thought, as though she didn't recognize him. Then she smiled.

Being Neville. What are you doing in my death dream?

"Your what?"

My death dream. Before the spirits of my people

vacate their physical forms, they come to this holy place to make a pattern of their dying with the threads of their life and weave it as a remembrance of what was, but will be no more. This realm exists in our communal mind. Some of our Wise have seen it in visions, but most of us view it only at the time of our death dream.

It was an odd concept, but no odder than many they'd come across in the Dungeon, Neville thought. No odder than many of the conceits of the various peoples who lived on his homeworld. Heaven and hell. Reincarnation. Karma. There were as many theories of what lay beyond life as there were cultures.

But here, at this moment, Neville wasn't interested in hearing any of it. He didn't want to hear Shriek speak of her dying. He wanted her alive and walking beside him, searching out their comrades, bringing their final judgment on the Dungeonmasters when they eventually caught up with them—as catch up to them Neville was determined they would.

For that to occur—for any of it to occur—he had to bring Shriek back with him. However that might be done.

"But you're not dead," he said.

He felt her smile in his mind. There was a beatific quality about her presence on the neural web.

I must be, she said, *or why would I be in my death dream?*

Neville thought quickly. Perhaps she was, but he wouldn't let her stay here. Not when there was a chance to bring her back. Only where to begin? How to convince her? For he saw that it was a matter of her point of view that had brought her to this place. If he could only convince her that she still lived . . .

And then he had it.

"It's another trick of the Dungeonmasters," he said. "Another play in their damnable game."

I don't think so, Being Neville. I have been in danger before, but never have I been in this place before today. I must be dead.

"Then am I dead too?"

That brought a puzzled look to her features. *I . . .*

"And if I am dead, then why am I here—in your afterlife, rather than in my own?"

You . . . Her shock passed like an electrical spark from her mind to his own. *You are inside my mind . . . ?*

Neville nodded. "I came to bring you back."

You don't understand. If you are here when the Gatherer comes to take me, you will be taken with me.

"I can't leave. I don't know the way back by myself. Show me the road."

But the Gatherer has already been summoned. I can feel Her breath on the wind.

There *was* a noticeable cooling of the air, Neville realized. He looked to the east and saw a darkness spreading across the orange sky.

"Quickly!" he cried. "Come back with me."

Shriek sadly shook her head. *Too late, Being Neville. The Gatherer comes because I've summoned her. My life web is almost done. She will take me home now—to the Beyond Beyond. And She will take you with me. . . .*

Neville looked at the eastern sky again. The darkness was spreading. And now he saw, in that blackness, a sense of enormous eyes, a cavernous mouth.

"Shriek," he said. "We must leave now."

Too late, too late, Shriek sighed.

The darkness was almost upon them now. Neville searched for some tie to his body, but the thread that bound him to his physical form was gone. He'd hoped, as a final measure if he couldn't talk her into coming back with him, to simply grab Shriek and use that thread to take them back to where their bodies waited for them.

But now he couldn't even return himself.

The darkness swallowed the orange skies until everything went a flat black. Only Shriek's web and the arachnid herself glimmered with a soft luminescence like phosphorus shimmering on water. Neville lifted his own hand before his face and saw that he too was glowing.

And then the Gatherer was there.

The only difference between the laboratory to which the Ren brought Guafe and Clive and the restaurant they had quit was that it had a banked wall of electrical equipment and other devices, and a huge mirror that was set a few feet out from another wall. Otherwise, it had the same sterile environment—white walls, expressionless Ren lab techs in their colorless suits—with nothing of a personal or cultural nature to be seen, no matter where one looked.

What made the lab yet more sterile, to Clive's way of thinking, was the bewildering maze of corridors that had led them to it—a stunning mishmash of alien cultures that Speaker Lena explained was a duplicate of a marketing satellite that served as a trade center for a number of space-faring races in a solar system far from the one in which the Dungeon was situated.

Clive was merely relieved to step from the confusion of stolen cultural artifacts in the corridors into the relative sanity of the lab.

"This'll just take a moment," Chary said as she went to confer with the techs. "I have to input our neural and physical characteristics."

Clive studied the mirror while they waited for her, a calm expression fixed determinedly on his features.

"I can go through first," Guafe said. "I rather relish the novelty of the experience. Knowing what to expect, I can study the changes as they occur."

"I'll be fine," Clive said.

But he couldn't stop the small twitch of uncertainty that arose in him at the cyborg's words. Of course Chang wasn't worried—not if he was allied with the Ren as the chessboard on the last level had seemed to indicate.

It was an unfair assumption of distrust, Clive knew, but it wouldn't leave him. Because what did he really know about the cyborg? Lord help him, what did he know of any of his companions, truly?

Annabelle had some physical resemblance to his lover Annabella Leighton, but he had no real proof that they *were* in fact related.

Smythe had been acting most oddly from when he first contacted Clive on the ship from England, disguised as a mandarin.

Sidi Bombay had appeared out of the African night—as if from nowhere. Perhaps from the Dungeon itself?

Neville . . . Neville was his twin, it was true, but with all the replicas that the Dungeonmasters could create, how could he ever be sure that the man wearing his form was truly his brother?

And the others. Shriek, Finnbogg, Tomàs . . . all he knew of them was what they had told him of themselves and how they had conducted themselves since they'd begun to travel together.

God help him, they could all be his enemies.

But this was exactly what the Dungeonmasters wanted, wasn't it? For some unfathomable reason they delighted in breeding mistrust amongst allies. Clive had the feeling that if he could simply understand some small aspect of the riddle—why they felt the need to foment this distrust, what was the importance of the Folliots—that the entire mystery of the Dungeon would begin to unravel for him.

Speaker Lena claimed they should be allies, that they could help each other. Would whatever responses she gave to his questions help solve the greater puzzle? Or would they make matters worse?

"Clive?"

Clive blinked at the mention of his name to see that Chary had returned from her conference with the techs and was waiting for him. She offered him her hand.

"We should remain in physical contact," she said. "It's not absolutely necessary, but it does make for a smoother run-through."

Clive shook his head. "That won't be necessary." He

walked toward the mirror and studied it without really taking in his own reflection. "What do I do? Just . . . ah, step through?"

"It's as simple as that," the male tech Howell said.

"You'll feel a moment of disorientation," Chary added, "but it won't last long. You'll be back here in just a few seconds."

Clive nodded. Steeling himself, he stepped toward the reflective surface, shivering as he passed through.

A momentary sense of vertigo caught hold of him. Warned to expect it, Clive still felt panic come bubbling up inside him. He reached out with those mental muscles awakened in Shriek's neural web, and a sudden wrenching sensation shook him, immediately followed by an unnatural calmness.

He felt as though he were floating in a vast gray sea. He held his hand in front of him but could see nothing. Only the grayness. The unending sea that spread out from him in all directions. The grayness both in which he floated and of which he was a part.

If he had a hand, if he even had a body anymore, in this strange sea it was invisible to his sight.

The Ren had said nothing of this.

The sense of calm that the grayness had given him began to unravel.

What if the source of this place was something other than the Ren?

He called out, not with a physical voice, for all sense of body was gone, but with a voiceless cry that went winging off into the grayness on the neural web.

And he was answered.

Not by Shriek. Not by any of his other companions who had shared her neural web with him. Not even by du Maurier. But he knew who it was all the same.

The voice that rang inside his mind—that flexed the invisible muscles of the gossamer spider's web that was now his mind—was one he would never forget.

It was the bodiless voice of the maze. The voice that had come to him but twice in his life—

No, he realized. He had heard it more than twice. He had heard it when—

At that moment the annoying flicker of lost memories returned to Clive in a rush. He remembered, remembered it all. Lord help him, how could he have forgotten?

Falling through the azure blue.

Stolen by the Dungeonmasters to a dream of London.

A dream of Annabella and their life made perfect with his receiving a promotion and therefore being able to propose marriage to her.

A dream that had gone sour when he had seen through its lies.

And then the Dungeonmasters had taken him someplace and erased the memories so that he would not be aware of their machination. Returned him to the blue void of the gate and let him arrive with the others, never realizing what he had experienced.

God, but he hated them.

And that voice he heard now—it had been there as well. He had begun to consider it not so much as an entity in its own right, but rather as the voice of his own subconscious. It had rescued him then.

What did it want of him now?

It is time, that voice said.

Time? Time for what? Clive asked.

Time for you to finish the journey on your own. Your companions—whether they play you true or false— will only hold you back now.

Who are you? Clive demanded.

Silence replied.

Damn you! Stop playing games. If you are one of the Dungeonmasters, then come out and face me like a man.

I am neither Dungeonmaster nor man—not a man as you know the term.

I'm not so easily shocked anymore, Clive replied. *God knows I've seen my share of odd beings since first entering this damned place. So step forward and show yourself.*

Though he fought to hide it, it shook Clive to the very roots of his essence to think that the Dungeonmasters had set him up as one of their gaming pieces from as early a time as his tenth year. For all he knew, from before his birth.

I ask you again, he said. *Name yourself.*

The ensuing silence was long enough that Clive thought the disembodied entity was again refusing to reply. But then a long sigh echoed along the neural web.

Had I lived, had I been born, the voice said, *my name would have been Esmond. Esmond Folliot.*

What!?

When our father's sperm first seeded our mother's egg, we would have been born as triplets. Bearing twins killed her. Had she carried all three of us to term, none of us might have survived, so I, as the youngest, was taken away.

Taken? By whom?

I don't know. I am simply here, in this place. I have been able to watch you both, my two brothers, but rarely has the veil between the worlds been thin enough that I might communicate with either of you.

And what of now? Clive asked. *How did you come to me now?*

I did not come to you, the voice replied. *You came to me—to the place of unborn souls; souls that should have been born, but were not.*

This is madness.

Perhaps. If you had dwelled here all the years I have . . . Perhaps I am mad. But I am still a Folliot. I am still determined that the creators of this place shall not have the better of us.

You know them? Clive asked. *Who are they? What is their purpose for entrapping us and all the others that have come to be imprisoned in this damned place?*

I don't know, Clive. I know only that you must go on alone now. It is in you that the hope of every prisoner of the Dungeon lies. But what you do, you must do alone.

I can't do that. I can't forsake the others.

Your loyalty will be your downfall.

What use winning, Clive asked, *if your method of doing so leaves your life a lie? I am the man I am. You say the hope of the Dungeon's prisoners lies in me. If I go on alone, if I forsake the others, then I will become someone else. Will I still prevail?*

There came a long pause. Then the voice sighed again.

You offer a formidable logic, it said finally.

Are you truly my brother? Clive asked.

Had I been born . . . then, yes. We would have been brothers.

It had to be yet another damnable trick of the Dungeonmasters, Clive thought, for surely this wasn't possible. How could he and Neville have an unborn brother?

But because this was the Dungeon . . . because here the impossible was not only possible, but probable . . .

How can you prove this? he asked.

This is a thing that can be accepted only on faith, the voice replied.

But an unborn brother . . .

He tasted the name in his mind. Esmond. Esmond Folliot. Damned if it didn't ring true.

When the others are safe, the voice asked. *Will you then do as I counsel?*

You'll help me find them?

A sensation very like a mental shaking of a head moved in Clive's mind.

I know only the whereabouts of you and our brother, the voice replied.

Can you at least lead me to him?

I can show you a road on the neural web that can take your thoughts to him.

A glimmering thread appeared in the grayness,

originating in the place where Clive sensed himself to be and leading off into the distance.

You have but to grasp it with your thoughts, the voice told him.

And if Neville's mind was on the end of this thread—what would that prove? Clive asked himself. That the voice was indeed that of an unborn brother named Esmond, or that of a Dungeonmaster with yet another of their mad ploys to play?

Will we speak again? he asked the voice.

I don't know, it replied. *You will have to come to me.*

Through a mirror?

There was no reply.

Wait! Clive cried. *Where have you gone?*

Still only silence.

And now the shimmering thread was beginning to fade.

Esmond! Clive tried one last time.

Still no reply, and now the thread was nothing more than a ghost, fading swiftly.

He caught it with his thoughts and let the thread pull him away, deeper and deeper into the gray.

CHAPTER TWELVE

Both Jack Casady and the feral child, who was introduced to them as Nacky, knew the way to a secret route leading to the underground city. Casady let the little *enfant perdu* lead the way while he walked with Annabelle and Sidi.

"I thought this was supposed to be some secret smugglers' route," Annabelle said.

"It is," Casady told her.

"Then how come everybody and his brother knows how to get there?"

Nacky turned and flashed her a toothy grin. "Frenchy likes to know everything that goes on in the Dives," she said. "You can't keep a secret from an EP— no way at all."

Frenchy, Annabelle thought. Right. Sidi and Tomàs had told her about him. A genetically altered Frenchman who now bore more resemblance to a giant caterpillar or slug than to the man he'd once been. Holding court over a gang of Peter Pan-like Borribles and smoking a hookah. More shades of Wonderland, with a little Barrie and de Larrabeiti thrown in for good measure. Were they going to run into Toad of Toad Hall next?

"And besides," Casady added. "There's nothing for a Diver down there anymore, anyway."

"What do you mean?"

"Getting out's easy; getting back in . . . well, even if you could, you couldn't hide out for long. Everyone's got an ID card—coded to their genetic makeup. You can't cheat with them. And if you try to sneak around, they've got all kinds of ugly little watchdogs running around there, just itching to round up a few strays."

"The zeros," Annabelle said.

Casady nodded. "Casey told you about them?"

"Oh yeah."

It was kind of hard to forget Casey's description of the simulacrum. Made up of fiber and plastic and metal, but with human brains housed in their synthetic bodies that were wired up to their computerized motor units.

"You ought to stay," Casady said.

"Can't."

"It's not so bad. We can fix you up with your own GBC so that, even if what you're wearing now does bite the bullet, you'll still be around. Or at least some of you will—the important parts. Casey told me you're a player. We've got a good scene happening in the Dives."

"You don't understand," Annabelle said. "We've got friends to track down still. And a score to settle."

"From everything I hear about the guys running this place, you'd have better luck being a black woman in the middle of a Klan meeting."

"It's still got to be done," Annabelle said.

"We don't really have a choice," Sidi added. "The Dungeonmasters appear to have a special interest in some of the members of our party. Even if we did try to find a refuge, they would come looking for us."

"Bummer."

Annabelle smiled at the word. "Right. A major bummer."

Nacky came dancing back through the rubble just then. "Found it!"

"Never thought you wouldn't," Annabelle said.

The EP led them down to the end of the alleyway and across the buckling pavement of a side street to where an old subway entrance stood. Its opening was choked with vegetation that proved to be easily pulled aside. Using one of the flashlights that Linda had given her, Annabelle pointed its light into the darkness.

The stairs leading down were in good shape. The air coming up to them was only slightly stale, with a hint of dampness in it.

"This is it," Annabelle said to Casady and Nacky. "End of the line for you guys. Thanks for the escort."

Nacky shook her head. "I'm coming."

"That's impossible," Tomàs told her.

"Can't stop me."

The Portuguese knelt down in front of her. "This is a very bad place we are going to, *muchacha*. There is no coming back from it."

"I wouldn't want to come back. Want to go with you and Sidi."

"And what of Frenchy?" Sidi asked. "Who would look after him?"

"He's got lots of other EPs."

"Yes. But I think you are a favorite of his."

The little feral face looked earnestly from him to Tomàs. "You think so?"

"*Verdad,*" Tomàs said. "I think so, *sim.*"

"You won't forget me, will you? Frenchy says that that's the only way you can live a long time—is by what people remember about you."

Tomàs enfolded her in a quick embrace. "We won't forget you," he said.

When he let her go, Sidi embraced her as well. "How could we forget one so brave and true?" the Indian asked.

When Nacky stepped back, she was chewing on her bottom lip. She looked around at the others, hesitating for one more long moment, then she lifted her hand in a quick salute and sped off into the ruins, disappearing almost immediately.

"I hate to leave her here," Sidi said.

Tomàs looked at him. "*Sim.* But where we are going . . ."

"It will undoubtedly be worse," Sidi said with a slow nod.

"That leaves you, Jack," Annabelle said. "You take care of yourself and thank Casey for us again—okay?"

Casady smiled. "You won't get rid of me that easily. I've got a hankering to see what the Chaffri've been doing with their digs since the last time I was there."

"A 'hankering'?" Annabelle asked with upraised eyebrows.

"I like country music—so sue me."

"But . . ."

"Look—anything happens to me, I just fade away and old Casey can call me up again. No problem."

He took one of the flashlights from her and started down. Annabelle shivered. This whole GBC business just gave her the creeps.

"I don't understand," Smythe said, stepping up beside her to look down the stairs. "One's either alive, or dead."

Annabelle nodded. "Yeah. You'd think so. But this is—"

"The Dungeon," everyone chorused.

"Right. Where any frigging thing seems possible."

"You coming?" Casady called from down below.

"We're on our way," Annabelle called back. She looked at her companions. "Well, kids. Ready for the next mess of bad-news craziness?"

One by one they followed her down the stairs to where Casady's flashlight was beckoning to them.

The Gatherer's features filled the entire sky. A darkness spread from the immense being, a deeper darkness within it that appeared to be the Gatherer itself. Neville didn't understand how he could discern differences in that stygian shadow, but he saw distinctions all the same. Within the cloak of blackness the Gatherer's features were like Shriek's, reflecting the beatific serenity echoed in Shriek's own visage.

As Neville stared up at the being, a sensation of utter peace settled in him. He understood now why Shriek had been content to pass on into the afterlife of her people. He understood, as well, why none among the living should be given a view of it.

Once tasted, who would not embrace his death?

He too, like Shriek, yearned to reach out and be taken in by the Gatherer. Vestiges of creatures his ancestors had been, drawn from the evolutionary ladder his race had once climbed, had him casting his own web of memory between the stones where Shriek hung. That the memories remain there, while he could go on.

Into the peace.

To be at peace.

Only . . .

A part of him rebelled.

Remember, he told himself. Death, peaceful though it promised to be, was not for them. Not now. Not so soon. Not with their companions still lost. The Dungeonmasters still unpunished.

"Wuh . . . wuh . . ."

He tried to speak but could not frame even the first word.

We cannot come with you. He sent the thought up to the Gatherer. *There is too much undone.*

Her voice, when she replied, was a breath of soft wind that made his soul shiver. *Others remain to do; your time is done.*

It was true, one part of him argued, yearning for what the Gatherer promised them. Let the others take up the battle. He and Shriek . . . they had struggled long enough.

Come with me.

Yes. It was that simple. Just let go of his last memories of life and go with her. Let her gather them in her peaceful embrace and take them away. . . .

Slowly Neville shook his head.

We cannot, he told her. *God help us, though every fiber of my being bids me to let go and come with you, we cannot.*

Someone must come with me, she replied. *I am like the sword drawn that must taste blood before I return to my sheath. One of you must return with me.*

We cannot, Neville repeated, for all that it broke his heart not to simply let himself go with her.

This is not a matter for discussion, the Gatherer said. *One must come with me—that is the law.*

I will come, Great Mother, Shriek said.

No, Neville said. *I . . .*

He would what?

The unselfish thought that had risen in him—that was related to the same impulse that had sent him here looking for Shriek—surprised him as much as it would have surprised any that knew him. He realized again that here, in this Dungeon, he was part of a group. It was not Neville Folliot who was most important in this place—it was the group as a whole. And their ultimate goal. To foil the Dungeonmasters. To see to it that as many of the party escaped as could.

His brother had already proved to be a better leader than he in this place. And he had not as much to offer to the company as did Shriek. So it was best for him to make the sacrifice.

Yes, but was that such a hard choice? a part of him asked. The Gatherer promises peace. Every part of your being yearns for what she offers. Is that such a sacrifice—to go with her?

But it was. For he realized that, no matter how much he yearned to go, he wanted to live more. It was not that he thought the Gatherer's peace a lie; it was that the impulse to live was stronger. But if his death would save Shriek, if it would help the others . . .

I will come with you, he told the Gatherer.

There is no need for you to sacrifice yourself on my behalf, Being Neville, Shriek told him. *I called her; I will go with her. Understand, Being Neville, if the Great Mother does not take me now, the peace that lies as a promise at the end of my people's lives will never be mine.*

You'll also be dead, Neville said.

It is my time, she replied simply.

Neville shook his head. But before he could reply, a new voice spoke.

I will go, it said.

Neville turned slowly. He saw his brother standing nearby.

Clive . . . ?

Clive here? How was it possible?

But before he could even begin to unravel that riddle, he realized it wasn't Clive who had spoken. Behind his twin there was yet another presence—no more than a ghostly shimmer at his brother's shoulder, but a presence all the same.

Clive had little time to puzzle out his own surroundings, or what Shriek and Neville were doing in this place. With as much surprise as evinced by his brother, he turned himself to see the glow hovering near him. But unlike Neville he had a name to put to that presence.

Esmond?

Yes, the glow replied. *It is I. Let me go with the Gatherer—allow me to find a moment's worth in a life that never was.*

Who is this? Neville asked.

Clive turned to him. *Our unborn brother, Esmond.*

Neville shook his head slowly. *Now I'm certain that we've all gone mad.*

Had he lived, Clive explained, *he would have been our brother Esmond. We were meant to be triplets, not twins.*

Clive, do you hear what you're saying?

It is the truth, Esmond said.

But . . .

Go now, Esmond continued. *Your bodies await you. You have tasks yet to perform. Let me do this thing.*

No, Shriek said. *This is my covenant to fulfill.* Then she turned to Clive. *I welcome this chance to say farewell to you, Being Clive. It does my heart good to see you still alive.*

You can't die, Neville protested.

I am as good as dead, Being Neville, she replied. *To go with the Great Mother is merely the final step in my journey. Go back to your lives with my blessing.*

No, Esmond said.

In the glimmering shape that was Esmond's presence, vague features began to form—as surely a Folliot's features as either Clive or Neville had ever seen. Their father was in them—and their mother, whom they had known only from portraits.

Esmond turned to the Gatherer.

Will you take me? he asked.

For a long moment the dark presence in the sky was silent. Clive could feel the tug of his body. He saw two flickering threads grow out of the darkness. One touched Neville's lower spine, the other attached itself to the centermost position of Shriek's chest, equidistant from the joints of each of her four upper limbs.

Come, the Gatherer said softly.

No! Shriek cried, but she was too late.

Esmond's presence lifted to float toward the Gatherer. The shadows enveloped him and began to draw away once more, leaving a swath of orange sky behind that was so bright after the darkness that it hurt the eyes of the three who watched from below.

No, Shriek cried again, but more softly now, her voice heavy with regret and promises lost.

Good-bye, my brothers. . . .

Esmond's voice whispered in both Clive and Neville's minds. The twins regarded each other.

He . . . Neville began. *That presence. Surely he wasn't . . .*

I can't explain it myself, Clive replied. *But I believe he truly was who he said he was.*

But that's impossible.

Clive nodded. *So one would think. I doubted him myself—but now, with his sacrifice . . . I find it hard not to believe.*

To have never lived . . . Neville said softly. *What would it be like, to be aware, but never actually living?*

Hard, Clive said. *Desperately hard.* He looked about himself. *What is this place?*

Neville started to shape the explanation in his mind, but suddenly the tug of his body was too strong. He felt the brush of Shriek's mind as it touched his, the neural web enveloping them, and then they were gone.

For long moments Clive remained behind, standing there in that alien landscape; then his body made its own demands on his spirit and he too was drawn away. . . .

■ CHAPTER THIRTEEN ■

"What's with Tomàs?" Annabelle asked Sidi.

The Portuguese was walking ahead with Casady; Smythe and Finnbogg brought up the rear. Sidi gave her a questioning look that was lost in the shadows.

"Wrong?" he asked.

"You know—he's acting almost human."

"I think Tomàs needed to acquire a sense of his own worth. You must remember that he comes from a time when a man such as he has no future and was considered to be of little value. One does not hear of the crews of those old sailing ships—only of the captains. And then only when they have accomplished some great deed of exploration or war.

"At first coming to the Dungeon did little to change that lack of self-worth in Tomàs. But now . . ."

Annabelle turned to look at Sidi, aiming the flashlight's beam up to his features. There was a thoughtful look in his eyes.

"And now?" she prompted.

The Indian shrugged. "I believe the more responsibility we give him, the more he will prove his value—not only to our company as a whole, but to himself as a human being."

Annabelle aimed the light back at the ground and nodded slowly. Made sense. And when she thought of how Tomàs had been saying good-bye to the little *enfant perdu* and how he'd been this past hour—helpful, easy to get along with—it seemed to be working too.

"Awfully modern psychology," she told Sidi, "for a nineteenth-century Indian."

"Your time isn't the only one concerned with the workings of a man's mind."

"I know. But with that caste system you guys've got . . ."

Sidi smiled. "I was born to the *varna,*" he said. "In India I would still be perceived as belonging to what I was born to. But I left India a long time ago. I left *varna* behind with it."

Their conversation came to a halt as they reached Tomàs and Casady, who were waiting for them. The stairs they had originally taken at street level had brought them down into a network of tunnels; now the tunnels had deposited them in a large open area.

"What's this?" Smythe asked as he and Finnbogg arrived as well.

"A disused Chaffri loading area," Casady explained. "Back when there was still trading going on between them and the Ren, they used to move the goods through this sub-subway system. The only goods being moved through it now are by smugglers."

"How far are we from the city?" Annabelle asked.

"Ten minutes."

"And the gate?" Sidi added.

Casady shook his head. "Don't know about the gate. Stands to reason that it'd be smack in the middle of wherever the Chaffri are thickest—seeing how they're the only ones using it."

"What about the Ren? How do they get to use it?"

"They've got their own gate."

"Figures."

Annabelle shone her flashlight around the large chamber. The light wasn't strong enough to reach its far walls.

"This war between the Ren and the Chaffri," she said finally, looking back at Casady. "It's not just about the Dungeon, is it?"

"You're asking the wrong guy about details. I've been in both sides of the city—a GBCer doesn't get to pick where he gets called up—and all I know is they've been at each other's throats for about as long as the

Dungeon's been in operation. And that's a long time, by any standard."

"Thousands of years," Finnbogg said.

Casady nodded at the dwarf. "What he said. Thing is, both sides are getting antsy now because there's a bunch of new players in the game. I've heard that they're another race entirely that stumbled on the Dungeon and want to take it over, but I've also heard that they're the original creators of this place and they want it back. They've got their own agents moving through the levels, getting things ready for some final showdown."

"Agents?" Smythe asked.

Casady grinned. "That's what the word I've heard says. Got it in both sides of the city. One's the Madonna, another's the Cloak, a third's a mismatched bunch of outsiders that follow a couple of guys named Folliot. . . ."

"*Christo!*" Tomàs said. "That is us."

"And let me set you straight, Jack. There's no way we're aligned with any of the Dungeonmasters," Annabelle said.

"I'm only telling you what I hear—not what I believe."

"I've heard of this Madonna in Tawn," Smythe said, "but not of the one you call the Cloak."

"He's supposed to be a little guy who makes a real good business out of hiding in the shadows, manipulating the people around him, just generally causing trouble. Supposed to have a pair of small horns growing out of his brow, and also goes by the name of the Lightbringer."

"Lucifer," Annabelle said.

Tomàs crossed himself.

"Close enough, I suppose," Casady said. "They got the Mother of God and the Big D. both working together against the Ren and the Chaffri."

"I don't understand," Smythe said. "Why the religious motifs? Why religions from our world, for that matter?"

Annabelle nodded. "Yeah. Why's there so many weird twists on the religions of our world? Everywhere we turn there's some new variation on the theme. It doesn't make sense. If they've got the whole universe to draw on, why center so much of it on our world?"

"Got me," Casady said. "I'm just passing on gossip."

"I wish we could find someone who *did* know," Annabelle said.

Casady shrugged. "My bet's that not even the Dungeonmasters really know what's going on anymore. I figure this started out as a game, and somewhere along the line it took on a life of its own and went right out of control. All they've been trying to do since, when they're not fighting with each other, is bring it back to what it once was—their own personal, private playground where they could get a kick out of messing with people's heads.

"See the thing is, they've got all this technology, but nothing's working quite the way it's supposed to anymore. They've had their agents out on the other levels, supposedly getting things back in control, but in reality, they're just setting up their *own* little private playgrounds. Place is splintering into so many different groups that you need a scorecard just to—"

He broke off suddenly.

"Kill the lights!" he told Annabelle and Smythe as he switched off his own flashlight.

"What is it?" Annabelle whispered.

"Thought I heard someth—"

They all heard it now—the quiet scrape of metal against stone. They turned slowly, studying the darkness around them.

Annabelle felt someone press in close to her. Her hand reached for the controls of her Baalbec.

"Zeros," Casady breathed in her ear.

She saw the red glow of their eyes now—three pairs, low to the ground.

Zeros. Right. She should have figured that there was no way they were going to get down to the next level without first having a run-in with these things.

"Too late for hiding," Casady said as he moved away from her.

He flicked on his flashlight. The beam stabbed the darkness, glinting on three forms made of metal and plastic. They were the size of German shepherds and stood on all fours, with torsos rising from where their necks should be. A head and a pair of arms were attached to each torso.

Little cybernetic centaurs, Annabelle thought looking at them.

Their heads were composed of a transparent plastic. Turning her own flashlight on them, Annabelle could see the human brains floating in some kind of thick liquid inside each head.

"Can they be reasoned with?" she asked Casady.

"Not a chance."

Annabelle nodded. "Okay, everybody back up slowly to the tunnel entrance."

They started to do so, all except for Annabelle and Casady.

"Annabelle," Sidi called.

She shook her head. "I can handle this."

"But . . ."

"No arguments, please, Sidi. I know what I'm doing."

At least I hope I do, she thought.

Casady switched his flashlight from his right to his left hand and drew his handgun from his belt. "You heard the lady," he said without looking over his shoulder.

"Is that going to do any good?" Annabelle asked.

"Against their armor? Not likely. But don't forget, I don't die, I just—"

"Fade away. Right. Well, let's try my idea first, shall we?"

"You're the boss," Casady said.

"Neville?"

The voice seemed to come from a great distance. It echoed vaguely in the fog that choked Neville's mind but seemed too obscure a sound to make any sense.

"Neville."

The insistent repetition of the word finally spoke through the fog. It was a name. Of course. *His* name.

"Neville."

It took an immense effort for Neville to open his eyes and focus on the concerned features of Alyssa and Fenil.

"Thank the Great Wind," Alyssa murmured. "He lives."

Neville sat up slowly, head spinning. "Sh-shriek . . . ?" he asked, then realized that he'd been sprawled across her chest.

He turned so that he was facing her and watched her many-faceted eyes flicker open to regard him. The beatific expression she had worn in her death dream had been replaced by a look of such utter loss that Neville realized a deep pang of regret himself.

She had been on the doorstep of heaven, and he had drawn her back. For what? Merely to continue this damnable struggle in the Dungeon.

I'm sorry, he said. *It seemed the right thing to do at the time.*

I understand, Being Neville, she replied. *But it is hard . . . to be back in this world of flesh and blood when that peace was almost mine.*

It will still be waiting for you.

For a long moment the archanid said nothing. Finally she sighed.

Perhaps, she told him.

What do you mean?

Can one touch that moment of utter peace more than once in one lifetime, Being Neville?

Gods! I . . . I never thought . . .

Shriek slowly shook her head. *Do not berate yourself, Being Neville. You meant to perform a brave and selfless deed.*

But if you've lost your chance at heaven . . .

Only the Gatherer knows if your brother has taken my place in the Beyond Beyond, or if there is still a place there, waiting for me. She paused, then added, *At least we now know that Being Clive is well.*

Yes, Neville said. *But—*

What's done is done, Being Neville.

As she began to sit up, Neville moved back from her.

"What happened?" Fenil asked. "Where did you go?"

"Go?" Neville asked.

He was only half-returned to the real world. The remainder of his being was still caught up in Shriek's death dream.

"He went inside," Alyssa said. "Into her mind."

"Inside?" Fenil regarded both Neville and Shriek with an odd expression. "What was it like?"

"It . . ."

Neville's brow creased as he remembered. Shriek's web of memories that she wove between those tall black stones. The Gatherer, filling the sky with her benevolent presence. The arrival of his brother Clive. And that other presence. The one who made the sacrifice. Supposedly his unborn brother.

Could such a thing even be possible?

Neville briefly described their experience.

"I have heard of such beings," Alyssa said. "Those spirits who lose their chance at birth are considered blessed in the eyes of the Great Wind."

"It seems so . . . so preposterous," Neville said.

Alyssa smiled and gave him an understanding look. "Many are the Mysteries of the world—but few exist who can unriddle them. If the Mysteries were so easily understood, they would scarcely be Mysteries, now would they?"

That wasn't what Neville wanted to hear at the moment, but he realized it would be all that he'd get. He had wanted Alyssa to tell him that it was impossible, that he could have no second, unborn, brother who would have been named Esmond. Who would sacrifice himself, as this entity had done.

Allow him the strength of his offering, Shriek said.

"Can you read minds as well as the thoughts projected from them?"

Hardly. But I've learned how to read the features of your people, Being Neville. Yours were what you would call an open book.

Neville nodded. He stood up and brushed from his clothes what he could of the dirt that had been ground into them, then helped Shriek to her feet.

"Remind me not to play cards with you," he said.

The arachnid was unsteady at first but slowly regained her sense of balance. She looked at the two dead giants, half-covered with rubble.

We dealt with them well, she said.

"Most permanently, madam," Neville said.

She turned to look at him to see, not that familiar mocking look that she expected, but a genuine smile on the Englishman's features.

"I'd offer you my arm," he added, "but I don't know the proper protocol among your people."

We spin a web, Shriek said, *to bind us close.*

"I believe I'll pass."

With Fenil and Alyssa's help the pair rejoined the rest of the party. The Tuan was waiting for them on the far side of the mountain created by the fall of the twin giants.

"Do we go on, my lady?" Captain Yoors asked.

"Indeed," Alyssa replied.

Yoors nodded. "I thought as much. I sent Thulen to scout ahead, and he came back with word that he's found a way into some new sort of tunnel—obviously man-made and more in scale to our size."

"Is it far?"

"A half hour—no more."

Alyssa regarded Neville and Shriek. "Do you need to rest, or can we press on?"

"Press on," Neville said. "Only God and the Dungeonmasters know what else is lurking down here in this sewer system. The sooner we get out of it, the happier I'll feel."

He glanced at Shriek.

I am weary, but I—she gave what passed for a smile on her alien features— *I vote that we go on as well.*

Neville was familiar with the concept of voting—the House of Lords ran by voting, while the Commons was elected by a limited, popular vote. Electoral reform was one of the great issues of his day. Neville wasn't decided yet on the finer points of the system, but while he generally considered it fitting enough for Parliament, he wasn't so sure that it was the best method of decision making for a military-styled unit such as they had at the moment.

It was Annabelle's influence, Neville decided, all this business with voting and the whole of a group having a say in what they did rather than following one leader. He admitted to the system's basic fairness but still believed that the most expedient procedure—in practical terms—was to have one man make the decisions. Otherwise the group could spend the better part of its time arguing among themselves rather than forging forward under their common goal.

On the other hand, the Dungeonmasters were a perfect example of the other extreme, so perhaps there was something to be said about democratic action even in a group this small.

Mounted once more, they set off with Thulen in the lead to show the way. The company kept their silvers to a slow pace to accommodate Shriek's slower gait, so it was closer to forty-five minutes before they reached the new tunnel that Thulen had discovered.

"It's a ventilation shaft!" Neville cried when he saw it.

Portions of the tunnel had worn away to show a join between two metal plates of what indeed had to be a ventilation shaft. Some beast had worried away at the join, pulling it apart enough to allow egress for beings of their diminutive size.

"The city below," Alyssa said as understanding dawned on her.

Neville nodded. "It would have to have ventilation. This will lead us directly to it."

There was no need to discuss what was to be done next. One by one they squeezed into the ventilation shaft's narrower confines. The floor of the shaft lay on a gentle gradient. Because the city they sought lay below, they took the downward slope.

Clive stepped from the mirror, feeling as disoriented as Shriek and Neville had coming from the arachnid's death dream. He would have stumbled had Chary not caught his arm and steadied him. He regarded her for a long moment. There was something wrong with her, some discrepancy that he couldn't quite focus on.

"Are you ill?" she asked.

Clive started to shake his head, but then he had it. "You've grown," he said. "You're the same size I am."

The tech smiled back at him. "It's more like you've come down to our size."

Clive looked about the room. It was true. Suddenly everything was in proportion once again. It was a dizzying sensation to look at it all—especially coming hard on the heels of his recent experiences as it did.

"It's so odd," he said. "I've been gone so long, but time seems to have stood still here."

No one appeared to have moved from the positions they had been in when he had left.

"So long?" Chary asked. "The procedure only took" —she looked at a nearby dial—"five point three six eight seconds."

"Only . . . ?"

Clive's sense of disorientation grew stronger.

"What is the matter?" Speaker Lena asked, concern plain on her features.

"Nothing. I just . . ."

He let his voice trail off. Time had passed at different speeds for him, while he stepped through the mirror, and for those who'd remained here. His mind was filled with the bewildering flurry of what he'd recently experienced—meeting his unborn brother, the rescue of Shriek and Neville, discovering the truth about his lost memories. . . .

It took a great effort to put aside the rage that came over him as he remembered what the Dungeonmasters had done to him. Going into his mind to rearrange his memories . . . that seemed the worst a man could do to another. For what was a man, if not the sum total of all he had been? Take some of that from him, and he is that much less the person that he could be.

Around him the Ren and Chang were still regarding him with varying expressions of worry and curiosity. Tell them nothing, he thought. For the moment, at least, he should keep what had occurred to himself. Knowledge was power—even when the owner of such knowledge did not yet know the best method to use it.

He let Chary lead him to a seat into which he gratefully sank. He watched Guafe step into the mirror and reappear moments later, returned to his proper size as well. The cyborg appeared to suffer no ill effects whatsoever.

"How did you find the experience?" Clive asked him.

Guafe shrugged. "It was over so quickly, it scarcely had time to register."

I am going mad, Clive thought. In my mind, I was gone at least an hour.

He recalled speaking to a man who had fainted from the heat once, who had told him that the experience seemed long enough for him to have been caught up in some long dream. His comrades, however, who had brought him around, assured him that he had been unconscious for only moments.

Perhaps this was similar.

All a dream.

When he thought of his experience with the voice from the maze—who claimed to be his unborn brother Esmond—that seemed the logical explanation.

But then he considered the realization that had come to him of how the Dungeonmasters had toyed with his mind, then manipulated his memories to forget the incident. . . .

Perhaps his mind had been manipulated again. The

Dungeonmasters appeared to be divided among themselves. Could one group now be playing him against the other with a new set of false or lost memories?

Madness or dreams? Both seemed too possible. Except what he had experienced had seemed so real. And Shriek and Neville . . .

When he finally found them again, he would ask them if they had ever been in that place he had seen with its orange skies and the huge dark face in its midst. Until then he *would* keep it to himself.

"Well, Clive," Speaker Lena said. "We've kept our side of the bargain and helped you. Will you return the favor?"

Clive shook his head. "Not so quickly. There's still the rest of our party to track down."

"That could take a very long time. Believe me, if they are in danger, then that danger comes from the Chaffri. Every moment you waste could be placing them in more danger. Help us, and we can help you."

Clive remained firm.

Speaker Lena argued further, but when she saw that Clive wouldn't budge from his position, she finally sighed.

"Very well," she said. Looking at Chary, she added, "Do what you can to find his companions—we'll be in the DSL."

"Which is?" Clive asked.

"The Data Storage Library. I want to show you some history."

She led the way out of the laboratory. Once they were in the hall, Guafe surreptitiously laid a hand on Clive's shoulder.

You do well to remain suspicious of them, the cyborg told him through the neural web they shared. *I don't believe they are telling us the entire truth.*

I thought you were on their side, Clive replied.

Hardly. It's simply easier to gain access to the information one requires by ingratiating one's self with one's hosts.

What have you learned, then?

That there is a war between our hosts and the Chaffri, and there is a third group in the Dungeon, but I believe that our hosts' motives to gain your help are not quite so altruistic as they would like us to believe. To use an analogy you will find simple to understand, we are all chess pieces in this Dungeon, but while most of us are pawns, there are some, such as yourself, who have a more important value.

Oh. I'm a king now, am I?

Guafe gave a mental headshake. *Not a king, but at least a knight or a bishop.*

And what do you suggest we do?

Wait. Watch and learn what we can. But take the first opportunity that arises to make our own way once more. The pressure of the cyborg's fingers increased slightly on Clive's shoulder. *Mark this well, Clive Folliot. The first opportunity either of us gets to escape— we should take it. I know I will.*

And what of the other?

We must hope to escape together, but if the occasion arises where I can escape only on my own, believe me, I will do so.

Before Clive could respond to that, Guafe removed his hand from the Englishman's shoulder. Speaker Lena turned to look at them.

"You're awfully quiet," she said.

"We have much to think upon," Guafe replied.

Much indeed, Clive thought. Such as Guafe's chess analogy. He thought again of that chessboard he had seen on the previous level—of the two pieces that wore a different color from that of the remainder of their party.

The cyborg and Sidi Bombay.

Whose side were they truly on? And if Guafe *was* opposed to him and the rest of their party, then what purpose did this last conversation prove? A moment of weakness for the enemy? Or was it simply an honest warning as to Guafe's own purposes?

Gods, but this place played havoc on one's sense of trust.

▪ CHAPTER FOURTEEN ▪

As soon as Annabelle began to approach the zeros, a low electronic growl rose from the voice boxes attached to their chins.

"You get the idea they're trying to tell me something?" Annabelle asked Casady.

Lips dry, heart thumping in her chest, Annabelle flicked on her Baalbec and continued her approach. As she took a couple more steps forward, the first of the creatures made a sudden rush at her.

Annabelle didn't hesitate.

Annie B., you're not operating on a full load, she told herself as she met the creature's attack.

The force of the zero's forward momentum knocked her off her feet, but before the Baalbec could kick in and fling the creature away from her, Annabelle wrapped her arms around it. The Baalbec's electrical force field, surrounding the creature as it was, exerted its terrible pressure. For one long moment the tableau held, electric charges ionizing the air about them, blue-white currents flickering up and down the creature's metallic body. Then the zero imploded.

Protected by the Baalbec, Annabelle wasn't hurt by the exploding metal and plastic. She was thrown back by the violence of the discharge, ears ringing, but stumbled quickly to her feet.

The remaining pair of zeros had begun their own approach. They halted now as Annabelle stepped toward them. The fluid surrounding their floating brains was agitated, bubbling into a froth inside its protective bubble. Their electronic eyes flickered like hazard lights. But they backed up as she continued to move toward them.

A moment later they turned tail and were gone.

"If I hadn't seen it myself," Casady said slowly, "I wouldn't have believed it."

Annabelle turned off the Baalbec and merely shrugged. But her pulse was drumming a rapid tattoo. Her heart felt as though it were rattling against her rib cage.

"You okay?" Casady added.

"Yeah. I . . ."

She wasn't about to tell anyone that she hadn't been sure her plan would even work in the first place. Giving Casady a quick grin, she looked at her handiwork. The creature lay in pieces all over the floor, and the adrenaline charge running through her changed into a flip-flopping nausea that settled in the pit of her stomach.

It was hard not to think of the human brain encased in the intricate cybernetic mesh of plastic and metal that had made up the zero's body. If she closed her eyes, she could see it imploding again. . . .

"I just feel a little . . . sick, that's all."

"Well, let's get a move on," Casady said as the rest of the party emerged from the tunnel behind them. "We hang around here any longer, and we'll have Chaffri all over our asses."

Annabelle nodded.

"That was a nice trick with the zero," Casady added, "but don't go getting cocky. The thing you just killed is only the smallest model they've got running around down here."

He looked around at the others, then led them quickly across the cavern to where another tunnel ran off toward the Chaffri side of the underground city. This one was wider than the one they'd just quit. The floor and walls, where their lights cut across them, appeared to be in better repair.

The city was ten minutes away, Annabelle thought as they hurried down this new passage. But she already felt as though it'd been an hour since they'd left the cavern behind.

"How much farther?" she asked Casady.

"Almost there."

Looking ahead, Annabelle could see a square of light ahead of them.

"Quiet now," Casady added. "This lets us out on a back street in a part of town that isn't being used anymore."

"Why's that?"

"Both the Chaffri and Ren are suffering from lower birthrates. Every year they end up abandoning more and more of their living and working space."

"But—"

"Later," Casady said.

He slowed their approach as they neared the square of light. They could see outside the tunnel now—a small plaza surrounded by buildings that had once been white but were now a dirty gray. Casady paused at the entrance and looked carefully out. The others waited impatiently.

"Okay," he said finally. "Looks clear. See that alley across the plaza to the right?"

Annabelle nodded.

"Head for it and take the second door you come to— on your right. We'll figure out the rest of your route once we get there. Out here we're sitting ducks for the first passing zero patrol."

Without waiting for them to agree or disagree, Casady left the entrance at a quick run. The others hesitated for only a moment, then followed. They got about halfway across the plaza when zeros stepped out of the side streets on every compass point.

Oh, shit, Annabelle thought.

Casady's warning had been well-taken. These zeros were five times the size of the ones they'd encountered back in the cavern. The brains floating in their plastic head casings were the same size, but everything else was multiplied. The new creatures bristled with projections that were all too obviously armaments of one kind or another.

There was no way her trick would work on these, Annabelle realized.

Casady had come to an abrupt halt. As the rest of the party joined him, they made a circle, backs to each other, facing outward. The zeros moved in closer, effectively cutting off their escape from any direction.

"I think we blew it," Casady said softly.

"No kidding." Annabelle said. "Try end of the road."

Oddly enough she felt utterly calm. Maybe it was because she'd never really thought that they'd ever get out of this place, that they'd ever have a chance to confront the Dungeonmasters—to beard them in their own den, as it were.

She flicked on her Baalbec.

"Well, screw 'em all," she said. "I'm going down fighting."

The ventilation shaft led Neville and his party along a gentle downward slope for long miles—or at least what felt like miles.

It was another benefit of their stature, Neville thought as he rode behind Alyssa. If their party had been of the same scale as those that this shaft serviced, they would have had to leave their mounts behind and crawl the length of the shaft.

They made a number of halts, during which one or another of the Tuan would scout ahead while the remainder rested. Shriek took full advantage of each of these interludes, snatching every moment of respite that she could before it was time for them to press on once more.

Neville dismounted from Alyssa's silver at each stop and sat beside the arachnid, lending her the comfort of his moral support. At their latest halt he joined her once more, squatting in front of her.

"How goes it?" he asked.

A sense of mild amusement sparked from her mind to his, tickling his thoughts.

I am not an egg, Being Neville, she said, *for all that you insist on treating me as one.*

"I'm concerned."

I know. I am doing better. I am not so much there *anymore.*

Neville knew exactly what she meant. Though the experience hadn't had the same intensity for him as it had for her—it was, after all, part and parcel of her racial background, not his—he could still empathize with her. Like the protagonist in Milton's famous poem he knew now what it was like to lose Paradise.

The memory sat in the back of his mind, rising up in the middle of the most mundane thought to remind him of what was now gone. Calm unclaimed. Peace lost. Solace thrown away. And for what? To struggle on in this hellish Dungeon.

It made one reconsider one's own sanity, Neville couldn't help but think at times.

What I fear the most, Shriek said, *is that we will have gone through all we have but never learn the why of it. Never to understand why it was we that were chosen . . . what the Dungeonmasters want with us . . . what any of this madness* means. . . .

She looked at Neville, and Alyssa sitting beside him. *Do you understand that fear?* she asked.

Neville nodded. "All too well."

Shriek continued to study him for a long moment. *You have changed, Being Neville,* she said finally. *And that change is not simply due to your meeting the Gatherer.*

"All men change," Neville said with a shrug.

He could feel her smile in his mind.

Yes. But not all change for the better.

They sat quietly for a few moments. The only sound was the quiet murmur of the Tuans as they spoke to each other, the fairy jingle of the silvers' harnesses when the animals shifted their positions. The light of their torches flickered, throwing shadows. The air within the shaft was basically fresh—far more so than it had been in the storm sewers—though it did have a very slight chemical scent to it.

"Among my people," Alyssa said, "it is the journey that is important, not the destination itself. When one seeks knowledge, the quest is the thing, not the final solution for which we aim. All too often that solution proves to be of far less import than what we learned on our route to reach it."

"Small comfort in our present situation," Neville said.

But Shriek was nodding her head. *I understand what you mean, Being Alyssa,* she said. *We have a similar philosophy on my homeworld.*

"I think it's a concept put forth by the philosophers of every culture," Neville said. "It's simply not what I want from this adventure. I want answers. I want satisfaction from those who have treated us as though we were nothing more than gaming pieces for them to move about on their game board. And one way or another I will have it."

"Brave words."

Neville looked up to find that Captain Yoors was standing near them.

"I mean what I say," he told Yoors.

"I don't doubt that you do."

Neville studied the Tuan's serious face. Yoors met his gaze. There was no give in him—not an inch.

"So you've finally decided to accept us?" Neville asked.

Yoors shrugged. "I'm not ready to count you among my friends—for all that, I know now that you are not ranked with my enemies."

A hard man, Neville thought. But they all needed to be hard if they were to survive in this place—men and women both.

"But when we do find these Dungeonmasters," Yoors added, "you will have to wait to have your turn with them, for they and I have the matter of an old debt to clear up first."

"They owe many debts," Neville said.

Yoors merely nodded, then returned to his mount and began to adjust its harness.

"We should ride on soon," Alyssa said.

Shriek rose wearily to her feet. *My body yearns for its nest, but I still have the strength to press on.*

Neville stood up beside her. Trouble made for odd fellowships, he thought. Here he felt closer to a creature that in England he'd be more likely to step on than attempt to speak with. Instead he counted her as his friend and gave little consideration to her bizarre appearance.

As for Alyssa—whose appearance left nothing to be desired—ever since the attack of the giant dogs she had exchanged her earlier flirtatious behavior for the responsibility of being the leader of her company. Surprisingly Neville found himself more attracted to her because of that. He had never considered it before, but it stood to reason that a man could do little better than to have a woman who stood beside him, rather than one who deferred to his wishes.

You have changed, Shriek had told him earlier.

Neville nodded to himself. He had, indeed. Far more than even she might realize.

"You look thoughtful, Neville," Alyssa said to him as he approached her silver. "Is something troubling you?"

"No more than troubles us all," he said.

He gave her a leg up. The Tuan who had been scouting ahead returned with no news except that the shaft continued with its gentle descent for as far as he could see.

"How deep does the city lie?" Neville asked.

There was no response from the Tuan until Fenil spoke.

"No one knows," he said.

Neville nodded. "Then we'll simply have to find out for ourselves, won't we?"

Fenil flashed him a quick grin.

When Neville was mounted behind her, Alyssa gave the signal to ride, and the company set off once more.

They rode quietly. Alyssa and Neville rode at the fore, with Shriek at their side. The rest rode single file. The only sound that accompanied them was that of the jingling harnesses and the soft click of the silvers' claws on the metal floor of the shaft. Their torches sent shadows scudding ahead of them.

Neville didn't mind the slowness of their pace. At this point it didn't matter to him how long it took them to reach the Dungeonmasters—just so long as they reached them.

He touched the hilt of his sword.

You'll have to be quick, Yoors, he thought, if you mean to collect your debt before I collect mine.

The Data Storage Library was like no library that Clive was familiar with in his own world. There were no club chairs and lights, no carpeting underfoot, no paintings, no sculptures. For God's sake, there were no bookcases—no books!

It was a long, rectangular room, garishly lit by overhead banks of lights, flanked on either wall by rows of cabinets. Desks ran down the central length of the room, dotted with computer stations that Clive recognized from their stay in Dramaran.

But where were the books?

"The data is digitally stored in CCs—compact cubes," Speaker Lena explained when Clive asked.

She went to the nearest cabinet and opened the drawer to show row upon row of small translucent cubes.

"One of these," she said, picking a cube at random, "holds as much data as a hundred books."

Clive let none of the surprise he felt show on his features. A hundred books on each cube? He began a quick calculation—the cubes in this drawer, times the number of drawers in each cabinet, times the cabinets —and gave up before he'd reckoned the amount of books that one drawer could hold.

"You said something about histories?" he said.

Speaker Lena replaced the cube and moved down

the room to another drawer. Taking a new cube from it, she sat down at one of the computer stations and beckoned the pair of them closer.

"History," she said as she inserted the cube.

She indicated that they should pull up chairs on either side of her. Once they were seated, she attached a cable running from the computer's main housing to a small socket on a plain metal bracelet that she wore on her wrist. Laying her hand flat on the table in front of the monitor, she moved her fingers in a quick, complex pattern on the tabletop. The screen came to life.

"This is the Dungeon," she said.

Clive gazed uncomprehendingly at the image on the monitor. It showed the vastness of space, constellations dotting the darkness in unfamiliar patterns—except for one that was too familiar, and that was the star pattern Clive remembered from when he had first entered the Dungeon. Close up was a large rock, floating in the center of the screen.

"What is this?" he asked. "What are you trying to tell us?"

Guafe explained what the image meant, then turned to the Speaker.

"Are you telling us that the Dungeon is an asteroid circling some unknown planet?" he asked.

"Not unknown." She manipulated her fingers on the desk once more and the view changed, from the asteroid to the planet beyond it. "This was Aralt—the homeworld of my people and the Chaffri. We discovered the Dungeon on our first manned flights beyond Aralt's atmosphere. All our subsequent technical advances sprang from what we found within it."

"You said 'was,'" the cyborg said, making a question of the statement.

Speaker Lena nodded. "Aralt was destroyed in one of our wars with the Chaffri. We have fought across the galaxies, leaving similar destruction in our wake wherever our forces have met."

There was no real regret in her voice, just a simple stating of the facts.

Guafe nodded slowly. "And then why does the Dungeon still stand unharmed?"

"Happily some part of the Dungeon itself has always intervened. But now . . ." She turned from the screen to look at Clive. "Our spies have learned that the Chaffri have cracked the coded seals on a Gannine weapons store. Once they have the weapons operational, they will move against us, then on through the gates to conquer other times and worlds."

"Gannine?" Clive asked.

"The original race who created the Dungeon."

"And just what *is* the Dungeon?" Guafe asked.

"The closest we can guess is that it is some form of space station—a giant laboratory that the Gannine used to study the various races they came across on their journeys through the vastness of space."

"And the Gannine?" Clive asked. "What happened to them?"

Speaker Lena shook her head. "No one knows. They were absent when our ancestors first commandeered the Dungeon, but lately it appears that they could be returning to reclaim their own."

"It seems curious that they should ever cast aside their work in the first place," Guafe said.

"We have always felt that they simply moved on to other endeavors," Speaker Lena replied. "The Chaffri held to the theory that they were sleeping—hidden somewhere in the vastness of the Dungeon—and that they would wake again. It appears that the Chaffri were correct."

Again she turned to Clive. "So you see our problem. If the Chaffri have gained the use of the Gannine weapons technology, we are all in equal danger. And if it is the Gannine returning—our danger is multiplied a hundred times."

"I still don't see what it has to do with me," Clive said. "I don't even understand the half of what goes on in this place, so how could I be of any importance?"

"You . . ." the Ren Speaker hesitated. "You are a

born leader. You can consolidate our forces, plan our attack. . . ."

Guafe leaned forward as though to study the screen more closely. He used the motion to disguise the movement of his hand that reached behind the Speaker's back to touch Clive's shoulder.

She's lying, he said on the neural web.

About what? It all seems preposterous.

Probably about everything except the fact that the Chaffri are a threat, that there is a third party out for both Chaffri and Ren blood, and that she needs you. The question is—what does she need you for?

Remember Annabelle's theory? Clive guessed. *It must have something to do with my Folliot blood.*

Yes. But what?

Guafe let his hand drop. Aloud he asked the Speaker, "Have you never searched for the Gannine before?"

"Oh, yes. That has always been an ongoing part of our research—both ours and the Chaffri's. Over the years we have had to conclude that, for whatever reasons they had, they simply abandoned the Dungeon to move on to other concerns. Left to its own devices, the Dungeon evolved on its own, factions forming and changing as the years went by. When we arrived, we took control of what we could—roughly an even division between the Chaffri and ourselves."

"And," Guafe said, "can we assume, by our own presence here, that both you and the Chaffri have continued the Gannine's work?"

"What do you mean?"

"Are we not here to be studied as well?"

"Oh, no. We each bring in new beings to foil the plans of the others. We have to. The Dungeon will not allow us to work directly against each other, so we must use intermediaries."

It *was* nothing but a game, Clive realized.

His fist clenched at his sides, but he kept his own counsel. Taking a deep breath to steady his anger, he reached behind the Speaker's chair to touch Guafe's shoulder.

We have to play along with her, he said.

I am not so certain that that is a wise course anymore, Guafe replied. *Better we put our minds to escape—and quickly.*

Agreed. But until that opportunity arises, we have to keep up a helpful pretense.

He dropped his hand from the cyborg's shoulder as Speaker Lena turned to him.

"I see now your problem," he told her, "and it *is* our problem as well. I will do everything I can to help you."

The Speaker's features beamed. "I knew you would help. I told the others you could do nothing else but help us, once you knew the truth."

I've yet to know the truth, Clive thought, but he doubted he would find it anywhere in the Ren's part of the city.

"Can you call up a map of this level?" Guafe asked. "I am feeling somewhat disoriented as to exactly where we are in the Dungeon."

Speaker Lena nodded. Manipulating her fingers on the desktop, she called up a series of maps. Clive and Guafe watched the levels go by—all those miles they had struggled through on foot, all those places of danger, flitted by in moments where it had taken them months to travel. Finally the screen stopped with a map of the eighth level.

"This is where we found you," the Speaker said, indicating a spot on the map displayed on the screen. Her fingers made another quick movement on the desktop. "And this is the city we share with the Chaffri. The demarcation line between our halves of the city is here."

Both Clive and Guafe leaned forward. They noted the position of the Data Storage Library and its proximity to the gate leading to the ninth level. The greater bulk of the Ren's part of the city lay between the two spots.

"Why do you use a gate such as this," Guafe asked, "when you have the teleportation device in your laboratory?"

"The device is something we made for ourselves—the Dungeon has its own gates, one of which is what you see here. We can't open or close them—they simply are."

"Do the Ren have similar teleportation devices?"

"Unfortunately, yes. Why do you ask?"

Both Clive and Guafe caught the sudden suspicion in her voice. Clive glanced at his companion.

Well? he thought. *Come up with something quickly.*

"If you were the only ones to have such devices, it would put you at a great advantage. It's advantages that we must be looking for, is that not true?"

Speaker Lena relaxed. "Exactly. And with Clive's help we'll be able to do just that."

"What exactly is it that you want me to do?" Clive asked again.

"I'll tell you that when we've rejoined the other Speakers. Have you seen enough in here?"

More than enough, Clive thought.

"For now," Guafe said. "We will most likely have to return for more data, once we have spoken with the other members of your council." He stood up from the chair. "Shall we go?"

While Speaker Lena disengaged the computer cable from her wrist and was returning the cube to its drawer, Guafe moved closer to Clive so that their shoulders brushed.

Keep her occupied, if you can, he said.

Do you have a plan?

Yes. I—

He broke off when the Speaker turned and moved away from Clive. Letting the two of them take the lead, he followed along behind.

"What luck do you think your scientists will have in tracking down the rest of our party?" Clive asked the Speaker. He spoke as much out of concern for Annabelle, Smythe, and the others, as he did to keep the Ren busy.

"We can ask after their progress as soon as we're finished with the council," she replied.

Clive immediately asked another question, wondering all the while what it was that Guafe had planned. When they reached a door that led back out into the Hub, both he and the Speaker found out at the same time.

Looking behind them, they realized that the cyborg was no longer with them.

The maps, Clive realized. Guafe had memorized the maps, learned what he needed of how the city was laid out, and was making his escape.

Wonderful. He was left here on his own amongst their enemies while Guafe went free.

An image of a chessboard arose in his mind—the pieces resembling Sidi Bombay and Guafe on the opposing sides of the board.

It had been a warning.

And now . . . Chang was gone, and the Ren would think he had played a part in the cyborg's escape unless he covered up his own part in the plan.

"Where on earth . . . ?" he began.

Speaker Lena regarded him coldly. "Where indeed?" she said.

Lifting her wrist, she pushed a small indentation on her bracelet and spoke rapidly into it. Clive couldn't understand a word of what she was saying, but he would have had to be both blind and deaf not to see the anger in her eyes or to hear the tightness in her voice.

Somehow he didn't think she was about to believe in his innocence.

▪ CHAPTER FIFTEEN ▪

Annabelle got ready to charge the zeros.

Maybe they were five times bigger than the little sucker she'd taken out back in the cavern, and maybe her ass'd be grass if she tried the same trick on these guys, but she was damned if she was going to just be docilely taken away again.

She was done with prisons.

Done with being played for a patsy.

Done with fighting for her life every second step of the way.

She'd had it up right to here, thank you very much, with this frigging Dungeon.

"Don't do it," Casady said as she took her first step.

"Screw you too," she said.

But then Casady grabbed her, and Annabelle's world just did another skidding flip-flop. She had the Baalbec turned on. There was no way—no *way*—he could grab her. But she could feel his fingers on her arm, his hand reaching through the Baalbec's field as if it weren't even there.

"You can't . . . that's impossible. . . ."

The Baalbec had to be malfunctioning.

Casady shook his head. "You keep forgetting—I'm not really here."

"But I can feel you. . . ."

He shook his head again. "It's a play on your senses. I'm just a collection of juiced-up molecules, made up to play Jack Casady. I feel real to you because your head tells me I'm here. I feel real to me because that's the way I've been programmed. But I'm just a glorified piece of playback, Annabelle, fired up with a high-tech AI program. Your Baalbec knows I'm not here."

"But your gun . . ."

"It's a real gun—fires real bullets."

"How can you hold it?"

"Because the molecules I borrow to make me exist can be as solid or permeable as I want 'em to be. I keep going just so long as the program's juiced up."

"And when the music fades . . ."

"I fade."

"Annabelle?"

So intent had she been on what the GBCer was telling her that she'd entirely forgotten the danger they were in. At Smythe's quiet call she looked up to find that the large zeros had closed in on them, leaving them no room to maneuver.

The cybernetic creatures made no move; they just boxed the group in, not allowing them any egress from the square. With their shining metal and plastic hides they looked like something an engineer might've designed on an acid trip in a hardware store.

Annabelle took a step forward, and a bright red laser cut the pavement before her feet, slagging the concrete. She quickly stepped back, not wanting to test her Baalbec's capabilities. Not when the GBCer could put his hand through its field. Didn't matter how reasonable an explanation Casady had to give, the experience had spooked her.

"Now what?" Annabelle said, staring one of the ugly suckers straight in the face. "So you got us. What're you going to do with us?"

A voice, its tone metallically nonhuman, spoke from the voice box under the chin of the zero directly in front of her.

"You will remain passive until an agent of authority arrives. Please be warned, any untoward movement will require the mobile tactical units to fire."

"At least they don't mean to kill us," Tomàs said.

Annabelle nodded without any enthusiasm. "Yeah, they want to save that pleasure for themselves. What'll it be this time, guys? A takeoff on an Inca sacrifice? Or maybe we'll get to play Christ on a cross."

"We've escaped from worse situations," Sidi said.

Annabelle regarded him for a long moment, knowing he meant well, but she was just too depressed to be able to find anything optimistic about their situation.

"Hooray," she said as she turned off her Baalbec and sat down on the pavement.

The lasers mounted on the bodies of the nearest zeros tracked her every movement. She turned her back on them.

One by one the others followed her example. Her foul mood was affecting them all. Finnbogg sat mumbling to himself. Tomàs looked more as she remembered him from before, sullen and with secrets brooding in his dark eyes. Sidi sat unsmiling with Smythe beside him; the Englishman was stoic as always, but grimly so now. Only Casady seemed unaffected.

Of course, she thought, he wasn't real.

He sat down close to Annabelle.

"You're doing this to them," he said softly.

"Doing what?"

But she knew. They were all picking up on her bad vibes, and the whole thing was just feeding on itself now.

"You're the leader," Casady said. "No matter what expertise the others might have that you do not, you have that one special quality to set you apart. They will follow you."

"Great. Look where it's gotten us."

Casady ignored her sarcasm. "Yes, look," he said. "All the way down to the eighth level of the Dungeon, whereas most prisoners don't even make it past the first few."

Annabelle shook her head. "You don't understand. We can't win this one on points. We either get to the end and win, or we end up like we are now—royally screwed."

"As your friend said—you've made it through worse."

"Yeah, but every time it takes a little more out of you until it gets to the point where you've got nothing left and it doesn't matter diddly anymore." She looked over at the zeros, then back at him. "I don't think you *can* understand. I mean, the worst that can happen to you is you run out of the juice that the music gives you, and you end up back on your card until somebody else comes along and calls you up—am I right?"

"Yes, but—"

"You've got this sixties mentality that you never grew out of—a weird combination of peace, love, and karma, and some kick-ass that you never left behind from before you got enlightened."

"So?"

All Annabelle could do was look at him.

So? Right. Maybe more to the point, so what?

It was like Philosophy 100 and "Why?/Why not?" Or that quote she'd heard about some traditional Irish musician who, when asked why he played so fast, simply said, "Because I can."

It was all in your attitude. That was what Casady was trying to say. Didn't matter if he was just a GBCer playing at being real, or a flesh-and-blood holdover from the sixties, marooned here in the Dungeon with them. What he said was true. It still came down to your attitude.

Think like a winner, and you win.

Why climb that mountain? Because it's there.

Like all that pop psychology bullshit that started up in the seventies and kept right on trucking, all the way into her own decade.

You can do it if you want to.

Think frigging positive.

But it was all a front. Most of the time, while you were playing smart and brave and on top of things, you were just scared shitless inside and feeling like a dummy. And it got harder each time, not easier.

She looked at her companions, at the circle of glum faces, most of which didn't even bother to look back at her. And sighed.

"I guess you remember sit-ins and be-ins—right?" she said to Casady.

He nodded. "Why do you ask?"

"My mom used to talk to me about them, about how people would just get together and not budge until something got done. About how maybe you couldn't change the whole world, but if you at least changed yourself, you were doing *something*. That kinda bull-shit."

Casady smiled. "I can see why you'd think that way. Sometimes we got our asses kicked, but sometimes . . . sometimes it worked."

"Yeah. I know. I got the point already. What I'm trying to say is thanks."

Before he could reply, she stood up and hauled Tomàs to his feet beside her.

"Christo!" he muttered. "Now what—"

She shut him up by starting to sing "We Shall Overcome."

Tacky, she thought, but hell. It had easy words and a nice, simple melody line.

Casady rose to his feet, pulling Finnbogg up beside him. Sidi and Smythe joined them. Arms linked, they all sang as loud as they could, cleaning the fear out of their hearts, just letting the music ring there, hard and sure.

If I saw this on the nightly news, Annabelle thought, I'd think we were all whacked out.

But it was a different world here. They were all feeling down. And damned if sometimes the old bullshit didn't cut straight through the new.

They were still singing when the Chaffri arrived.

When the torches finally gave out, Neville's party lost not only their source of light, but their means of measuring time as well. Knowing that each torch had lasted for twenty minutes made it easy to reckon how long they had been traveling and to schedule rest stops. With the last torch gone they were reduced to feeling their way along the shaft, slowed down to a snail's crawl, and time lost its meaning.

In the darkness a minute and an hour took on too similar a denotation.

They made slow progress—even if, with the endless similarity of the ventilation shaft, it seemed as though they made no progress at all—and they all began to suffer from a mild sense of claustrophobia. It was not until their third rest stop after the torches ran out that they began to perceive a difference: that chemical scent in the air, faintly detected when they first entered, seemed somewhat stronger now.

And then a scout brought back the welcome news that he'd spied light ahead.

Though they had been resting only a few moments, they were all so heartily sick of the shaft, of the darkness, of their interminable journey through both, that they immediately mounted once more and set off to find that source of light.

It proved to be a grating that looked out on an immense city.

Neville marveled to look out on it—such an expanse of streets and buildings, all nestled here underground, lit by long banks of lights on the cavern roof above that were too bright to look at for long. It seemed a great waste to him that, with so much knowledge and ability in their hands, the Dungeonmasters used it for no more than vexing the prisoners that they kidnapped and placed in the game-board maze that the Dungeon was.

What a man could do with what they had!

"Thank the Great Wind," Alyssa said. "We've done it."

The grating was so small that only three of them could stand shoulder to shoulder and look out at one time. They each took their turns, studying the streets below them. Like the city above this place appeared to be deserted as well. But here there was no rubble, no sense of decay or destruction. Simply an emptiness.

"How to get down from this shaft," Neville said. "That's our problem now."

I could spin a line, Shriek said.

Neville nodded, remembering what he'd heard of an earlier descent that she and the others of her party had made from one level to another.

"Perhaps," he said. "Though first we'd have to get through this grating. . . ."

But the spacing between its bars was too small to allow them egress. And the immense screws locking the grate to the walls of the shaft were too large and too firmly in place to budge, even when they tried two at a time on one screw.

"So we travel on," Fenil said.

"And a good thing too," Neville said quietly as he looked through the grating once more.

"Wha—" Alyssa began, but Neville laid a finger across her lips.

"Look," he said softly.

On the street below them a pair of monstrously large creatures had appeared, pacing slowly down the smooth pavement. They were like the cyborg, Chang Guafe, Neville thought. Some combination of metal workings, fused with a living creature. Mechanical centaurs—if one exchanged the horse and man for a dog and dwarf.

Of course their large size was a matter of scale, Neville realized. To his party they were giants—as every other creature had been on this level except for the Tuan—but in relation to the buildings and streets below, they were the size of large terriers.

"What are they?" Alyssa asked.

"I don't know. But we had a member of our party— human in shape—that reminds me of them."

Guafe, Shriek said.

Neville nodded. "Still, I wouldn't be so likely to trust these creatures as I would our erstwhile companion."

They waited until the creatures had traveled the length of the street and disappeared from view before moving on themselves. Their own route was easier now, for the gratings were spaced regularly enough so that the darkest it became was at those places equidistant between two apertures, and there it was no more than the deep twilight just before night that Neville remembered from his homeworld.

Making good time, they reached a branching in the shaft about an hour later. Part of the shaft continued on at the same level; the new branch led downward at a sudden steep angle. After some discussion they chose the route that would take them down.

The claws of the silvers scraped and slid on the metal floor of the shaft as they made their steep descent. Eventually it grew so difficult that Shriek had to release a line from her spinnerets. She attached one end to the wall of the shaft where they were, then took the lead on the way down, playing out the sticky thread behind her. The silvers, once the Tuan showed them how to walk on the thread, soon picked up the knack of using it for a brake for the remainder of the descent.

At the bottom of the shaft they had a choice of dozens of new routes. Through the gratings here they could see inside the buildings. The shaft they chose eventually led them into one of the buildings. Here they found shafts that led them straight into the casings of a number of large machines that reminded both Neville and Shriek of the computer banks they had seen on previous levels.

"We can get down to the ground now," Fenil remarked the next time they paused to take stock of their surroundings.

He indicated a spiraling descent created by loops of cables inside the machine where they were resting. At the floor level they could see that there was enough space between the sides of the machine and the floor to allow them to creep through.

"True enough," Neville said. "But this part of the city appears to be deserted. We might as well continue through the shafts until we reach a peopled area."

"If there is one," Yoors said.

"Oh, there will be one," Alyssa said. "I can *feel* other presences."

She closed her eyes, then with a loose wave of her

arm indicated the direction in which they were already traveling.

"That way."

Neville gave her an odd look. Was she going to prove to be a psychic now? But then he remembered that she was the priestess of these Tuan, as well as their secular leader. Who knew what a Tuan priestess was capable of? In this Dungeon he had seen too much that was strange simply to dismiss such a thing.

Being Neville has the right of it, I believe, Shriek said. *Once we reach a peopled area, we will have a safe vantage point from which to spy on them in these shafts.*

"And we can take further counsel at that point," Alyssa said.

The only drawback that Neville saw to this, even if it had been his idea in the first place, was that he was soundly tired of feeling like a mouse or a rat, scrambling about inside these walls.

"And if we can't descend from the shaft in those peopled areas?" Yoors asked.

"It's a trade-off," Neville replied. "No question about it."

"But a chance we will take," Alyssa decided.

There was no argument from the Tuan once she had made her decision.

Counsel taken and their course determined, they set off again.

For the second time in as many days Clive found himself connected to the Ren's truth detector, the electrodes attached to each of his temples, his wrists, his ankles, and his chest. Once again three Speakers sat at the desk before him. Speaker Lena was not amongst them. She sat to one side of the desk, glaring at him. There were three guards present—standing watch behind Clive—and two techs to run the machines.

"I don't believe you had anything to do with your friend's escape," Chary told him in a soft voice as she and Howell were connecting him to the machine.

Clive gave her a weak smile. That was small comfort when the truth detector would proclaim his lies.

Damn Guafe for putting him in this position in the first place.

He was in for it—no question about it—unless . . . Clive nodded to himself. Unless he told the truth. Not enough to incriminate himself—just enough to keep the evaluator from setting off its alarm, or whatever it was that it did to tell the Ren that its subject was playing them false.

Chary turned on the machine, and it began to hum on its trolley beside Clive. That odd buzzing sensation that he remembered from his previous experience with the evaluator returned. It traveled the length of his spine, spreading out to every nerve end while an unnatural sensation of warmth settled in the base of his spine.

"How many of us are sitting at this table?" the centermost Speaker asked him.

He was the same one who had been present the last time. His name was Kian, Clive remembered. The other two Speakers had been introduced as Ovard—he was on the left, yet another short, dapper man—and Berna, a red-haired woman with cold gray eyes. Speaker Lena appeared to be merely observing the proceedings this time.

Speaker Kian frowned. "I asked you—"

Lord, this infantile test again, Clive thought, but he replied before one of the guards behind him jabbed him with the muzzle of his weapon.

"Three. Four if you count Speaker Lena."

"What is the color of our robes?"

"Blue."

"Are you a native of this world? Please answer in the affirmative."

"I am."

With each reply Clive made the evaluator hummed at his side, sending that curious buzz to follow the traceries of his nervous system. He felt a sense of disorientation creep over him. His surroundings took on a surreal quality, while his mind seemed to sharpen. It was almost as though he could see *within* the objects about him.

The stark furniture blurred as though it were slightly vibrating. The Ren were still human shapes, but their features and bodies had clouded into smears of swirling color.

Clive blinked away the sudden sheen of perspiration that dripped into his eyes.

Speaker Kian glanced at the techs.

"Can we continue?" he asked.

"Adjustments have been made," Howell said. "You can question him now."

Speaker Ovard steepled his fingers and gave Clive a long, serious look. "What is your purpose in this Dungeon?" he asked.

Clive made an effort to concentrate on his reply. But it was difficult. The Speaker's words appeared to issue from his mouth as both sound and swirls of color.

"To find my companions and to escape," Clive said.

The buzz whined through his nerves.

"And?" Speaker Berna asked.

"Have our satisfaction from the Dungeonmasters for how they have treated us."

Again the machine's hum. Again the quiver running the length of his neural system.

"Are we your enemy?" Speaker Kian asked.

Clive blinked as more sweat pooled in his eyes. The entire room seemed to be shimmering.

"I . . . I don't know."

That appeared to perplex them, for the three Speakers at the table bent their heads close together and whispered amongst each other for a few moments.

"Where has your companion gone?"

"I don't know."

"Why did he abandon you? What is his purpose?"

"I presume the same as all of us—to escape."

Each reply Clive made intensified the evaluator's response on his nervous system. He felt as though his

entire body were humming along in concert with it—
each cell vibrating. Faster and faster.

Lord, he thought. What is happening to me?

"I ask you again," Speaker Kian said finally. "Do you
perceive us as your enemy?"

It took a long moment for Clive to gather his
thoughts. It was increasingly difficult for him to concentrate on any one thing for longer than a moment.
As soon as he focused on an object or a thought, his
entire being appeared to spin about it.

"I don't know what you want with me," he managed
finally. "If you are asking me, do I trust you"—he
paused to let the swirling room slow down enough for
him to complete his sentence—"then the answer is
no."

"He is speaking the truth," Howell said. His voice
was so clinical that it cut through the blur affecting
Clive, giving Clive a momentary respite.

Speaker Ovard pursed his lips. "And your companion? Why did you help him escape?"

"I . . ."

Then it happened again. There was a hissing and
popping sound from the evaluator beside Clive as it
shorted out. The room became a plummeting mael-
strom in which he bobbed helplessly like a piece of
flotsam, tugged free from some safe harbor. Dimly he
could hear voices crying out in alarm.

"The evaluator—it's feeding back again!"

"Cut the power!"

Blue fire ran through Clive's nerves. He could feel
Chary plucking the electrodes from his skin. They
popped free with sounds that echoed in Clive's mind.

"I told you we shouldn't have used this on him
again," she was saying. "Something in his neural system sets up a feedback and shorts everything out."

Clive lolled in the chair, head on his chest, eyes
rolled backward. Once again he lost all awareness of his
surroundings and went traveling through a gray mist.

Esmond, he called into the fog, but there was no
reply.

Of course there wouldn't be. Esmond, if he had ever existed, had sacrificed himself and been taken away by the Gatherer of Shriek's afterworld.

Free-falling in the mist, his thoughts coalesced into a more orderly form. With only the grayness about him his mind was no longer confused by the bewildering input of surreal data with which it had been forced to contend.

That machine of the Ren. Lord help him, what did it *do* to him?

An oval clearing appeared in the grayness. Drifting directly before it, Clive found himself looking into a Victorian sitting room—just as he had the previous time that the evaluator had sent him into this place— only this time the room was empty.

He leaned as close to the oval as he could propel himself.

"George?" he called softly.

From his vantage point he could see what he supposed was du Maurier's desk. The green blotter held a scatter of manuscript pages and half-completed pen-and-ink drawings. Clive's shocked gaze centered on one almost-complete drawing.

It was that of a woman, obviously attending a fancy dress ball. Her costume was that of Little Bo-Peep, illustrating, Clive realized, a poem of the same name that lay on the desk beside the drawing. But it was neither costume nor poem that drew and held Clive's gaze.

It was the woman's face.

Those familiar features.

God help him. A pen-and-ink Annabella Leighton looked back at him from that drawing. Du Maurier had used her as the model for that piece.

Clive knew such a pang of loss that all he felt was a bleak emptiness inside. He already knew, from what Annabella's own descendant Annabelle had told him, that he had never returned to England. Never returned to Annabella, pregnant with their child.

But he had once—in that damnable dream that the

Dungeonmasters had forced upon him. Perhaps, he thought, despair lying thick on him, he should have closed his mind to the lie of it. Perhaps he should simply have remained in that dream because, for the first time since coming to the Dungeon, the fact hit home that he would never actually escape this damnable place.

All that he had been, all that he might have been, had been stolen away by the machinations of the Dungeonmasters—God curse their souls!

He tried to turn his gaze from the drawing but could not. He reached for it, through the oval opening, but it was as though he were outside a window, looking in. His fingers were stopped by invisible glass.

The door of the room opened then, and Clive finally dragged his gaze from the drawing to see du Maurier enter the room.

"G-george . . ."

Du Maurier stopped dead in his tracks and stared at him. The shock of familiarity ran across his features as he recognized Clive.

"Don't leave so quickly this time!" he cried as he hurried toward the oval opening.

But already Clive could feel the Dungeon pulling him back—away from the oval that allowed him to look upon, but not touch, the England he had lost. Away from his old comrade.

If he could just pass a message to Annabella through him . . .

"Tell her," he began.

The pull of the Dungeon grew too strong, dragging him back into the gray mists.

"Clive!" du Maurier cried. "For God's sake, man! Don't go."

"Tell her . . ."

But the gray mists washed over the oval, shutting it from view like draperies being drawn across a window, and the hole that let him look into his old life was lost again.

The fog settled in his head, clouding his mind.

"Tell her that I love her still," he said. "That I always will."

But there was no one there in the mist to hear what he said.

When he finally regained consciousness, it was to find himself back in that chamber modeled on the Victorian world he had lost, the same chamber he had awoken in when the machines had malfunctioned the first time and sent his mind spiraling away into the grayness. Chary and Speaker Lena were both sitting there, watching him.

He sat up slowly.

"I apologize," Speaker Lena said. "The evaluator shows you spoke the truth. You knew nothing of your companion's plans."

"I told you things would work out," Chary said.

Clive realized that the female tech was interested in him—as a man, rather than simply as a subject for her labs. But with that pen-and-ink drawing of Annabella still fresh in his mind, he knew he would not reciprocate her feelings.

He swung his feet to the floor.

"Tell me what it is you want me to do," he said to Speaker Lena.

"I'm so sorry about the accident with the evaluator," the Speaker said. "But you must understand. We are surrounded on all sides by enemies. Without assurances—"

Clive was rapidly losing all semblance of patience.

"Didn't you hear me?" he said. "Tell me what you want done, and I will do it. Not tomorrow. Not when your Speakers can bring themselves together long enough to convene some new council. But now."

Speaker Lena regarded him for a long moment, then quickly nodded her head. She rose to her feet.

"Come with me," she said.

▪ CHAPTER SIXTEEN ▪

Annabelle's first impression of the Chaffri was that they looked like a bunch of Mardi Gras Indians, all decked out in colors so bright it hurt her eyes. She'd been leading her companions through a version of the Wailing Men's "Anger's Not Enough"—a moldy-gold hit from 1991—and their voices all trailed off at the newcomers' approach.

There were a half dozen of them, two women, the rest men, all of them white-skinned, but everything else screamed color. Serapes, trousers, and baggy shirts painted day-glo bright, headdresses and vests of multihued feathers, faces daubed with garish makeup thick as war paint—exactly the kind of whacked-out madcap inventors who would put together cybernetic machines like the zeros with their metallic bodies festooned with what looked more like decorative additions than anything serviceable.

But, she reminded herself, those decorations on the zeros hid laser mountings—lasers powerful enough to slag the concrete at their feet. Who knew what the hell the Chaffri had going for them under their feathers and gear?

She started to flick on her Baalbec, but then thought twice about it.

Right. Real compassionate of you, Annie B. Stand here cocooned in the Baalbec's force field, all nice and protected, while her friends had to face their captors with nothing but their clothing and skin to protect them. Because ever since their escape from the prison in Q'oorna, the Baalbec was no longer operating at its full potential. Time was she could have held them all in its force field. Since then it just barely worked on herself and—considering what had happened with Casady —she couldn't even be sure of that anymore.

She let her hand fall back from her bodice.

"Which of you is the Folliot?" the foremost of the Chaffri asked, speaking the patois of the Dungeon with a stiff accent.

"Depends," Annabelle said after a pause that was a heartbeat long, "on how true-blue you want the blood."

The Chaffri's gaze shifted to her, eyes narrowing. "You are a descendant?"

Annabelle shrugged. "Got the blood—that's all I know. Can't show you a pedigree, but of course you folks already know that."

"What is that supposed to mean?"

"Well, it's because of you that Clive never got back to England to make an honest woman out of my ancestor —not that any Leigh ever really gave a shit about that kind of a thing."

The Chaffri continued to study her. Finally he nodded.

"My name is K'cholik," he said. "We will require your assistance in a matter of great urgency."

He started to turn away.

"Say what?" Annabelle said.

K'cholik turned back to look at her.

"Is your hearing impaired?" he asked.

"Not as much as your brain is, pal. Who the hell do you think you are, ordering me about? And what makes you think I'm going to help you anyway?"

"It is not a matter of whether you are willing to or not," another of the Chaffri replied—one of the women this time. "It is something that must simply be done, or you will suffer the consequences."

Annabelle shook her head. "I don't believe you guys. What is it? Something in the air down here that makes you crazy? I'm not doing diddly until you straighten out a few items—starting with sending away your watchdogs here."

"Impossible," the woman said.

K'cholik turned to her. "There is no need to argue with them, Unaa. The zeros will bring them along for us."

Annabelle glared at him and took a step forward, fists clenched at her sides. A laser immediately burned the concrete at her feet once more, filling the air with the reek of burnt ozone.

She stepped hastily back.

"We brought you here," Unaa told her. "You are ours to do with as we will."

"Uh-uh," Annabelle told her. "Nobody owns us."

A third Chaffri joined the conversation then—a slender man with soft dark eyes and lips so thin they were almost nonexistent. He wore his feathered headdress like some archaic punk's Mohawk.

"It won't hurt to explain," he said.

"Don't begin that old argument, Peotor," K'cholik told him.

Peotor ignored his companions. "We require your help against the Ren and Gannine," he told Annabelle. "They have joined forces recently and are moving against us."

"The Gannine?" Sidi asked.

The Chaffri's gaze shifted to him. "The Ren woke them when they finally broke the codes on one of their arsenals."

"Fascinating, I'm sure," Annabelle said. "Only who or what are the Gannine?"

"They created this gaming board—the Dungeon."

"*You're* not the Dungeonmasters—you and the Ren?"

"We were—until the Gannine woke. Now that they *are* awake, it's anyone's guess as to who will come out ahead. If they have joined with the Ren, as our spies tell us . . . we have no hope of standing against the Gannine weapons without your help."

"And just what kind of help is that, guv'nor?" Smythe asked.

Peotor blinked in surprise. "Why, blood, of course. We need the Folliot blood to power our ghosters."

"You want to drain my blood?" Annabelle said slowly.

"You won't feel any pain," Peotor assured her. "And we'll store your mind pattern and a cell sample so that we can regrow you after the final battle is done."

All Annabelle could do was stare at him. "Ghosters?" she said finally.

"Both we and the Ren have been developing them for years—it's all we have that will stand against the Gannine's superior technology. At least we hope it will. Unfortunately they require a certain rare blood type that we have, after searching hundreds of worlds, found in only one family—the Folliots."

"You're kidding—right? This is some kind of weird joke?"

"Probably not," Casady said from beside her. "Neither the Chaffri nor the Ren have any morals—and they're both experts in cybernetic construction."

The Chaffri woman named Unaa took a small tube from her pocket and pointed it at Casady. "That will be enough," she said.

Casady shrugged. "Hey, I'm only trying to tell it like it—"

When the woman pressed on the tube, there was the sound of a small whuft of displaced air. A tiny projectile struck Casady. His entire form shimmered and crackled, like the picture on a TV screen going haywire, then he literally disappeared. All that remained was the gun he'd been holding, which fell to the pavement with a loud clank.

Annabelle bent quickly to pick it up, but a zero's laser slagged the weapon before she could touch it.

"Damn GBCers," Unaa muttered.

Annabelle just stared at the place where Casady had been standing, her face registering the shock that had frozen her thoughts.

She'd known that he hadn't been real—that he was some kind of projected image, an AI program that fed on sound—but knowing and actually accepting it were two different things. Intellectually she'd known. But emotionally she'd seen him as a flesh-and-blood human being. A real person that the Chaffri had snuffed out of existence the way someone in her own world would change a channel.

"You bastards," she said as she slowly rose to her feet. "It'll be a cold day in hell before I help you."

Peotor shrugged. "Whether you want to help us or not is immaterial. We'll use your blood, with or without your consent."

"Take them away," K'cholik ordered the zeros. "Keep them in storage while we prepare the ghosters for an infusion of her blood."

"It has to be fresh, you see," Peotor told her, his voice sweet, his thin lips shaping an unpleasant smile.

"We will fight them," Tomàs said softly from behind her.

"Just say the word," Smythe added.

Fight them? Annabelle thought. Yeah, right. Like they had a hope in hell of taking more than one step forward before the zeros cut them down.

"No fighting," she said. "We don't have a chance."

She turned to look at her companions, her eyes adding, Not here. Not now. Let's wait for better odds.

And if they never got better odds?

Annabelle refused to let herself think about that.

You're the leader, Casady had told her. They will follow you.

If she held up, if she put forth a strong faith, kept hope alive, then it would at least stop her companions from despairing.

"How pleasant to see you coming to your senses," Peotor said. "This whole experience could be quite invigorating, you know. Imagine the new body you'll have. If you like, you can design adjustments, which we'll see are implemented before it comes to term. Would you like smaller breasts? Gills? A penis? It can all be arranged. And naturally your memories will all remain intact."

Annabelle looked down at the slagged handgun—all that was left of Casady—then slowly raised her gaze to meet Peotor's.

Hope, she reminded herself. Keep the faith that we'll pull through again.

She smiled at Peotor. "Before this is all over," she said, "I'm gonna have a piece of you, sweetheart."

Her companions ranged closer to her. Finnbogg started to hum under his breath "We Shall Overcome."

Annabelle glanced at him and ruffled the hair on his head. Hard to remember how pissed off she'd been with him once.

"You've got it, Finn," she said.

She turned back to face the Chaffri and held out her hands offering up her wrist. "So, are you going to chain us up or what?"

"That won't be necessary," K'cholik said. "We have a holding cell prepared for you."

Annabelle's eyes narrowed at that comment. They had a cell prepared already? So who the hell had told the Chaffri that they were coming?

"Take them away," K'cholik said.

No one in Neville's party was entirely certain as to what exactly they were looking for. They were all agreed on a confrontation with the Dungeonmasters and discovering a means of escaping the Dungeon itself. Shriek was determined to seek out the missing members of their previous company. Yoors wanted simple revenge—he no longer cared about escape himself. Alyssa was determined to understand the whys and wherefores of the Dungeon and to learn what part the Tuan had to play in it.

Neville was in basic agreement with them all. He wanted to find Clive and the others. He wanted satisfaction from their captors. And he wanted to understand.

Only where to begin with any of those courses? It was over that, that they were constantly arguing.

"We've been wandering aimlessly for hours now," Yoors said as they rested once more.

"And found nothing," another of the Tuan guards chimed in.

Fenil nodded. "No inhabitants to this place—only those machines."

"I know," Alyssa said, "but what else can we do?"

"Capture one of the machines," Yoors said promptly.

Alyssa frowned.

And do what with it, Being Yoors? Shriek asked. *They might not even be sentient. What if we put the entire party at risk to capture one of them, only to find that it is no more than a machine and can tell us nothing?*

"Machines don't move in random patterns as these things do," Yoors said.

"I disagree," Neville said. That earned him a glare from Yoors. "The Dungeonmasters are perfectly capable of creating machines that are sentient. Lord, Shriek. Think of Guafe. He wasn't created by the Dungeonmasters, but I'd call him more machine than man."

Shriek nodded. *It's true. He is a hybrid. And those creatures we've spied do appear to have some form of organic matter housed in their head casings.*

"So," Neville said, "while we have our differences"— he glanced at Yoors—"I also agree that if we don't come upon some human inhabitants soon, we should attempt to capture and question one of the creatures."

That earned Neville a glare from Alyssa.

"And how do you propose to do that without putting us all terribly at risk?" she asked.

Neville sighed. "Every moment we are in this Dungeon we are at risk."

"Yes—so why call it down upon ourselves, when it comes unasked for all too often?"

She looked from Neville to Yoors. The Tuan captain remained silent—no doubt, Neville thought, because

Yoors knew that Neville would argue the case, saving Yoors from yet another argument with his leader.

"Sometimes the risk is necessary," Neville said. "We need information, and I see no other method of gaining it."

Alyssa said nothing for a long moment. She looked out the nearby grating, gaze fixed on the interior of the warehouse through which their shaft was presently traveling, but Neville doubted that she saw anything. She was looking within.

"How?" she said finally, turning back to look at them. "How will we bring it down? We know nothing of its defenses. For all we know it could be linked to some central agency—by its mind, by radio, by who knows what. In some small building in the center of the city's defenses, there might well be men and women using their advanced equipment to look through the eyes of those creatures to see everything that they see."

To relatively primitive technological societies such as Neville's own, or ones that had no technology to speak of such as the Tuan's, the mechanical marvels of the Dungeon were still unfamiliar enough for them not to take every aspect of them into consideration. It was too easy to forget just what the Dungeonmasters' creations were capable of, but they had all seen enough on the previous levels for Alyssa's warning to strike home.

Such things are possible, Shriek said.

Neville nodded glumly. "All too possible."

Though he was reluctant to do so, Yoors had to agree as well. "But that still doesn't solve our problem."

"No," Alyssa said. "My suggestion is that we follow the next of these creatures we spy."

"But they move too quickly," Fenil said. "We're no more than bugs to them. How could we keep up?"

I could keep up with them, Shriek said.

Neville shook his head. "It's too soon since your ordeal."

I am much recovered now, Being Neville, though I thank you for your concern.

"Would we wait for you here?" Alyssa asked.

No. Travel on. I will find you when I have need to.

Through the neural web they shared, Neville realized.

He caught Yoors regarding Shriek and himself with
new suspicion, but he said nothing to allay the Tuan's
worries. The wise man didn't show all his cards.

They traveled on then, through length upon length
of the ventilation shafts, following the bewildering network until they found one that brought them out of the
building they were in, to a place from which they had a
view of the streets once more.

"There!" one of the Tuan called softly.

Below, a pair of the curious mechanical creatures
were moving down the street. They walked one to a
side, staying close to the buildings that reared up tall
beside them.

Shriek immediately sped back the way they had
come, heading for the descent to ground level that
they had passed inside the building. Neville and the
Tuan remained at the grating, taking turns watching
the mechanical creatures fare the length of the street.

"She's too late," Fenil said.

"Don't speak too soon," Alyssa said.

She pointed to where the tiny figure of the arachnid
had just reached the street. Shriek hurried down the
pavement, pausing at the corner to peer cautiously
around it. They saw her look back in their direction for
a brief moment; then she turned the corner and, like
the creatures she followed, was lost from sight as well.

"And now?" Yoors said.

Alyssa glanced at him. "Now we go on."

"I would still like to know how she will find us again,"
the Tuan captain said. "It seems odd to me that she
would be able to do so with any ease—unless, of course,
she knows this city well."

He turned to look at Neville, who merely smiled
back.

How are you doing, Shriek? he asked the arachnid,
broadcasting his thoughts to her on a narrow beam so
that only she could hear him.

Well enough, came her reply. *They do not appear to move too swiftly. I should have no trouble keeping up with them.*

Be careful.

I will.

Call in your position at the first sign of trouble, and for God's sake, keep out of their way.

You worry too much, Being Neville.

"I was speaking to you," Yoors said.

Neville blinked at him. "I hadn't realized it was a question."

"I want to know how your companion can find her way so easily about this city."

Neville sighed. "I can sympathize with your loss of your brother, Yoors," he said, "and I understand that you're far from home and frustrated that you can't do anything to strike back at those who have put us in this position. But I grow increasingly weary of your glares and bad humor."

Yoors growled something unintelligible and reached for his sword, but Alyssa's hand was quicker. She caught his wrist. But before she could speak, Neville leaned closer.

"You can go on by yourself," he said. "Pick any direction that suits you, and I'll go the opposite way."

"No," Alyssa said. "We will continue on together."

Neville ignored her, all his attention fixed on the Tuan captain.

"I too have lost companions who might well be dead, for all I know. I too want satisfaction from the dogs that brought us here. But while there's little I can do about either of those except for pressing on, I'll be damned if I'll put up with any more from you."

For a long moment no one spoke. Then Yoors surprised them all. He nodded slowly and reached out a hand to Neville.

"I . . . I'm sorry," he said.

Neville looked down at the proffered hand, then lifted his gaze to meet the captain's own guileless eyes.

Well, I'll be damned, Neville thought. Unless Yoors

was a better poker player than himself, it seemed the Tuan was genuinely sorry.

Neville took Yoors's hand in a firm clasp.

Perhaps he was being a fool in doing so, but Neville believed at that moment that one trust deserved another.

"We speak," he told the Tuan, "my companion and I —we speak mind to mind."

"Our agents acquired the design from the Chaffri," Speaker Lena explained.

Clive stared at the thing. It stood as tall as he did himself, but on four legs, and appeared to be made entirely of clear crystal. It had a head like a dog's— streamlined, powerful jaws, clear eyes set to either side of its face above the muzzle. Its body was a combination of an ape and a large hunting cat—a tiger or a lion. The limbs were flexible, talons on the end of each articulated finger, opposable thumbs on front and hind paws. The torso, the powerful chest and shoulders, were that of a lion.

"Acquired?" Clive said with a trace of mockery in his voice.

As Speaker Lena began a complicated explanation of just how the blueprints had fallen into the Ren's possession, Clive stepped closer to the construct and ran his fingers along its smooth skin. It was housed in yet another of the Ren's labs, deep inside their innermost complex. Most of the chamber was taken up with what Clive assumed was the apparatus with which they had created the thing that stood before him; but one wall showed the flat surface of what first appeared to be a mirror, except that it gave back no reflection.

Mostly it showed a grayness as unrelenting as that in which Clive had found himself when the evaluator malfunctioned again. But from time to time places appeared—unfamiliar views that seemed so realistic that the glass surface could only be a window looking onto each separate scene that was shown. A jungle, a city street, a frozen arctic waste, the surface of an asteroid such as the one the Dungeon was purported to be, a coniferous forest, the interior of some form of ship that moved through the dark void between planets—Clive believed that either Chang or Annabelle had once identified such ships to him as spacecraft.

The images remained for only a few moments before the grayness swallowed each in turn.

It was a gate, Clive realized. Either some new mirrored gateway that the Ren controlled, or that Gannine gate that led from the eighth level down to the ninth.

He made sure that he gave the glass no more than a curious glance before turning to study the construct that Speaker Lena had brought him here to view. But he continued to steal surreptitious glances at it as each new scene appeared. The number of different views appeared to be finite, for Clive soon recognized repetitions. The scenes passed by in the same order each time.

"What is this thing made of?" Clive asked when Speaker Lena fell silent once more.

He tapped the construct with a fingernail.

"Ordolite," Chary explained. "It's a form of plastic that's strong enough to withstand anything up to and including a direct laser hit, but flexible enough to allow complete mobility. The Gannine created it."

"The construct?"

"No. The ordolite. The Chaffri created the construct."

"They call it a ghoster," Speaker Lena added.

"I see. And what does it have to do with me?"

"All the construct needs now is to be fueled," Chary went on. "Through advanced biotechnology the fuel will replicate itself infinitely. As everything about the ghoster was constructed of ordolite, once it is operational, it will never need to be serviced again."

"And what will you use to fuel it?" Clive asked.

Chary hesitated and glanced at Speaker Lena.

"It will require your death," the Speaker said.

Somehow Clive was not surprised. All that did surprise him was how calm he felt.

"I see," he said. "And that answers my earlier question as well."

"It's not what you think," Speaker Lena hurried to assure him. "It's true this body you are wearing will die, but we will save your brain pattern and reinstate it in a new body once we have grown you one. Your new body can be exactly the same as the one you now wear, or modified to your own specifications."

"You mean to clone me, then," Clive said, the unfamiliar word coming easily to his lips.

Chary shook her head. "Not exactly. It's true that your new body will be cloned from cell samples that we will take from your old one for that purpose, but your brain pattern and personality—everything that makes you *you*—will be the original. When we bring you back, you will feel as though you're just waking from a long sleep. There will be no discomfort."

"This thing needs my death to fuel it?" Clive said.

"Your blood—yes. Folliot blood."

"Why Folliot blood?"

Both Chary and Speaker Lena shook their heads.

"That is how the Chaffri designed it," Chary said. "But as they probably stole the blueprints from the Gannine, who knows why it will work only in this fashion. We have tried other blood—but without success."

"So it will work only with my blood, or my twin's?"

"With anyone who has your blood—such as your descendant, Annabelle Leigh."

"Why didn't you merely bleed one of us when you captured us on the various other levels? Or does it require a willing sacrifice?"

"Oddly enough," Chary said, "that's exactly it. According to the data we've acquired, if the donor is not a willing participant, it will set off an imbalance in the blood, and the ghoster will not function."

"Why haven't you used any of the clones you've made of us?"

"Again," Chary said, "for all that a clone is an exact replica of its subject, only the original will work."

"Or so say the design plans we acquired," Speaker

Lena said. "We have experimented with everything except an original Folliot—all without success."

"That does not sound promising," Clive said.

"There's no need to be afraid," Speaker Lena assured him. "Even if the experiment proves to be another failure, we can still reinstate you in a new body with everything about you intact. You risk nothing."

Clive frowned, thinking. "If the ghoster's fuel can replicate itself infinitely, why must you kill me to fuel it? Why not take just a few pints?"

"Because," Chary explained, "the initial fueling requires ten pints—which is about as much as you have in your body at any given time."

"I tell you again," Speaker Lena assured him. "You risk nothing."

Nothing? Clive thought.

He looked at the ghoster construct again.

What of his soul?

For that appeared to be the flaw in their reasoning. How could their machines transfer a man's soul from one body to another? Thoughts and memories . . . After all he had seen in the Dungeon since he first arrived, with the way the Dungeonmasters had so easily manipulated his memories, he could see how thoughts and memories might be successfully transferred. But not a soul.

And that was the key to this ghoster construct, he believed.

It didn't simply require his original Folliot blood to function—it required his soul. And that was too dear a price to pay.

Not that he had ever had any intention of helping either the Ren or the Chaffri in the first place. He meant to bring them low, plain and simple, and to take down the Gannine while he was about it. They were monstrosities—all three races.

He laid his hand on the construct's smooth synthetic skin once more, then slowly turned to his companions.

"When do we begin?" he asked.

Speaker Lena appeared taken aback for a moment, but she quickly recovered.

"Why, immediately," she said. "It will take us a few moments to set up the proper procedures. . . ." She glanced at Chary.

"We can be ready to go in fifteen minutes," the tech said.

"That quickly?" Clive said.

Speaker Lena turned back to him. "You are absolutely certain you wish to go through with this?" she asked.

"Oh, yes."

"Then I'll take you to a more comfortable place where we can wait while the techs ready their equipment."

"I'd prefer to wait here," Clive said, laying his hand on the ghoster's shoulder once more. "To meditate with my . . . I suppose we could call it my descendant, couldn't we?"

"I suppose you could," Speaker Lena said with a slow nod. "Chary, will you see to the preparations?"

"Right away."

Clive waited until the tech had left the room. Once he and Speaker Lena were alone, he turned from the ghoster to look at her.

"You must think very badly of us," she said.

Clive found a smile. "Not at all." He stepped away from the construct, closer to her. "You are fighting for survival—it's a very understandable reaction."

"I knew you would understand."

"As I hope you'll understand this," Clive said.

Before the Speaker could move to escape him or sound an alarm, he struck her with a roundhouse blow in her solar plexus. Speaker Lena dropped like a felled ox. Clive darted for the mirrored wall.

"N-no!" Speaker Lena cried from where she lay.

Clive turned to see her struggling unsuccessfully to regain her feet.

"I'm fighting for survival too," he said.

He glanced at the gateway. Damn, he needed more

time. The view of the city street was just disappearing. That meant the next one would be the arctic tundra, followed by the asteroid—at least two views before there was another suitable one, which would be the forest.

He could hear someone at the door.

"Those are . . . are Randoms pictured there," Speaker Lena said, obviously fighting nausea. Her eyes implored him not to step through.

The gate showed only grayness.

Clive heard a sound at the door.

Damn them all, they were coming back too soon.

"Randoms are . . . they are . . ." Her throat convulsed as though she were holding back bile.

The door opened with a crash, armed guards appearing in its threshold.

The grayness of the gate changed to the arctic scene.

"They are only . . . Gannine fictions. . . ." Speaker Lena managed.

Clive didn't know what she meant by either Randoms, or fictions. All he knew was that he had this one chance to escape. He would get no other.

"D-don't!" Speaker Lena cried.

But Clive was already stepping through.

▪ CHAPTER SEVENTEEN ▪

The Chaffri's holding cell turned out to be an area of general confinement where they locked up both their own criminals, and trespassers into their half of Downside. Of the two dozen or so others who were their fellow prisoners, most were humanoids, Annabelle noted as she was pushed inside with the rest of her party. But there were a few of the truly alien beings that she'd run into more than once in the Dungeon.

She spotted one, with a chitinous skin and six limbs, that reminded her of Shriek, though the arachnid had two more limbs; in another corner a ball of fur unrolled enough so that a pair of eyes could examine them, before whatever creature it was rolled itself up again.

She turned back to look at the Chaffri as the cell door closed behind her.

"We will be coming for you soon," Peotor told her as he locked the door. "You'd do best to compose yourself —the ghoster requires your willing participation."

In their feathered finery and day-glo clothing, with the gaudy face paint on their white skin, the Chaffri reminded Annabelle of nothing so much as clowns.

Right. Clowns, she thought. Make that death clowns.

"You'll rot in hell before I help you," she told him.

Peotor smiled. "I know you mean that, but you'll come willingly all the same. It's that, or we'll take your friends apart in front of you—one piece at a time."

"You—"

"Really, you have no reason to be so upset. Help us, and your friends live, and you will come out of this with a new body."

Before Annabelle could reply to that, he turned and joined the remainder of the Chaffri who were leaving the holding cells.

"I'll have your balls, you lowlife!" Annabelle shouted after them, but the metal door locking the holding cells from the remainder of the Chaffri's security complex had already closed with a large clank.

She sighed and turned to look at her cellmates again. When three familiar figures rose from among the strangers, she blinked with surprise, her anger momentarily forgotten.

"Jesus—how'd you guys get here?"

Facing her were two of the Japanese from New Kwajalein, back on the Dungeon's first level—Sergeant Nomura, who had been in charge of the Japanese fighter plane, the Nakajima 97, and Chuichi Fushida, the sergeant who had been in command of the raiding party that captured Annabelle. But the one who took up her immediate attention was the cyborg, Chang Guafe.

"Where's Clive?" she asked. "And the others?"

"You are the first of our party that I have seen since Clive and I were separated in the Ren half of this city," Guafe replied. "I was making my way to the Chaffri gate when I was captured."

Smythe pushed closer. "What about Clive?" he demanded. "How is he? Damn it, man, *where* is he?"

"Still with the Ren. He has . . ."

The cyborg hesitated—an unusual action for him, Annabelle realized with a sinking feeling. Whatever he was going to say, it was going to be very bad.

"He's what?" she asked, not sure she even wanted to hear it.

"He has joined forces with the Ren."

"But they are our enemies," Tomàs said. *"Christo!* Surely he is just pretending to help them?"

"I hope so."

"You don't sound so sure about that," Annabelle said.

Guafe shrugged—another unfamiliar gesture. "He did not confide his plans to me."

So just how did they get separated? Annabelle wondered, but she decided that now wasn't the time to get into it. If Guafe had wanted to talk about it, he'd have told them.

She turned to the Japanese. "It is good to see you both again," she said, giving them each a quick short nod of her head. "Fushida-san, Nomura-san."

The Japanese seemed very happy to see a familiar face. "We are pleased to meet with you again, Sacred One."

Annabelle sighed. Christ, not this again. But she didn't have the energy to argue it with them.

"How did you get here?" she asked.

"These people—the Chaffri," Fushida said. "After we recovered the Nakajima from where you abandoned it—"

"Oh, yeah. Sorry about that."

"—the Chaffri raided New Kwajalein to steal it from us."

"What do they want with that old plane?" Annabelle wondered aloud.

Nomura shrugged. "They have not confided in us, *neh?*"

"We were working on a new fuel system," Fushida went on, "when the Chaffri attacked. They had a machine that swallowed the Nakajima whole—with us in it. The next thing we knew we were in this city. When the Chaffri discovered us, they locked us up in these cells, and we have been here ever since."

"They will tell us nothing," Nomura said.

Fushida spat on the cell floor. "They have no sense of honor."

"They don't have much of anything worthwhile," Annabelle said. She was about to question them further when they were approached by one of the other prisoners.

He was tall and lean, skin a dark mulatto that told Annabelle that he wasn't a renegade Chaffri—not unless there was more to them than the bunch who'd captured her. This man had the look of the street about him—quick eyes that took everything in, a stance that left him ready to move in any direction. A careful man. But when he spoke, Annabelle couldn't help but put him down for yet another lunatic.

"He called you the Sacred One," the man began.

"Yeah, but he—"

"You must call them down to help us. The Chaffri aren't just sending us up to the Dives anymore. They're building zeros like crazy, and it's our brains that are going to be sitting in those frigging ordolite heads."

"Call who?" Annabelle asked.

"The Gannine. You *are* the Madonna, aren't you?"

Annabelle had to laugh. "Me? I don't think so, pal. I never could hold with that virgin birth crap."

"No, no," the stranger said. "I'm not talking about mythology. I mean, the Madonna of the Gannine—their agent."

Another man approached then—shorter, hair curly as a corkscrew, slight of frame.

"She might not know, Kan," he said.

The first man turned to look at the newcomer. "What do you mean?"

"Remember what the Cloak told us?"

The man named Kan nodded slowly. "I see."

"Yeah, well I don't," Annabelle said. "Would someone tell me what the hell's going on here?"

"Well, you see—" the second man began.

"Hold on—what's your name? And what are you guys doing in here?"

"I'm Sordiam and my friend here is Kan. We're Divers. We got picked up on a smuggling run."

"Okay." Annabelle made the introductions around her own party. "So this Cloak you were talking about—he's an agent of the Gannine?"

She remembered Casady talking about the Cloak, something about how he was also called the Lightbringer—Lucifer.

Sordiam nodded. "Only he didn't know it until very recently—when he was contacted by the Gannine and taken down to the ninth level."

"If he was taken down, how did he come to speak to you about it?"

"We were there when they took him," Kan said.

"What did he look like?" Annabelle asked.

Now she was afraid that if they thought she was the Madonna, someone might decide that Clive or Neville was this Cloak. If either of them had been taken down to the ninth level by the Gannine, she might never see them again.

"Better yet," she added before either man could reply, "what do the Gannine look like?"

"We don't know," Sordiam replied. "It happened in a back alley, Topside, where it was dark as shit and all we could hear were the voices."

"And the Cloak?"

"He's a black man."

Sordiam went on to describe a figure that seemed very familiar to Annabelle.

"That sounds like Baron Samedi."

Kan nodded. "That was the name we knew him by."

"But he's dead. We saw him die on the seventh level."

"Several times," Sidi added.

"Those were his clones that died."

"Oh, Jesus," Annabelle said, rubbing her temples. "When are things going to start making sense?"

She looked at her companions and saw the same mix of bafflement and exasperation on their faces.

"We heard what the Chaffri pig said to you," Sordiam went on. "He wants to bleed you to fuel their ghosters—right?"

Annabelle nodded. "He said they'll run only on Folliot blood."

"I've heard that name before," Kan said.

"Where?" Smythe asked eagerly.

"From the Gannine, when they were talking to the Cloak—Baron Samedi. They made it sound like Folliots and the Gannine were one and the same thing."

"Makes sense when you think about it," Sordiam added. "The Chaffri stole the design of the ghosters from the Gannine. Why wouldn't it take Gannine blood to make them run?"

"Now wait a minute," Annabelle said. "There's no way I'm related to the people running this place. I'm not their Madonna, Folliots are Englishmen, not Dungeonmasters, and—"

The door to the holding cells clanged open and Peotor was there with a pair of zeros, each the height of a human. Further conversation died on their lips as they nervously regarded the Chaffri.

"Such a fascinating discussion," he said.

"Listen, you—" Annabelle began, finding her voice, but Peotor cut her off.

"Have you made your decision? Do you come willingly, or must we take apart a few of your friends first?"

"I . . ."

Sidi stepped close to her side. "Don't worry about us, Annabelle."

"*Sim,*" Tomàs said, flanking her on the other side from Sidi. "We will stand or fall together."

Smythe and Finnbogg ranked themselves beside her, as did, much to her surprise, Guafe and the two Japanese. Sordiam and Kan each took a step away from her and watched the proceedings with interest.

"Sorry, guys," Annabelle told her companions. "But I've gotta go."

Because she couldn't stand by and watch anyone die for her. No way. It would serve no purpose.

Was this the position that Clive had found himself in? she wondered. Forced to join their enemies—or at least pretend to join them—until the chance arose for his own escape?

"No," Sidi said. "You can't—"

But Annabelle just shook her head. "I've got to," she said. "I . . . I'll see you around sometime. Say hello to Clive and the others if you run into them."

"Do not trust them," Tomàs said. "They will kill us anyway—turn us into"—he glanced at Sordiam and Kan—"into those zeros, as these men have told us."

Annabelle just shook her head. Turning from Peotor's view, she gave them all a wink and lifted her hand to her bodice, reminding them of all it would take to activate her Baalbec.

"I'm taking the chance that they'll keep their word," she said.

"Of course we will keep our word," Peotor said.

While his zeros kept their lasers trained on the prisoners, the Chaffri unlocked the cell door and ushered Annabelle out.

"If you will follow me," he said, once he had relocked the cell.

Annabelle lifted a hand to her friends, then the door shut behind her, and she was in a long hall with Peotor and the zeros, the holding cells lost from view. The sound of their passage echoed hollowly down the corridor.

Neville was attempting to describe a London theater to Alyssa when he finally heard Shriek's voice in his mind once more. He and the Tuan had traveled through miles of ventilation shaft—miles by the reckoning of their size, at any rate—since taking their leave of the arachnid. Through all that time there had been no word from Shriek, and Neville had hesitated in contacting her himself for fear of interrupting her at some crucial moment when she might need all of her concentration.

As the hours had passed, he couldn't help but worry.

Being Neville?

I hear you, Shriek, he replied, the relief obvious in his voice. *Have you run into trouble?*

Not yet. But I have found others who need our help.

Others?

Neville could feel her smile in his mind.

The missing members of our company, she told him.

You have? How are they? Where are they? Have you spoken to Clive?

Shriek hesitated for a long heartbeat before replying.

Your brother is not among them, she said.

Where is he? What happened to him?

I do not know. I do not see the Guafe being either.

An image suddenly filled Neville's mind, and he realized he was seeing through Shriek's eyes. It was a fly's view of a hallway down which marched the various members of their erstwhile company. Annabelle and Smythe, Sidi and Tomàs, loyal Finnbogg. They were obviously the prisoners of the cybernetic creatures and gaudily clad humans who walked with them.

The latter, Neville realized, must be the elusive inhabitants of this city.

Where are you? he asked.

From the strength of your voice I believe we are fairly close to each other, Shriek replied. *I will keep our mind link open so that you can use it to home in on my position.*

We'll be with you as soon as we can, Neville said.

He opened his eyes and looked at Alyssa.

"Shriek has found my companions," he said.

"Where are they?"

"Not far. The Dungeonmasters have them prisoner." He rose to his feet. "Will you come with me?"

Alyssa nodded and stood as well. "Of course," she said, adding to her people, "To mount!"

In moments the Tuan were mounted and riding their silvers at a swift pace through the ventilation shafts, following Neville's lead. Twice they ran into dead ends and had to backtrack, but they were quickly gaining on Shriek, for her mental voice continued to grow stronger in Neville's mind.

A word of caution, Being Neville, she warned him at one point.

And that is?

There is an enormous size discrepancy between ourselves and the others of our party.

What do you mean?

But even as he asked, Neville already knew what she would say. He'd guessed it himself. Somehow that mirror they had traveled through to reach this level of the Dungeon had altered their size.

We would fit into the palms of their hands, Shriek replied.

Wonderful, Neville thought. Tiny as they were, how could they even hope to effect a rescue of the others?

The ventilation shafts continued to unwind beneath the quick pace of the Tuan's silvers.

They've stopped now, Shriek called back to Neville. Again his mind filled with images of what she saw.

A prison cell, Neville said.

Shriek gave a mental nod. *And I see the Guafe being. But not my brother.*

I will wait until their captors leave before approaching them.

No, Neville sent back. *Wait for our arrival instead. If one of the other prisoners mistakes you for a—pardon me, Shriek—a bug . . .*

I will contact them through mindspeaking.

I still say wait for us. Who knows? Perhaps their captors can communicate mentally as well. If you mindspeak while they're present, we could all end up prisoners.

Then come quickly, was all Shriek said in response.

Alyssa picked up the company's speed when Neville had conveyed the latest conversation to her, but it still took them the better part of a half hour before they reached the holding cells that Shriek had shown Neville. He and Alyssa peered down through the nearest grating to look at the prisoners. Shriek clung to the other side of the grate.

"I don't see Annabelle," Neville said.

They've taken her away. She hesitated, then added, *They mean to kill her.*

"Do you know where they've taken her?"

Shriek shook her head. *No, but I can follow the trail of her thoughts.*

"Contact the others," Neville said. "See if they can get us out of this damned shaft."

The confusion that Shriek's sudden appearance evoked in their companions would have been comical to behold if the situation hadn't been so serious. Guafe was the first to recover.

"Clive and I came through as giants," the cyborg said.

"Nothing strikes me as impossible anymore," Smythe added.

With a boost from Guafe, and using the buckle from his belt, Smythe pried loose the screws that held the grating in place. One by one he carefully passed Neville, the Tuan, and their silvers down to the waiting hands of the others.

"Madre de Dios," Tomàs muttered. "What will they do to us next?"

Sidi quickly filled Neville in on what had befallen Annabelle and Clive.

"He's in the other half of the city?" Neville asked.

"He was when I last saw him," Guafe replied.

"Annabelle is the more immediate concern," Sidi said.

Neville nodded slowly. "But what of Clive?" he asked. "If these Ren mean to use him in a similar fashion . . ."

"I know, sah," Smythe said, obviously troubled himself. "But Annabelle is closer."

"I'll grant you that," Neville said. He glanced from his perch in Smythe's hand to the prison's bars, then to the cyborg. "Can you get us out of here, Guafe?"

"I can try."

The cyborg crossed the cell to the bars. Bracing himself, he took ahold of a bar in each metallic hand and began to exert pressure on them. For the longest time nothing appeared to happen. Unlike the features of a man Guafe's face showed no sign of the strain he was undergoing. His metallic brow remained dry, his features showed concentration, but little else.

Placing Neville down on the floor, Smythe went to give a hand. A moment later Sidi and Tomàs joined him, soon followed by the two Japanese and the pair of smugglers, Sordiam and Kan. With that many backs put to the task, there was no question as to their success.

Slowly the bars began to give.

When the space was large enough to allow a man egress, they fell back from the bars and gave a short cheer. Neville went into Smythe's breast pocket, Shriek perched on his shoulder, Alyssa and her mount in one side pocket, another Tuan and silver in the other. The rest of the Tuan were quickly tucked into the pockets of the others. Then they made their way through the bars to the hallway beyond.

"Now this door," Tomàs said.

Unlike the cells this door was solid metal, top to bottom, except for a small window set just at eye level. Guafe peered through the window.

"The hallway is clear," he said.

Before anyone could ask how he meant to get through this door, he placed one hand on the top doorjamb and hoisted himself into the air. When he was high enough, he broke the window with the heel of his free hand, then thrust his arm through. A moment later they all heard the door's lock snick open.

Guafe lowered himself back down to the floor. When he gave the door a push, it opened silently onto the hallway. Guafe stepped out, glass crunching underfoot.

"Why didn't you break out sooner?" Smythe wanted to know.

The cyborg shrugged. "I arrived no more than a half hour before you did," he said. "I was merely waiting for an opportune moment."

He glanced at the tiny Shriek who clung to Smythe's shoulder.

"Which way now?" he asked.

The arachnid closed her eyes for a moment, then pointed to their left with one chitinous forelimb.

That way.

∎ CHAPTER EIGHTEEN ∎

The place Peotor took her to was an enormous chamber—easily a quarter the size of a football stadium. Annabella stopped in the doorway and stared across its immense distance, the two zeros flanking her on either side, eyes tracking her every movement. Slowly she took in the amazing view.

One full wall was taken up with what she assumed was some kind of video screen. Mostly it showed a pattern of unrelieved gray, but images appeared on it in a regular rotation, separated from each other by those times when the entire screen went gray again. She saw the bleak surface of an asteroid, fade to gray, a coniferous forest, deep and thick as those in upper New York State, fade to gray, the interior of a spacecraft. . . .

Lining another wall, their crystalline ordolite surfaces highlit by the flickering video images, was a long line of the ghosters that her blood was going to awake. Annabelle didn't look at them long. They obviously existed solely for the purpose of war, and the fact that something in her was going to make them operative just left her with a sick, empty feeling inside.

But what could she do?

The Chaffri were going to kill her friends if she didn't go along with them—*willingly* go along so that the chemical balance of her blood would be just right to make the ghosters function. Yet what kinds of destruction would these machines cause? Would the Chaffri settle with just taking over the Dungeon? Once it was in their power, wouldn't they just move on to all those worlds from which they stole their prisoners—all those poor souls who were no more than gaming pieces in the Chaffri's senseless struggle with the Ren and Gannine?

She imagined these ghosters coming to her own world—wreaking destruction there. . . .

She thought of her daughter, Amanda. Of the members of her band. Of her friends and family. Of all the people that made up the crazy confusion that was her planet. Of all those hundreds of millions of beings on all those various worlds and times from which the Dungeonmasters had gathered their cannon fodder.

How could she be responsible for all their deaths?

Because it would be her blood fueling those damned machines.

She would be a part of the ghosters.

She *would* be responsible. . . .

She had always had a certain streetwise toughness, something that the Dungeon had brought to the fore, more and more, the longer she was trapped in it; but she'd never been a hawk. Never rooted for war. Though she was willing to fight for what she believed in, she took no delight in instruments of pain. Things that existed only to cause destruction.

And those ghosters . . .

On the large screen a jungle scene appeared, faded to gray.

Her gaze drifted across the wide expanse of the floor to the opposite side of the room from the ghosters. Her eyes lit up as she saw the Japanese Nakajima 97 standing there with a deflated hot-air balloon, a curious machine that looked like the proverbial saucer-shaped spacecraft, and some other winged machines that she didn't recognize but assumed were planes of one sort or another.

"What are those doing here?" she asked Peotor.

The Chaffri shrugged. "Sometimes when we bring people through, they've come in vehicles. We let them keep them, so long as they're not operative, but if they can get them to work, we have to take them away."

Annabelle remembered something that Clive had told her about his time in Dramaran. "What about those air scooters that the Dramaranians have?"

"We confiscate only those vehicles that can reach a certain altitude. The atmosphere in the Dungeon isn't the same as it would be on a world such as your own. It thickens the higher you get. We're afraid that a craft such as the Nakajima might irreparably rupture the sky."

The gray video screen cleared to show a crowded city street, alien creatures bustling along its length, strange vehicles moving slowly where the sidewalk would be in Annabelle's world, the pedestrians walking down the middle of the street.

The image faded to gray.

Annabelle looked at the Nakajima, remembering her flight in it. The green paint on its fuselage and wings was chipped and fading; the red circles on the wingtips and near the tail assembly were in as bad a condition, but the craft still looked splendid to her. Here was something made for war but that need not necessarily be used for war.

On the video screen a view of an arctic waste appeared. Annabelle just caught a glimpse of some figure on the ice, but then the image was gone, fading to gray.

"What are those images?" she asked, pointing to the screen. "Some kind of—what?—video meditation or something? They keep running through the same pattern, the same views repeating. . . ."

"That is the gate to the ninth level, where the Gannine have wakened," Peotor told her. "We'll be sending the ghosters through it once they've been activated."

"All those different places are on the ninth level?"

Peotor shook his head. "Not exactly. Those images you see are Randoms—a multiple of pocket worlds that the Gannine have created on the ninth level to confuse our calibrating machines when we make the jump between the levels. The images have been increasing day by day—soon there won't be any gray left at all, and then the ninth level will be closed to us through this gate."

"When the screen's gray, then the gates are opened to the ninth level?"

"That's correct."

The asteroid surface was back, fading to gray.

"So these places they show aren't real?" Annabelle asked.

"Oh, they're real all right—we just don't know *where* they are."

"But surely with your tech you've got your own gates in operation by now?"

Peotor nodded. "Yes, but something about the ordolite that we use to make the ghosters and our zeros won't allow them to jump through anything but the gates created by the Gannine."

On the screen the grayness became the coniferous forest, faded to gray again.

A tech approached them from the side of the room closest to the door they'd come through. Banks of electronic gear and other apparatus stood there, with gaudily clad Chaffri bustling about, busy as ants.

"We're ready for her now," the tech said.

Peotor took her arm. "Remember," he said as he led her over. "You must do this willingly."

Annabelle just looked at him. "Willingly. Right. Give up my life so you can use my blood to fuel all those monsters, just so's you guys can kill more efficiently."

"Not all of them," Peotor explained. "Just one. Each takes ten pints of Folliot blood to fuel initially."

"So you're going to need other Folliots to fuel the others?"

Peotor nodded. "We're already working on that."

Oh, Christ, Annabelle thought. What if they go after Amanda?

"But," Peotor said, "one is all we need functional for the moment."

Annabelle glanced at the ghosters and fought back a shiver. The arctic waste image caught her eye on the video screen. Just before it faded to gray again, she realized that there was a man out there on the ice. And not only could she see him, she could recognize him.

It was Clive.

The screen faded to gray.

Annabelle turned to the Chaffri holding her arm. "Out there on the ice," she began.

"I know," he said. "It's your ancestor. A pity we couldn't have gotten to him before he was swallowed by a Random, but we're not about to risk ourselves going after him. To cross over is easy—getting back is something else again."

"But—"

"At least the Ren don't have him. I just wish we could say the same for his brother. . . ."

All the while he spoke, he was leading Annabelle to where the techs were getting ready to transfer her brain pattern into their computers and then harvest her blood to fuel the ghosters.

"You're a real bunch of sons of bitches, aren't you?"

Peotor made a tut-tutting sound. "Willingly, now," he said. "Don't forget. Or your friends will suffer."

Willingly.

That was a laugh. And who was to say they'd let the others go anyway?

As she was surrounded by smiling techs, all ready to wire her up to their machines, she realized that this was really the end of the road.

Annie B., you are in deep shit, she told herself.

What a brilliant realization. She thought about Jack Casady, about positive thinking, about all the pop psychology that said, yes, you too can be a winner, if you just *believe.*

Somehow she didn't think singing a song was going to do that much good right about now.

The first zero they came upon was more surprised to see them than they were it.

Guafe was in the lead when they came around a corner to confront the dog-sized creature. Before it had a chance to train its lasers on the party, Guafe closed the distance between himself and the creature. He brought a metal fist down upon the protective covering that housed the zero's brain.

His first blow cracked the transparent covering; the second broke it. Fluid spilled out over the creature's body, sizzling and sparking on its electrical components. The brain collapsed in its housing. One unaimed laser sprayed a wall, nearly reaching Smythe and cutting him in two, before the zero's systems shut down and the creature collapsed.

"Right," Kan said. "I'm out of here."

The other smuggler, Sordiam, nodded in agreement. "Another few minutes and this place will be crawling with zeros—big suckers, not like this."

We are very close to where they have the Annabelle being, Shriek said.

"That's okay," another of the prisoners said. "Chase after her if you want, but I'm with Kan. No way I want to head down to the ninth level."

Kan nodded. "If you folks are smart, you'll come back up into the Dives with us."

"Staying here will be suicide," Sordiam added.

But Smythe merely shook his head. "I'm going on."

"As am I," Sidi agreed. He looked around at the other prisoners. "You are free now—make your own choices."

When they finally moved on, their company was composed of only Guafe, Smythe, Tomàs, Sidi, and the two Japanese. In their pockets, and on Smythe's shoulders, rode Neville, Shriek, and the Tuan with their mounts. Guafe remained in the lead, carrying one of the downed zero's laser mountings, complete with its power pack. It made for a bulky burden, but they all felt safer for having it with them.

"Lord, what a ragtag band of ruffians we make," Smythe said.

We must hurry, Shriek urged them. *I can sense the Annabelle being growing more agitated.*

"*Ahora bien,*" Tomàs said. "Tell her we are coming."

Is anyone aware of the Chaffri having telepathic

abilities? Shriek asked, worried as to whether her contacting Annabelle would give their enemy warning of their approach.

The wail of a distant siren ended the need for any caution. It was obviously an alarm, and that meant that the Chaffri were already warned.

"Run!" Guafe cried, and he broke into a quick trot, Smythe running at his side.

As they approached a sudden widening in the corridor, Shriek called out:

This is it. The Annabelle being is beyond those doors.

Zeros appeared at the far side of the corridor—human-sized, their lasers swiveling in their housings to train on their party—but Guafe cut them down before any of them had a chance to fire. Then he aimed the weapon on the door in front of them and fired again.

Shriek's warning came just as the techs were attaching the first electrode to Annabelle's temple.

Being Annabelle! Do not let them hurt you. We are on our way.

They were on their way?

For one long moment Annabelle went blank. That was Shriek's voice in her head. Shriek, who, along with Neville and Clive, was still unaccounted for. What was she doing here?

Then her sense of self-preservation kicked in.

"Got an itch," she said.

She reached up as though to scratch and activated the Baalbec. The tech attaching the electrode was thrown back as the Baalbec's force field cut in. The tech hit the banks of equipment hard enough to shatter the glass on VU meters.

"What the—" Peotor began.

He grabbed at her, and he too was thrown away from her. He collided with one of the zeros, and the two fell in a tangle to the floor. The other zero immediately opened fire.

"No!" Peotor shouted.

Too late. The laser's beam skidded off the force field

and struck the banks of equipment. Plastic and metal were slagged. Sparks erupted and smoke billowed from the machines.

The other techs took long moments to recover. As a warning siren cut in, they ran for weapons. The zero fired again at Annabelle. This time the deflected laser cut down two of the techs, and the air was suddenly filled with the too-sweet stench of cooked meat.

The other zero had recovered, and it too opened fire, but as had happened with its mate's shots the deflected laser beams did more damage to Chaffri equipment than to their prisoner.

Then the door to the enormous chamber burst open, and Annabelle's companions were there.

"Go through the screen!" Annabelle cried to them. "When it's gray, it'll take you down to the ninth level."

The zeros turned to meet the new attack, but Guafe's laser cut them both down. Peotor was caught in the swath that the laser beam fanned across the room. He was cut almost in two, blood fountaining from his torso as he fell.

And what about you? Shriek asked.

"I'll follow," Annabelle told her.

She ran toward the Nakajima.

Guafe cut down the remaining techs and their whole party headed for the screen. The jungle scene appeared, its sun-bright glare sending strange shadows scurrying across the room, before it faded to gray.

Being Annabelle? Shriek called to her.

Annabelle had reached the wing of the Japanese plane and was climbing up to the cockpit. Once she'd slid open the glass canopy, she looked over to where her friends were all gathered near the screen that was in reality a gate.

Where the hell was Shriek? she thought.

What are you doing? the arachnid asked.

"I'm bringing the plane!" she called back. "Get going —I'll meet you on the next level."

Peotor had told her that it might be impossible to get out of one of the Randoms once you were in. No way everyone should risk their ass in there, but no way she was leaving Clive on his own either.

But . . .

"Just do it!"

She was inside the cockpit now. As she slammed the canopy closed, she could see the screen go to gray. Her friends hesitated for a long moment. Annabelle started up the Nakajima. Its engine whined, broke into a cough, before it snarled like some living animal and steadied into a throbbing hum.

She started the Nakajima rolling toward the screen.

More zeros appeared in the doorway Guafe had burst through—the big ones this time, Annabelle saw.

Get going, she willed her friends.

As though they'd finally heard her, they went through, all in a group, the grayness swallowing them.

Now there was just Annabelle and the zeros.

She knew the Nakajima was made for combat, but somehow she didn't think it would take too many direct hits from those lasers.

She turned the plane to get the best run she could get in the huge room. When she faced the screen again, she forced the engine to give her all it had to give. The Nakajima taxied toward the screen, picking up speed. She just got the nose up as the scene of the frozen waste appeared, the small figure of Clive standing out in the tundra.

It's got to be now, she thought.

The zeros' laser blasts exploded all around her. A number hit the plane but didn't cause enough damage to stop it from lifting off the ground.

And then she was through.

Airborne over the frozen tundra, no sign of the gateway behind her. On the ice fields ahead of her the figure turned at the sound of her engine. High above him, rotating slowly in the bright twilight sky of the tundra, was a spiral of stars that Annabelle recognized. It was the same as the symbol tattooed on the back of Horace's hand. The same as the stellar formation that

Clive had described to her, the one that had heralded his arrival into the Dungeon.

What the hell . . . ? she thought.

No time to think of it now, she realized as she banked the plane and came swooping back. The spiraling stars now at her back she checked the sky ahead of her. Wherever the gateway she'd come through was, it wasn't visible from this side.

Don't worry about that either.

She turned her attention back to the figure on the ice below.

Here I come, Clive. Let's just hope the hell I can get us out of here again.

The following drawings are from Major Clive Folliot's private sketchbook, which was mysteriously left on the doorstep of *The London Illustrated Recorder and Dispatch*, the newspaper that provided financing for his expedition. There was no explanation accompanying the parcel, save for an enigmatic inscription in the hand of Major Folliot himself.

Much to our great despair, we arrived on this level of this blasted Dungeon with our party fragmented. Into four groups we were split, and some of us with our proportions drastically changed! And what a wretched place we find ourselves in.

It is owed to some small good fortune that we were reunited. Thus, we forge on, strengthened by our numbers, in our search for an escape from this peculiar and frightening place. *If* and *when* we return, will we ever be the same?

SELECTIONS
FROM THE SKETCHBOOK
OF MAJOR CLIVE FOLLIOT

ALYSSA, THE SONG
OF THE WIND,
AND HER
PARTY RIDING
THEIR SILVERS.

MR. JAKE,
WHO GUIDED
ANNABELLE, FINNBOGG,
AND SMYTHE IN
THE DIVES.

CASEY'S PLACE
A TYPE OF TAVERN
WITH MUSIC.
FROM
ANNABELLE'S
DISCRIPTION,
IT IS A LESS
THAN RESPECTABLE
ESTABLISHMENT.

SIDI AND TOMAS
ALMOST FELL PREY
TO THIS MULTI—
JOINTED CREATURE,
BREZHOO.

POOT, ONE OF LES
ENFANTS PERDUS,
WHO SAVED SIDI'S AND
TOMÀS'S LIVES WITH
HIS EXCELLENT SHOT.

THEY MADE THEIR
NARROW ESCAPE IN
THE BALLOON.

I WAS INTERROGATED BY THESE THREE "SPEAKERS."
THEY WISHED TO DETERMINE WHETHER I WAS THE
TRUE CLIVE FOLLIOT!

FRENCHY — MENTOR OF
LES ENFANTS PERDUS.

THE PROPHET
SUFFERS A
TERRIBLE FATE.

NEVILLE AND SHRIEK, HAD THE UNFORTUNATE
EXPERIENCE OF MEETING THESE TWO GIANTS,
TRAVESTIES OF NEVILLE AND MYSELF—OR
OF REVEREND DODGSONS TWEEDLEDEE
AND TWEEDLEDUM?

Shriek, as Neville found her in the death dream; awaiting the Gatherer to bring her to her destiny.

These creatures with human brains and glowing eyes were the watchdogs of the underground.

ARALT, THE HOME PLANET OF THE REN,
AND AN ASTEROID BELIEVED TO BE
THE DUNGEON.

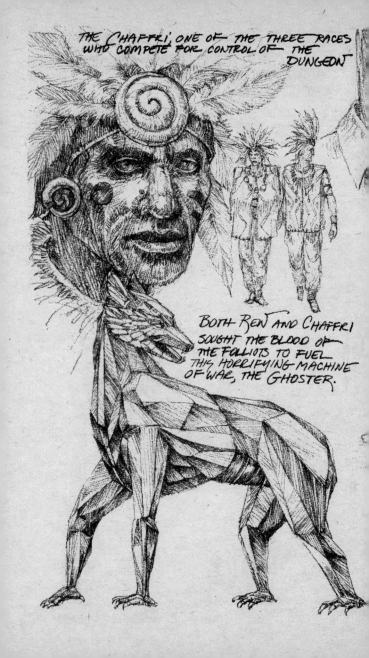

THE CHAFFRI, ONE OF THE THREE RACES WHO COMPETE FOR CONTROL OF THE DUNGEON

BOTH REN AND CHAFFRI SOUGHT THE BLOOD OF THE FOLLIOTS TO FUEL THIS HORRIFYING MACHINE OF WAR, THE GHOSTER.

THE POWERS OF THE DUNGEON
HAVE REDUCED SHRIEK AND NEVILLE
TO MINIATURE.

ESCAPED TO THE
XT LEVEL THROUGH THIS SCREEN.
NABELLE ATTEMPTED TO FOLLOW ME IN THE NAKAJIMA!

Here is a sneak preview of
THE DUNGEON,
Volume 6

THE FINAL BATTLE

by Richard Lupoff

Clive Folliot and his intrepid band have escaped yet another level of the intricate Dungeon that has confined them for so long. Have they reached, at long last, level nine—the final circle? Is freedom at last in view, or will Clive, Neville, Annabelle and the others find themselves facing opponents this time impossible to defeat?

They still do not know whose machinations brought them to this place, or what it might take to escape the Dungeon forever. They can only pit themselves against whoever and whatever might challenge them. For freedom is just a level away, and freedom has never seemed so sweet. . . .

For a moment he was too dazzled by whiteness to notice anything else. Not the cold, not the wind, not the clouds that swirled overhead like living things. All of these he would notice—but not yet.

Clive Folliot clasped his hands to his eyes.

It was as if he had been struck by a solid mass of light, a pure essence of undifferentiated color so overwhelming that it forced its way past the irises of his eyes and filled his whole skull. His brain reeled before the dazzling onslaught. He grew dizzy, felt himself stagger, folded onto his knees.

Instinctively he dropped one hand, resting his knuckles on the hard surface to give himself a sense of balance, to assure himself that he would not fall prone. If he permitted himself to do that, he feared, he might slide, tumble, roll into nothingness.

His sense of direction had been snatched away from him.

He had no inkling of east or west, of up or down. He felt as if he might plunge into the earth itself, or into the sky.

He forced the fingers of his other hand apart. Between them the whiteness still smote him, but he was able now to control it somewhat. And his eyes were adjusting. Recovered from the initial shock of unbearable whiteness, they were beginning to provide him with a fuzzy image of the world into which he had fallen.

Whiteness in all directions. Whiteness above and below.

And now he began to notice other things. Now he noticed the cold, and now he noticed the wind that stung his cheeks and hands, and now he threw back his head and squinted at the sky above. Shards and fragments of cloud still swirled overhead, chasing one another like ferocious beasts in cannibalistic pursuit.

Was this the ninth level of the Dungeon? A wilderness of windswept, frigid whiteness? His mind returned to his first entry into the Dungeon, that strange world (or series of worlds—he could never be certain even of that) where he had wandered for he knew not how long.

His first entry into the Dungeon had occurred in the Sudd, that mystery-laden swamp north of the equatorial lake country where he had sought the answer to his brother Neville's disappearance. Neville, who had set out to find the headwater of the White Nile and vanished from the continent of Africa and the face of the Earth.

Traveling with Quartermaster Sergeant Horace Hamilton Smythe and the ancient and wizened Sidi Bombay, Clive had found himself tumbling through a rock like a great shining diamond with a heart of pulsing ruby, into a world of blackness and mystery. The Sudd had been a place of prostrating heat, and the Dungeon . . .

The first level of the Dungeon, the World of Q'oorna, had been a world of blackness. Black earth, black vegetation, black landscapes through which black rivers wound beneath eternally black skies. Overhead the enigmatic spiral of brilliant stars.

Clive had made his way through eight levels of the Dungeon, and now he found himself in what seemed to be the ninth. The ninth: this world of blinding whiteness and numbing cold.

The wind keened in his ears, but somehow through that keening he heard another sound, a sound like the buzzing of an engine. He was able to scan the sky, by this time, without recoiling in pain from the sheer burning brilliance of its whiteness. He turned slowly on his heel, scanning the sky until he caught a glint.

It came again.

He was able to identify it with the source of the buzzing.

And now he was able to see it as a black speck against the grayish whiteness. A speck that grew and took shape. It resembled a cross, and for a moment he feared that he was going mad, was experiencing a religious hallucination, but then as it grew larger he was able to make out a tail structure, and a whirring disk at its front end that he knew was an aerial screw. A propellor, his great-granddaughter Annabelle had called it.

It was an aeroplane, its configuration and painted markings identifying it as the same Nakajima 97 in which Annie had escaped the Japanese encampment at New Kwajalein Atoll back on level—he couldn't even remember which level of the Dungeon they had been on when they had encountered the Imperial Japanese marine detachment.

The Nakajima waggled its wings.

Clive spun and saw something that looked like a child's spring-driven toy moving across the ice toward him. At first glance it appeared tiny, but as it approached him more closely he realized that it was neither tiny nor toylike, but was in fact larger than he. The clicking sounds had come from the contact of its metallic feet with the surface of the ice.

"Clive Folliot! Being Clive Folliot!"

The voice was mechanical and uninflected, but Clive recognized it at once and felt his heart leap with joy. "Chang Guafe!"

"It pleases me to see you still functioning, Being Clive!"

"And it pleases me to see you as well, old friend. I feared that I was alone, stranded here on the ninth level of the Dungeon. Chang Guafe, did you see the aeroplane with Annie in it?"

"Is that where we are—the ninth level? No, Being Clive, I saw no aeroplane."

Clive turned slowly, surveying the unbroken vista of whiteness. If only Chang Guafe had arrived minutes earlier, even seconds earlier, he could have verified Clive's sighting of the Nakajima. He might have been unable to prevent its subsequent disappearance, but at least he could have told Clive that he was not mad. "The ninth level," Clive muttered, "where else could we be?"

Chang Guafe lifted his shoulders in a hideous parody of a shrug. When Clive had first encountered the alien cyborg, it had been able to change its shape almost at will, extruding new mechanical parts and reconfiguring its organic components to suit the needs of the moment. The Dungeonmasters, those enigmatic manipulators of the destinies of uncounted victims, had crippled Chang Guafe's ability. But perhaps Chang Guafe had overcome the handicap. A being of the immense will and intelligence of Chang Guafe might overcome almost anything. Almost anything. Almost, almost . . .

"A good question, Being Clive." Chang Guafe nodded his head, artificial sensors reflecting the whiteness. Although the sun was not clearly visible through the cloud cover, it could be seen as a glowing patch of brightness not far above the horizon. "We learned that the Dungeon is of nine levels, and we traveled together through eight of them. It would seem to follow, then, that we have reached the ninth and final level. Is it, then, a featureless wilderness of whiteness? That seems an unsuitable anticlimax to our long adventure."

"But if this is not the ninth level . . ." Clive swung one hand in a circle, taking in their white surroundings with the gesture. "If this is not the ninth level of the Dungeon," he resumed, "then what is it? Where can we be? Why were we brought here, and what can we do about it?"

A violent shiver ran through him, making him realize for the first time how very cold he was. He blew on his hands to warm them, then drew another breath and released it. The exhalation plumed away like a streamer of smoke. He wore only the clothes he had worn on the eighth level of the Dungeon—

hardly an adequate costume for his present icy environment.

What ignominy, if he should die here, alone, of exposure to the cold. If he should die here of exposure after all the perils of the Dungeon, the battles with men and with monsters and at one point with the very demons of Hell . . .

But an idea struck him. "Chang, you are the possessor of senses varied and keen beyond the human. Do you think . . . ?"

"That somewhere," Chang Guafe continued Clive's thought, "maybe even somewhere nearby, there is more to this world than featureless whiteness?"

"Exactly! Something, perhaps, hidden by the glare."

"Stand by, Being Clive. I will see what I can see!"

"Have you regained any of your ability to change yourself?"

Chang Guafe emitted a hideous grating sound. The portion of the alien that Clive thought was a mouth curved into what Clive thought was a smile. "You have seen Hell itself, Being Clive, and you know something of the torments of the damned. Compared to the pain of my recovery, my friend, the torments of the damned are the pleasures of a spratling's outing. But yes, Being Clive, I have overcome the affliction placed upon me. And I shall avenge every twinge of pain that my recovery cost! But for now—behold, my friend!"

Before Clive's eyes, Chang Guafe underwent an amazing transformation. He spread his mechanical limbs like a giant spider—like the alien Shriek, Clive realized with a pang of loss—and steadied himself on the ice. Like a telescope extending, Chang Guafe extended his neck up and up until it towered twice the height of a man and then some.

Strange devices were extruded from Chang Guafe's head, feathery filaments like the antennae of African moths, and glittering, multifaceted viewers like the astonishing eyes of a fly or a honeybee.

Slowly Chang Guafe rotated his head, turning it in a manner that would have been impossible for any ordinary living creature but that seemed effortless and natural to this being who was as much machine as he was organism.

At last the head completed its rotation and came to a halt. The telescoping neck retracted until the strange configuration of organs and devices that passed for Chang Guafe's face was approximately level with Clive Folliot's own.

"You were right, Being Clive." Chang Guafe nodded solemnly. "Beneath our feet the ice extends far downward until it comes to water little warmer than itself. But yonder"—and he raised a limb, using a clawlike extrusion as if it were a pointing finger—"the ice rises as tall as a bungalow. It is as if an iceberg had been captured and held in place within this great ice floe. And within that iceberg—"

"Is what?" Clive could not contain his eagerness.

"I could not tell in detail, but my sensors indicate an irregularity of density."

Clive was crestfallen. "An irregularity of density, Chang Guafe. And what does that mean?" Clive clutched his fists in his armpits, trying to avoid frostbitten fingers. He stamped his feet to keep them from freezing. He could last a while longer here on the ice, but only a while. And then . . .

"I will put it another way," the cyborg grated mechanically. "If the iceberg were a solid block, there would be very little variation in its density. Instead, I detected great variation. It is my inference, then, that since this variation includes zones of greater density than ordinary frozen water, the iceberg contains objects, artifacts, or even creatures frozen within itself."

Chang Guafe drew its legs up beneath its body, raising its torso and head above the ice so that it glared down into Clive Folliot's haggard face.

"The iceberg also contains pockets of far lesser density than ordinary frozen water. Pockets of so little density, I infer that they actually contain air. They may be either caves or rooms."

Caves or rooms! The iceberg might contain a means of contact with humanity, with civilization. Perhaps with the Q'oornans or with the greater masters of the Dungeon: the Chaffri, the Ren, even the most powerful and mysterious of all, those beings known as the Gennine—said by some to be the actual creators of the Dungeon.

If not—well, at least it might provide temporary respite from the chill and the wind that swept the ice floe. It might provide a few more hours of survival for Clive Folliot, hours that he and Chang Guafe could apply to trying to figure out a means of escape from this terrible place. If Clive and Chang Guafe could survive their present chilling dilemma, they might make contact with Annabelle Leigh—Clive's many-times-great-granddaughter—and with Horace Hamilton Smythe, with Sidi Bombay, with whatever members of their beleaguered party who still survived.

But Annabelle Leigh had already made contact with them! The sun-glittering aeroplane that she had obtained from the Imperial marines at New Kwajalein—what had happened to it? Where, now, were the Nakajima and Annie?

"Come along then, Chang Guafe! You point the way, and let's get us to that wonderful iceberg of yours!"

Chang Guafe settled down between twin rows of long, metallic limbs and clattered in a direction that coincided with that of the glowing blob of the sun.

Clive fell in beside the alien cyborg. The pace that the cyborg set was a rapid one, but Clive was able to keep up and was grateful for the exercise that warmed his limbs. He knew that the cold was sapping his reservoirs of strength and that the same exercise that provided warmth simultaneously drove his reserves of energy toward exhaustion. But there was nothing to be gained by remaining behind and passively awaiting the end.

Rage at destiny! Fight to the end! Then, if death must come, he would at least have lived his life to the full, to the last breath of his lungs and the last beat of his heart.

Clive staggered and reached one hand to clutch at Chang Guafe. The cyborg had detected Clive's growing weakness and had offered once to carry him, but Clive had recognized in Chang Guafe's manner the fact that the alien, too, was growing weak. His power was immense, but so also were his needs for energy. And with neither food nor fuel, struggling across the face of this ice floe, both of them were approaching exhaustion.

"Being Clive," Chang Guafe said.

Clive clutched one of Chang Guafe's metal-sheathed limbs near the point where it met his body. He knew that the metal would be devastatingly cold, but his own hands were by now so numb that he was unable to tell by feel.

"Being Clive," Chang Guafe repeated. "Battle onward! Our goal is within reach!"

Clive raised a hand to shade his eyes. They were walking straight into the blobby sun. The bright, fuzzy circle had hardly moved in all the time they had walked toward it. It seemed neither to be rising nor setting, but merely waiting for them, a quarter of the way up the sky, perpetually at late afternoon or early morning, nor had Clive Folliot any way of telling which.

Could he reach his friend George du Maurier or any of his other acquaintances in London, from his sweetheart Annabella Leighton to his editor, Maurice Carstairs of the *London Illustrated Recorder and Dispatch*? He lacked the mental energy and power of concentration needed even to make the attempt.

He could only struggle onward, placing one foot in front of the other, holding his hand against Chang Guafe's metal carapace for guidance, hoping to reach the iceberg. He blinked, and could not be certain whether he saw the sun and the sky and the ice that surrounded him and his alien companion. There was so much whiteness, so much cold and whiteness—was he seeing it all, or had he become blinded by the glare, a victim of snow blindness?

He held his free hand before his eyes and was able to distinguish his spread fingers as black silhouettes against the gray-white glare of the ice. At least he was not blind! At least—not yet!

"Courage, Being Clive!"

"You can say that, Chang Guafe! You're as much machine as—"

"This is not mere bravado," the cyborg interrupted. "Look ahead, Being Clive!"

Clive Folliot halted for a moment and raised his eyes from the ice beneath his feet. Towering above him, silhouetted a darker gray-white against the glaring gray-white of the sky, loomed the iceberg.

Together, Clive Folliot and Chang Guafe managed to cover the final few rods of their trek. Clive stood, staring up at the iceberg. From this distance, he could see that it was as tall as a small tenement. If only he could enter its confines and climb the stair to Annabella Leighton's cozy flat!

But that was out of the question.

With a new burst of energy he began edging sideways, circling the iceberg. Within it he could make out vague and shadowy forms.

"Here!" he heard himself shouting hoarsely. "Here, Chang Guafe! A doorway! A doorway! We are saved, Chang Guafe! It is a doorway!"

Without waiting for the alien to catch up to him, Clive staggered through the man-high opening in the iceberg. He found himself standing in a room-shaped vacuity within the ice. It appeared to be featureless, filled with a weirdly shifting gloom, the feeble light filtering in part through the opening through which Clive had himself entered and in part through the living ice itself.

As far as Clive Folliot could tell there was nothing in the room save himself. No furnishing, no chair or table or couch, no stove—oh, what he would have given for the warmth of a merrily flaming oven or hearth!—nor closet nor bed nor any other furnishing or sign of habitation.

He circled the walls, peering as best he could into the shadowy world of the living ice until he came to —a figure that suggested the human form! He strode forward and pounded his fists on the ice, forgetting all his cold and fatigue, his mind filled suddenly with the excitement of his discovery.

"A man! A man! Come out! Tell us your story! Tell us—" He stopped. How far was it into the ice, to reach this man? And was he indeed alive?

He did not speak, he did not move. Had he been frozen into the ice when a ship was blown off course and its passengers and crew died on the polar cap? Worse yet, had he survived the shipwreck and then been trapped by some horrid happenstance, in the ice, and frozen there alive?

Clive shuddered, half from his own coldness, half from terror at the thought of what might have happened to this mute, anonymous, unmoving stranger who seemed to gaze unblinkingly at Clive from his place deep within the ice, even as Clive gawped at him.

From behind Clive came the clicking and scrabbling sounds that meant Chang Guafe had followed him into the opening.

"Chang Guafe—" Clive motioned, "—come and see this." He spoke the words without turning away from the terrible sight that held him mesmerized. The longer he stood before the frozen figure, the more details he could make out.

The man—for he seemed clearly to be a man— loomed well above Clive's own height, and Clive was a person of goodly size. The frozen one's shoulders were broad, his head tall and hatless but surmounted by a generous mane of black, unkempt hair. His face was of an unmatched pallor; whether due to a natural lack of pigment or to the cold, Clive could not tell.

The figure wore an outfit of matching jacket and trousers, tattered and threadbare and of a dull black material. His collarless and uncravated shirt was of the same color. So huge was the man that neither the sleeves of his coat nor the cuffs of his trousers reached their normal place, but rode high above wrist and ankle. His shoes were thick-soled and heavy.

"You have made a discovery, Being Folliot," Chang Guafe's voice grated.

"Indeed I have," Clive replied. "Indeed I have!"

"Have you a plan to propose?"

"Chang Guafe!" At last Clive turned so as to face the alien. "In all your repertoire of tools and organs, do you think you could find something that will permit us to free this fellow from the ice?"

"Free him?" Chang Guafe asked. He scuttered forward to stand close to the wall of ice, peering into it with an extruded sensor that looked for all the world like a sea captain's telescope. "Free him?" Chang Guafe asked again. "How do you know he lives, Being Folliot? And if he does live, how do you know that he will do us good rather than ill?"

"I don't know that he lives. I merely suspect it. And as for doing us harm—how can our plight be made worse than it is? As things stand now, we shall both perish. If we free this prisoner, who knows what favors he may perform for us, out of sheer gratitude? I think, Chang Guafe, that this strange pale fellow is our last, best hope. But the way to find out whether he lives, and whether he is benevolent or malign, is to liberate him from his icy prison. The question is, Chang Guafe, can you do it?"

Chang Guafe emitted the shuddering, grating sound that reminded Clive Folliot of a piece of chalk vibrating shrilly against a polished slate, that he knew passed with Chang Guafe for laughter. "Can I do it, Being Folliot? Of course I can do it!"

"Then in the name of all that is holy, Chang Guafe, do not stand there dithering!"

Clive stepped aside to give the alien better access to the wall of ice that contained the towering human figure. He watched in awe as the alien shifted and strained. He seemed not merely to be rearranging the metal parts that made up the mechanical portions of his body, but in some miniature machine shop contained within a cavity of his body to be fabricating the very parts and mechanisms that he would shortly call into play.

At last, Chang Guafe extended toward the wall an instrument that resembled a rotary saw blade.

The blade spun.

Chang Guafe pressed it against the ice.

An ear-splitting scream split the air, a scream that came from no throat of human or beast or alien but from the living ice itself as the saw blade marked its path against the wall. Chang Guafe guided the blade first in a vertical path, cutting a line so straight and true that Clive Folliot was unable to distinguish it from the perfection of a plumb bob.

Extending one of his telescoping organs, Chang Guafe drew the line he had scored as high as the top of the frozen man's head and then a bit higher as if allowing for good measure. Then he rotated the blade so that it spun in a horizontal plane and continued to cut the ice until it was time to turn the blade once again and draw it downward toward the icy floor of the cave.

In due course Chang Guafe had carved from the living wall a gigantic ice cube in which the frozen form of the giant was imbedded like a fly in amber. He hefted the cube out of its niche in the wall, laid it on the floor so that the giant's frozen eyes glared at the roof of the ice cave.

While Clive Folliot gazed in awe, Chang Guafe fabricated from his internal machine shop a weblike metallic filament that he strung about the gigantic ice cube. There was a humming sound. The filament glowed first rose, then red, then white-orange.

With perceptible speed, the ice block began to melt.

Water dripped from the block of ice, puddling up and then refreezing on the icy floor of the cave. Soon a cloud of steam formed around the block, obscuring the figure that lay within. But in the last moment before the immobile giant disappeared, Clive felt a bolt of psychic energy pass through his body.

He had caught the eye of the frozen man—or the frozen man's glance had caught Clive—and the glare of pure malice that passed from the giant to Folliot was the source of that psychic bolt!

THE FINAL BATTLE by Richard Lupoff goes on sale in June 1990 at bookstores everywhere. Don't miss the amazing conclusion to the adventure that began with The Black Tower—*in the final volume of Philip José Farmer's The Dungeon!*

PHILIP JOSÉ FARMER'S

THE DUNGEON

"A vast and richly layered recreation of
the Merlin legend...full of careful detail and brilliant
flights of hallucinatory images."
—*The Kansas City Star*

The Coming of the King
Nikolai Tolstoy
Volume I of The Books of Merlin

"Here Nikolai Tolstoy, the descendant of Leo Tolstoy, has
created a masterful, imaginative epic, bringing Merlin fully
to life. **The Coming of the King** is a comp' x blend of myth,
history and fantasy, with elements of medieval life richly
detailed. Readers of Arthurian literature, fantasy and British
history will eagerly await the next volume."
—*The Cleveland Plain Dealer*

"Plan to read this book when you have time to savor the
descriptive passages, to ponder the actions of the principal
characters and to appreciate the misty philosophies and
strange beliefs of bygone generations. Tolstoy presents a
Merlin alive and energetic, far different from the Merlin of
fairy tales."—*The Pittsburgh Press*

"In classic, heroic style, and with wit, tragic sensibility, and
poetry in the bardic tradition, Merlin's story is gathered up in
masterly fashion....Once tasted, never forgotten."
—*Publishers Weekly*

Buy **The Coming of the King** now on sale wherever
Bantam Books are sold.

GUARDIANS OF THE THREE

For centuries the feline people of Ar and the powerful Lords of
the East have been at peace. Legends surround the Eastern
Lords and their servants, the liskash—lizard warriors—but
few have ever seen them. This series tells the exciting story of
the sudden rise and devastating assault of the Eastern Lords
against the people of Ar, the catlike Mrem. The Council of the
Three—a group of powerful Mrem wizards—must fight with
their every resource to protect their vulnerable world.